SONG OF THE HEART

As children on the island of Phetray, Minn Macfee, a cottar's daughter, and Ewan Mackinnon, the minister's son, are bound together by the accidental drowning of Ewan's sister. When Ewan is blamed and Minn shunned, they must go their separate ways grieving. Years later, Ewan returns to Phetray and is enchanted by Minn's frail beauty. Then the Second World War breaks out and, separated by miles and weighed down by tragedy and misunderstanding, their love seems destined to die...

In memory of my 'Purple Granny',
Catherine Maclean Fleming. She'll know why.

SONG OF THE HEART

by

Helene Wiggin

Magna Large Print Books
Long Preston, North Yorkshire,
BD23 4ND, England.

British Library Cataloguing in Publication Data.

Wiggin, Helene
 Song of the heart.

  A catalogue record of this book is
  available from the British Library

  ISBN   0-7505-2592-4
  ISBN   978-0-7505-2592-3

First published in Great Britain in 2004 by
Severn House Publishers Ltd.

Copyright © 2004 by Helene Wiggin

Cover illustration © Andy Walker by arrangement with
P.W.A. International Ltd.

The moral right of the author has been asserted

Published in Large Print 2006 by arrangement with
Severn House Publishers

Magna Large Print is an imprint of Library Magna Books Ltd.

Printed and bound in Great Britain by
T.J. (International) Ltd., Cornwall, PL28 8RW

Acknowledgements

Readers who know the Inner Hebrides will recognize echoes of Tiree in the island I have called Phetray. I have stolen some of its beautiful scenery as a background but none of its history or people. Phetray is populated by fictitious characters and the wartime events there are of my own making.

I would like to thank Harold Smith for sharing his wartime experiences on a Scottish island and Donneil Kennedy for help with some Gaelic phrases.

PART ONE

Blow the wind southerly, southerly, southerly,
Blow the wind south o'er the bonnie blue sea;
Blow the wind southerly, southerly, southerly,
Blow, bonnie breeze, my lover to me.

They told me last night there were ships in the
  offing
And I hurried down to the deep rolling sea
But my eye could not see it, wherever might be it
The barque that is bearing my lover to me.

One

Kilphetrish, 1930

The girl scampered over the grass, stubbing her toe on a stone, hopping on one foot, cursing into the wind like Uncle Niall when the cow caught him on the nose. Her mother, Eilidh, was standing in the doorway of the stone house waving a cloth, yelling angrily after the child,

'Mind what I'm telling you, Minn Macfee ... away for whelks and limpets, a full pail or it'll be a thin stew we'll be getting for the dinner. No dreaming and no singing! We've enough bad luck in this house to last us a lifetime without you calling on the sea witches! And mind, the eye of the Lord sees all, lassie!'

'I hate you! I hate you!' Minn shouted into the wind with her fingers crossed. The sting from her 'admonition' was still throbbing on her thighs. She had spilled the precious milk from the cow, broken an egg when she tripped over a stone. Mother had taken the strap to her legs.

'If you won't slow down then you'll be made to slow down, *mo ghaoil*, it's for your

11

own good.'

It was one of Mother's black days when the mood hung like thunder clouds in the rafters of the crofter's cottage. Now she must find some seafood or there would be another admonition. School was out so at least she was free from the chores in the smoky house. The rain was only dripping and the shore wind was light. It was time to greet the old seal, sing to the mermaids and spin stones into the sea. She could fill a pail in minutes and then go search for eggs in the machair to soothe away Mother's gloom.

Minn knew where a hen was laying away, and that secret hoard was usually her own spending money. Only Dan the *buth* knew about this little arrangement, swapping eggs for liquorice dabs and pan drops in his shop, but today she must find a speckled brown egg for Mother's tea.

She was making her way down to the old ruined dun, the old fort on the rocks where the limpets clung to the shoreline in clusters. She was good at smashing them off the rocks and scooping up all she could find into her pail whilst brushing away the flies from her ankles.

The seaweed under her bare foot was like dead man's hands clutching her toes. Sometimes the pot was thickened with carrageen; she hated it slithering about but when she was hungry anything that filled her belly full

12

was swallowed with her nose scrunched up.

Now it was time for the 'Colonel' to make his appearance. He lived somewhere under the rocks and when she sang he would bob round into the small bay to admire her performance. He was just an old grey seal with a kindly eye but he always came when she called. Today she was going to sing in English to him: one of the songs they were learning at the school: 'Mary of Argyll'.

In her heart she knew that Gaelic was the real sound of music but she liked the sad ballads and the jingles about the lords and ladies who always ended up in the kirkyard dead.

If only she could practise her songs in the house, but music was forbidden. She used to practise in the cow's byre but once Mother caught her singing on the Sabbath to the cow and she beat her mercilessly.

'I'll have no blasphemers of the Sabbath in this house! And in English too! We have to beat the dark spirits out of you for your own good.'

Minn took her admonitions without a murmur but her heart was full of rage at the injustice. She had only been singing a school hymn. Mother would not hear a sound of music indoors or in the kirk.

'Music is devil's work, ma girl. Don't you forget it ... no matter what the Dominie says or yon fancy minister in the manse. God prefers the spoken word, the silent prayer to all that caterwauling and tonky tunes they have in they hymn books. Music incites the flesh to lust. My word is spoken on the matter.'

'But the bagpipes, Mother?' Minn argued.

'What of them? The call of the pipes brings only sorrows to a home and to those that follow them.' There was no arguing with Mother when her black moods filled the kitchen, when she sat in darkness spinning like a *cailleach*, muttering curses into the wool. Her face was leathered and lined like old boots and her hair was white, her hands were gnarled and coarse. Minn could never imagine her young or having the beauty that Uncle Niall, her brother, once spoke of wistfully. Eilidh Macfee never smiled.

Minn just had to sing. It bubbled and burst up through her in ripples of phlegm from her chest. She liked to stand square and lift her voice loud into the wind. Let it echo around the rocks. If she cupped her hand like a shell on her left ear she could hear the voice echoing back into her head. Sometimes she could hear the fiddles in her head at the ceilidhs and danced around the beach like a dervish spinning until she fell dizzy and laughing.

'I have heard the mavis singing
His lovesong to the morn;
I have seen the dewdrop clinging
To the rose just newly born
But...'

14

Minn was shouting by the edge of the shoreline but for once Colonel Blimp didn't oblige. Instead a canoe edged round the rocks with a boy grinning as he paddled towards her, his black hair flopping over his eyes.

'How now brown cow... Is that Minnie Macfee scaring the shoals away again?'

'Shut your mouth, Ewan *dubh*, you've scared away the Colonel with your paddling. Is your sister coming out to play the now?' She shook her fist at him. Trust Ewan *dubh*, the dark one, to spoil her game. He was her friend Agnes's big brother and son of the Manse. He won all the prizes in the school and would soon be off to the mainland to college for a proper education.

Ewan spent his holidays helping the fisher-men or living rough on the small off-shore islands in his canoe, fishing and camping like a boy scout. Agnes said there was nothing he didn't know about the waters, the tides, the secrets of the shoreline, and he drew all the sea birds for her. He even ate seaweed for the fun of it.

Agnes Mackinnon was her special friend and lent her storybooks in English to read from her own bookshelves. Minn wrapped them in scraps of oilskin and hid them under the boxed bed, for Mother did not approve of 'Noo ... vells', as she called them. They

15

were of the devil too. At home there was only the big black Bible for Sunday reading.

Everything was of the devil in their small cottage on the edge of the machair. Uncle Niall Macfee, on leave from the ships in his cap and dark reefer jacket, took no interest in Minn's upbringing but sucked on his clay pipe and looked into the peat fire. His hands were tanned on the outside and pink on the inside from years working in salt water. Sometimes she thought she saw him look upon her kindly with a sigh.

'Poor *caileag*, born to shame and no father.' But that was usually when he was full of the drink from the boat or the bothy where it was purchased in secret by even the Elders of the Kirk when the spirit moved.

At least Agnes saw no shame in knowing her and Ewan just laughed and teased her making her red faced with fury.

'Want a hand with the pail?' he asked, lifting his paddles.

'No, thank you, I've nearly finished,' she replied.

'There's some good ones round the corner. You can squeeze in the back and I'll take you.'

Minn hesitated but the truth was she was afraid to get aboard in case the canoe might turn over and she'd be flung into the sea. The truth was she couldn't swim and feared the water. Had it not flung Uncle Erchie

16

from his lobster boat one tide and thrown his body ashore the next dashed on the rocks?

Far worse, had it not stolen her father away before his wedding, shaming her mother and giving her the black moods, making Minn a bastard? She was sure he must have drowned at sea, for no one would ever speak of him.

There was always hushed silence around her birthing day when she, 'conceived in shame and born in fear', as Mother always reminded her, had clung on to life by a whisper: a frail scrap of pink flesh with a pulsing heart through its ribs that refused to be stilled. She was a summer child who was kept indoors in a wooden crate for a cradle until fit to be seen.

Mother took praying fits ever since that time but no Bible words could ever comfort her sorrows. Everyone knew that Phetray men were all for the sea: they called it the grey widow-maker and Phetray women bore the wind and the weariness on their faces.

'Come on, I won't bite you, Minnie Mouse.' Ewan laughed at her reluctance.

'Don't call me that. I canny swim,' she confessed. Ewan smiled, his dark eyes sparkling warmly. As big brothers went Agnes was lucky to have such a gem. 'I'll teach you both then,' he replied with a grin.

'But I'd get wet and I'll no be swimming in

ma nothings.' Minn could feel herself blushing at the very thought.

'I should think not. I'm sure Aggie will lend you one of her knitted efforts. She can learn too. Everyone should be able to swim if you live by the water. It makes sense.'

Minn shrugged her shoulders. None of her kin could swim. No one went into the water unless to wash off winter's muck and smoke. There were too many dangers in the water, sea *cailleachs*, sirens and evil sprites waiting to lure innocents to their end, and most of them were female. Minn knew all the superstitions.

'I have to go back with this pail or I'll be for a skelping.' Minn backed up the shingle to the tide line and the flies, the machair. There was just time to search for an egg. She was not going to make a fool of herself in front of Ewan *dubh*, of that she was certain but she didn't know why.

Next to the Struthers, the minister and the dominie were almost gentry. They were the undisputed leaders of Phetray. Ewan would be expected to follow in his father's footsteps: away to university and away from the island.

All the clever ones took that path to freedom and few came back. Only crofters' sons and fishermen stayed. Cottar children with no prospects had little choice in the matter. Even at ten Minn sensed her family's place was at the bottom of the midden heap, last in line for a decent education. They had been pushed to the edge of the sea with just a few chickens and crops, to live from the sea as best they could. Somebody had to stay on the island and do the menial jobs, kelping, field work, road mending, fishing and waiting on. That would be her fate, however bright she knew she was.

'Yon lass's as quick as a weasel out of a dike,' Uncle Niall would laugh about her as he sat by the lamplight filling his baccy pipe.

If she collected every hidden egg on the island her savings would never be enough to get away from Phetray. Mother said Macfees were cursed if they left the island, but Uncle Niall could go and come as he pleased. It was his stone cottage with the turf roof weighed down with stones and nets that sheltered them from the gales that whipped across the island.

The message was drummed into her skull and beaten into her thighs: those that were conceived in fear and born in shame must never leave this shore.

Balenottar Point

Ewan Mackinnon kept his promise to the cottar girl and on the next fine day he brought his sister, Agnes, down to the shore to meet Minn, teaching them both to swim. There was lots of screaming and splashing around for the girls were fearful of the waves and the cold sea. 'Move your arms like me,' he demonstrated, prostrate on the sand, aping the breaststroke and kicking frog-like shapes with his legs, sending grains and shells in all directions.

The girls giggled as they practised their strokes in the sand. He took them to the safe open bay with a long slope into deep water where they could wade and feel their feet on sand. The sea was blue and inviting and the waves were just ripples. They changed modestly in the sand dunes, the heat of the summer sun stinging the soles of their feet.

Minn Macfee was already a head taller than Agnes Mackinnon. Ewan could not help but notice the tiny breast buds filling out her knitted swimsuit where Agnes was still flat and undeveloped. Patiently he trawled each in turn through the water so they could practise their leg strokes and then he clasped them round the waist. Then it was time for the girls to jump on to the water and thrash towards his waiting hand. In deeper water he held them by the chin so they could feel the buoyancy of being held up by the sea.

Agnes was not so well coordinated as her friend and trembled at the thought of letting go of his grasp. She thrashed and sank, afraid to float.

'You must let go...' he urged her. 'Float on your back and let your arms gently paddle.

You are the boat and your arms and legs are your rudder. If you can float you will always be safe in calm water. Go on, Minn, you can do it.' Ewan was shouting encouragingly, holding on to her tiny waist.

Minn lay back stiffly. 'I can't, I can't!'

'Look ... I'm hardly holding you.' Her teacher was lifting her like a waiter holds a tea tray. 'Just float out of my hands. Head to the sky.' He watched Minn's eyes, distrustful at first, blinking back her fear. 'See, you can do it!' She was fixing her gaze trustingly on his own dark eyes. 'I'm watching you ... you're floating now.'

Her silver-blue eyes stared intently at him hardly believing she was afloat, gently bobbing away from his arms.

'Me next...' yelled Agnes breaking the spell between them. 'It's my turn now.'

The moment his attention turned to his sister, Minn capsized, gulping in a mug of salt water. 'You made me sink!' She managed to turn and thrash back to safety.

Agnes wanted his attention, making Ewan grab her knitted costume straps like a harness. 'Come on, you can do better,' he yelled.

Over the weeks he watched them both grow more confident swimming a little further each time so their feet no longer touched the sand. He warned them never to swim unsupervised or in any other place than the safe shelving shores of Kilphetrish

Bay. The Phetray coast was treacherous and the currents unpredictable. Once they could swim Ewan felt it was safe for them to come out in the dinghy alongside him.

Minn kept whining that she had never left the island and begged for trips further out to sea. 'I can swim back to the shore,' she boasted.

'You'll do no such thing. There are jagged rocks hidden under the surface at high tide waiting to trap you. Have you never heard of the sea hags of Ardnag Point? They lie in wait to lure silly girls on to the rocks who disobey orders. Just because you can swim does not mean you can outrun the tides,' warned Ewan.

Then his father, the Reverend John Mackinnon, took his son to task for spending so much time with two young girls: his moustache twitching as if there was something faintly indecent about these activities.

'You mustn't single out one of my parish poor, giving her ideas above her station. It has come to my attention you have been seen cavorting half naked over the sands, and you almost a man now, sprouting bodily hair.' The minister was wagging his finger as if he disapproved that Ewan's height was already outstripping his own.

'I'm just teaching my sister and her friend to swim,' Ewan argued. 'Where's the harm in that, sir?'

22

'Whatever for? They're not going to be fishermen.'

'I would have thought all civilized people need to know how to swim, especially on an island.' Ewan felt his cheeks flushing at this dressing down.

'Your mother doesn't want Agnes near boats. Her chest is weak and exercise will exhaust her. It would not be wise to continue these lessons for your own good. If you must go down to the sea, make yourself useful on the harbour. Help collect in the lobster creels. Do I make myself plain? Stay away from the Macfee girl. She was born to trouble, that one!' John Mackinnon wagged his pulpit finger again.

'Yes, sir.' Ewan bowed his head to his father's will. What was wrong with Agnes's friend? Minna might only be a rough cottar child but she had shown courage in overcoming her fear of the water. Now she swam like a mermaid, with trailing white hair. She made Agnes rock the boat with laughter when she sang to the seals. He could see no harm in their friendship at all.

Three weeks later, towards the end of the summer, Ewan was rowing off Balenottar Point checking the lobster pots when he spotted the two girls on the shore waving to him, beckoning him to heave to. He had been careful to obey his father's wishes, leaving his sister to her games. Now they were playing tag on the shingle and jumping out of the sand dunes in a makeshift slide, dancing and waving.

He paused to watch them, envying them their friendship for he had always been a loner. No one wanted to play with the minister's son. Each time he had made a friendship his father moved on to another parish and Ewan was forced to start all over again.

He found companionship amongst fishermen in boats, watching the sea creatures and birds, sketching them in charcoal in his sketch pad.

The water around his boat was calm enough but further out he could sense the sea was strengthening and soon breakers would be forming. He could read the wind and the waves and he was uneasy. Ewan watched the girls stripping off their skirts and shoes, racing towards the water leaving clumps of clothing dotted along the beach.

Minn was shouting, 'We're coming in! We're going to walk on water like Jesus!'

'No! Not here... Go back at once! It's further than you think,' he yelled out to them, standing up, forcing his voice above the swell, rocking his own boat in his anxiety to warn them.

Their two heads bobbed in unison as they ploughed towards his boat against a racing tide. Ewan's heart was pounding with fear as he watched helplessly. They hadn't the strength to swim against the tide to reach his boat; the stupid pig-headed kids. Had he not warned them? 'Go back now!' he screamed into the wind.

His arms were burning as he rowed like a galley slave, letting the current push the vessel inshore, trying to race the glassy heaving swell. Balenottar Cove was edged with fingers of rock and steeply shelving. The Atlantic rollers roared and crashed on to these rocks when the sea was angry. Each rise of the swell pushed him further out of reach of them. 'Go back! Agnes... Go back!'

Ewan's seagull screams were useless. He was praying out loud but the God of the swelling tide was deaf to his pleas. The roar of the rising water in his own eardrums drowned out any voice he might have.

The girls were in deep water now and tiring fast. 'Float on the water... For God's sake! Let the tide take you back!' he willed them to hear his command.

His arms were useless propellers against the current. He strained to keep their heads in view but the waves were breaking over them and the white spume engulfed them and they kept disappearing.

There was no time to panic, for a huge unexpected wave crashed over his boat, hurling him into the water, throwing him up into the air and flinging him helplessly towards the shore. He could feel the grit under his feet and stood shaking to see where the girls were heading.

In slow motion he saw the dark head of his sister bobbing helplessly, drifting to the finger posts of jagged rocks. He saw in horror her tiny body thrown up on to the rock like a limp rag doll as over and over the waves played with their toy, dashing it against the rock until it disappeared, wedged in some gully out of reach.

He thrashed out in that direction but his arms were like lead weights and would not turn. His strokes were powerless to propel him forward. He was thrown once more on to the sand where he gasped for breath. Why was there no one on the shore to help him? Where was Minn?

Then he saw the girl rise up on the crest of a mighty wave, propelled lifeless on to the shore. He was half crawling with exhaustion, dragging her from the edge to safety. He pumped the water from her lungs.

'Live you stupid *caileag*,' he prayed, hoping he was lost in some nightmare. He turned her face down, lifting her arms in the only way he knew until she coughed and sicked up the seawater. With relief he saw her face was turning pink and she gasped for breath. He left her to recover, yelling for help. Surely someone was around?

Then he caught sight of his own upright

boat coming in on the angry tide, unbroken, and he threw himself in the water to launch himself towards the rocks where Agnes had last been seen. He was crying with panic,

'I must find her!' She might still be wedged safely into some rock. 'Agnes, I'm coming.'

Ewan bobbed up and down on the water in pursuit of his boat; the damn thing was elusive, drifting beyond his grasp, but he swam on like an automaton, using every last ounce of strength in his body, until he grabbed the side and hauled himself in. Then the sky went dark and he could no longer feel his limbs.

He lay too exhausted to care if he lived or died at the mercy of the cruel tide.

Then there were voices and arms and other strong hands pulling at him, dragging the boat back to the shore.

'My sister. I have to find her ... over there... *He fooar!* So cold.' He was too weak to point or raise his head, so cold as a blanket fell over his shoulders. He could see the heads shaking and knew it was too late to save her.

Little Agnes's body was recovered the day after the accident. She was washed up naked on the white sands of Ardnag Point, bruised and battered, tiny in death, her black hair tangled in seaweed, tossed by the tide, barely recognizable. She was wrapped quickly in a blanket of jackets to hide her disfigurement and carried back to the Manse.

Ewan sobbed as the little bundle was lifted from the cart. His mother lay sedated in the darkened bedroom and his father stood like an alabaster statue trying to compose his features as he viewed what remained of his child. He had barely spoken one word to his son since that dreadful evening when Ewan was brought home shivering by Doctor Murray. Now the parson must contain his fury and find words for an elegy of hope for his only daughter. He laid into his son only when they were alone.

'What have you to say for yourself? I forbade you to take those girls in the water. Her death and our sorrow are on your hands.' John Mackinnon's words were like ice on his skin. 'The other bairn is saved, I hear. Trust the sea to deliver back its own. I hold you solely to blame.'

How could he offer anything in reply? He sat in his room for days unable to eat or sleep. What was the point of telling them the honest truth that he had come upon them purely by chance or that Agnes had disobeyed his warnings when she answered Minn's challenge to 'walk on water'.

'No one walks on water but the Lord! Blasphemers will be punished,' his father would have answered. How was the Macfee girl supposed to know such sophistry? It was not the child's fault. She was too young to know that no one challenged the sea, too innocent of the ways of water and tide, too ignorant to realize its treachery, for the ocean's ways were cruel and its heart was ice cold.

Someone must take the blame for the accident so it might as well be him. It was his fault for teaching them to swim in the first place, for taking away their natural fear of water. He had killed his sister.

He sat watching the silver-grey waves crashing on to the shingle in the darkening light, the breaking water pounding the sands. Once he had found comfort in watching the power of wind on water, but there was nothing romantic in its bleakness, only the hypnotic thrash of the waves on shingle.

A great emptiness filled his heart knowing he must watch the battered remains of his sister being placed deep in Balenottar kirkyard; the agony of his mother trying to be Christian about this terrible tragedy. There was no sleeping as the nightmares of guilt haunted his dreams. He kept swimming out into that black endless sea without a shore, trying to catch Agnes's arm to save her from the rocks.

How many nights had he woken in a sweat of 'if only's', seeing Agnes drowning over and over again? Did she gulp in salt, her eyes bursting, limbs thrashing, alone and terrified? The sea was a fickle mistress in snatching one to its bosom with cruel fingers yet casting the other unharmed ashore. He had prided himself on his knowledge of the cruel sea, but who could sound its unfathomable deep? There was no peace in the running waves, memories like waves tumbling over each other, scratching his mind like grit between his toes. How could he live knowing it was all his fault?

For days after the drowning Minn woke screaming with terror, choking and sweating, but she could never recall the nightmare. All she could hear was the waves pounding in her ears, the water over her head and her struggle to reach the surface for breath. All she could see was Ewan's face looming over her, shouting her back to life. The rest was a blur. There was no comfort back in the croft.

'You bring shame to our clachan. To swim in a rough sea, to challenge the witches of Ardnag Point...' Mother paddled the treddle of the spinning wheel with peat-stained boots as if she didn't care.

'It is a thrashing you'll be getting when Uncle Niall returns, you wicked girl. Your wilful disobedience was the death of the minister's child!' That was the moment she found out that Agnes was drowned and it was all her fault. Not one ounce of sympathy was given to the shivering child.

She ran to the rocks to hide from the silence and the stares, throwing boulders into the water in fury. The sea shimmered like polished silver in the moon's pale light. It looked calm and inviting but she knew underneath raged wicked spirits brewing another cauldron of boiling water especially for her this time.

Everyone hated her and for a second she wondered if she must jump into the sea and join Agnes for ever in *Tir nan og*.

No, not yet, whispered a little voice inside her head. You have to stay on this dry land for ever.

If only they had played on the dunes and ignored Ewan's presence. If only she had not tried to be clever and show off to him. Minn knew behind all the excuses there was always this wish to impress the boy, to show him she was as good a swimmer as he was now. Pride was her undoing. It was all her fault and she must be punished.

There were whisperings in the cottage doors as she passed by. 'What do you expect from a bastard Macfee? That's the cursed one, that bairn with the silver hair and mermaid's tail. Don't play with her or you'll die!' shouted the children, running away from her.

'I'm no going to school,' Minn whined, backing away from her morning walk down the coast track to Kilphetrish. 'My guts is churning.'

Eilidh Macfee was deaf to her pleas, shoving her roughly on her way. 'You'll go and take your medicine. I'm no having one o'mine shaming us anymore than you have. On yer haunches and walk!'

Minn crept slowly to the play yard, pausing to wait at her usual spot where Agnes was dropped off the cart for school. What was the point in hovering for a cart that did not appear? In that instant she knew Agnes would never play with her again, and Minn was alone.

The teacher, Mr Macpherson, was stern faced and said, 'Minna is not to be blamed for the tragic accident. The ways of the Lord are strange to our blinded eyes and we will not question His holy judgement in choosing one to be saved and the other lost. It is up to Minna to prove herself worthy of such a mercy.'

They sang, 'There's a home for little children above the bright blue sky', which was Agnes's favourite hymn, and said lengthy prayers.

The teacher said she was not to blame but his cold eyes told Minn a different story. They could not hide his doubting.

The children gathered at the manse door with wild flowers and wreaths but none of them was let indoors to pay respects. Agnes was not for public viewing. Agnes was buried in the churchyard by the men of Balenottar.

Minn wept by the shore but no one comforted her. For months afterwards she was shunned in the playground and after school.

There was no volunteer to take Agnes's place as her friend. Ewan disappeared from school to the mainland and Mother decided to walk three miles further down the coast to join another kirk with a stricter congregation.

Sometimes when the blanket of gloom was wrapped tight on her shoulders she would spit at Minn. 'I canny bear to look upon that poor minister's sad face knowing it's all my bairn's doing: devil's child that you are: conceived in lust and born in fear. From now on you will wear black weeds to mind you of your sin and disobedience, to bring you to salvation. Why did the sea no take you to its bosom instead of that angel child?'

Minn had wished that on many a tide but said nothing. The years would roll on until it was time to put books away and be at the mercy of a poor girl's fate. Her punishment was to stay on the island for ever.

Two

The Crannog, 1933

'Don't you step out of that scullery, lassie, until you've shed every one of those rags, ma girl! Off with they sacks and skirts, down to your semmet. What's the world coming to

33

when I have to train up a wee bastard of Eilidh Macfee?' The cook sighed, her bosoms heaving at the sight of the ragamuffin standing in a pool of dirty woollens, her eyes like blue enamel saucers. 'Still, you canny help yer birthing, but shove that mop of straw hair in this cap. Who knows what'll jump out of yon wild lugs and bite me?'

Minn shivered in her knitted underwear, her bare feet were not used to stone-flagged floors. There was a dark chill in the store-room with its grey-painted shelves high to the ceiling, stacked with brown crock pots and stone jars. To her left was a walk-in pantry where rows of dead creatures swung in the cool breeze from the wire mesh window. On the sink board a fish with glazed eyes was staring at her with its guts ripped open. This was a place of death and mutilation, and she was expected to make her home here?

'Take this overall and the pinny, wrap it round and see to that bucket of vegetables. We'll give you a good scrub later. Go on ... sharp to yer duties, lassie! I want all they carrots and tatties scrubbed and peeled, no black bits left. And take yon footstool to reach to the sink. You've still a few years growing in you by the size of you.'

Minn stood awestruck by the rattle of orders. She bobbed and bent her head.

'Well? Say "Yes, Mistress Lamont" to me. Rules is rules here. This is no the schoolyard

34

now, Macfee. You're here to watch and learn, follow me like a shadow, silent and respectful, for you never know the time or the hour when that bell will clang and I'll be needed upstairs.' Susan Lamont was examining the specimen before her like a lump of butcher meat, hardly the size of tuppence halfpenny, a sharp-jawed little madam in the making, if ever there was one. The girl's bottom lip was trembling.

'None of yon soor dooks mouth on you. Stick that bonnet straight and find a kirby grip in the jar to tidy away yer wisps. We keep a tight ship in ma kitchen even though it's no the Queen Mary it once was. We must do our best for Lady Rose, so not a peep out of you until that bucket is emptied.'

Minn stood on the stool to reach into the sink, tears plopping on to the peelings. This was not what she'd hoped for on leaving Kilphetrish school: to be sent for a skivvy to the big house, stranded on the island. At the end of her first long shift she ran home across the damp grass to the cottage on the shore.

'Well?' said her mother as she sat knitting, making the most of the evening sunshine.

'I'm no going back there again ... I hate it. It's full o' dead things! I want to go back to my schooling.' Minn sat on the grass, feeding the wool from the basket to her mother like a machine.

'Wheesht ... wheesht, *mo ghaoil!*' Mother

replied as she drew an arc of spun wool like threads of gossamer into the air. 'It's an honour for the likes of us to be serving at the big house.'

'No it's no. Even I know fine that the best servants go to Glaschu to seek their fortune. Why does it take so many people to look after one old woman? The Lady Rose Struther hardly leaves her bedroom. I hate it and I'm no going back the morrow.' Minn stared out to flat sea glinting like green glass. It wasn't fair to have to leave the school.

At the summer prize giving at Kilphetrish school, Lady Rose had arrived in a pony and trap, her silver hair tucked under a flowery straw hat. She was escorted by the minister to the platform in the yard before the assembled school, the wind whipping up her long gauzy skirt to reveal layers of silken petticoats and white calfskin boots. She was so thin she curved against the force of the breeze in a C shape, her shoulders hunched and rounded.

Minn joined the queue for her leaving certificate and a small prize for knitting and mending. The minister's son had taken all the best prizes alongside Johanna Macallum, the factor's daughter. She had won the Struther scholarship to a Glasgow college.

Minn hung back at the unfamiliar sound of her Sunday name, Mairi-Minna, until she felt the fist of the dominie in her shoulder-blades propelling her forward to bow to

Lady Rose.

'You should be proud to be fished out of the pond, honoured that you were specially asked for at the Crannog. Was it not you who never once missed a day's schooling? Who won the prize for the neatest spinning and mending?' Mother nodded with satisfaction, thinking her task well done. There was little else to offer a child with such an unfortunate history.

'Why did ma father drown at sea before your wedding?' Minn screamed like a sea-gull. If only they could read into her soul how she longed to go to the mainland and study for a teacher or smooth the sick brows of the fevered ones like a Florence Nightingale or even row madly into the storm like her heroine, Grace Darling.

Now she must rise at dawn and walk down the white sandy tracks to the grey stone house that glowered out of the early morning mist, a stern old granite keep softened by a fancy front full of windows to catch the sun. It was turreted like a fairy castle, but she must take the back gate of the Crannog, keeping out of sight of the front windows and garden path just in case Lady Rose might catch a glimpse of a rough servant at her chores spoiling her view.

'No more of such devil's talk! It is the will o' the Lord that he places you where he wills you to do his duty.' Her mother lifted rough hands together in prayerful thanksgiving. 'Let us thank Him for His mercy that He places you safe amongst us as a dutiful servant to your betters. You will learn fine manners and they'll give you your daily bread and it's one less mouth for me to feed from our small pot. Mind… You'll speak English to your betters and we can hold our heads in the clachan here. So be a good girl, attentive to your mistress. Don't lose your chance of betterment.'

It was one of those days when Mother was speaking like a Bible so Minn shrugged her shoulders and sighed. There was no changing her fate. It was only what she deserved, but she would not give in without a fight.

'It's no betterment! This back-breaking, rough work with chapped hands, fingers pickled like vegetables and aching legs from stretching on tippy toe,' Minn argued.

If only she was taller, prettier or cleverer. It was not fair that her friends could go to the mainland for an 'eddycashun'. Then Minn paused in full flow, thinking of her only true friend lying in the graveyard, and shuddered. This must be her punishment so she must make the best of it.

For months Minn saw only the scullery and the kitchen range, the pantry and the outhouse, the laundry and the backyard where she fed the scratting hens and put Lady Rose's smalls to blow dry in the gale. There was the endless steeping and boiling, starching, ironing, all to be done to Mistress Lamont's strict instructions. The skeleton staff had many extra jobs: the annual stock-taking, spring cleaning and preparations for any summer visitors, who thankfully brought their own staff to see to them.

When there were strangers in the house there was such rivalry and much tut-tutting from the English maids, who found life on Phetray no picnic, girning about the weather, the wind, the lack of gas and electricity, tele-phones and wirelesses, whatever they were. Sometimes they would leave behind maga-zines with pictures of their ladies in the sea-son, at the Court balls and the races. Minn would drool over the beautiful clothes and ballgowns with jewels and sumptuous fur wraps

There were pictures of the little royal prin-cesses with their nanny. How she longed to go to London to see it all for herself. Every-one gossiped about the good old days before the Great War when servants were two a penny and the house rang with laughter. There had been shooting parties when Lord Struther's coterie of cronies landed for the season in a motor car that was hoisted off the steam packet on a crane and driven up to the Crannog in a sandstorm of white dust.

Then the war took the Phetray men away to sea, to watery graves far from their homes. The few that came back to tell their tales wanted more for their sons than service. The widows and mothers struggled to keep the croft fires burning. Young Lord Struther was killed early in the war. His wife caught the Spanish flu in London and only his sister, Lady Rose, returned from her ambulance driving, with a bunch of wild harum scarum women who wore no corsets and cropped their hair like men.

Some had been in prison and were exhausted, sickly, and for a while the place echoed with their girly chatter. There were rumours flying around the island of strange goings on at midnight when they gathered in a circle trying to speak to their long dead. Mistress Lamont whispered with a sniff that they were tempting the very devil himself!

Later the Crannog fell silent for months on end, boarded up, covered with dust-sheets until Lady Rose returned in 1930 to live permanently in seclusion.

It was rumoured that she had been disgraced at Court but no one knew the details and there was no one left to care. She lived among the hebes and the red hot pokers in the high-walled garden that stood firm against the worst of the westerly winds, writing her memoirs and reliving lost joys.

Minn grew accustomed to the ways of the household, so different from life on the seashore. She got used to having a bath and brushing her fair hair until it shone, tying it back in a bun, mending her uniform, pressing it firmly into shape. She no longer needed the footstool as her legs lengthened and her shape filled out with all the leftover plates of food she wolfed down. Sometimes Mistress Lamont trusted her to poach the salmon, stir the sauces and prepare the afternoon teas neatly on the butler's tray with a starched cloth and gleaming silver teapots while she dozed in her armchair by the range.

Then came that fateful day when Effie Brown was sick and there was no maid to see to Lady Rose. Minn was ordered into the cotton print day dress with a broderie anglaise apron and sent upstairs to see to her mistress.

She slid up the staircase silently with her wooden tray to prepare the fires in the bedroom, counting the portraits on the wall slowly, dour faces peering out of wigs with haughty expressions knowing full well that she was novice.

She was to see to the rooms while no one was in the house but a shrill voice called from the bedroom.

'Brown? Is that you?' Minn froze. Should she disappear and ignore the summons or reveal herself? Curiosity got the better of her fear and she tapped on the door.

'Brown is sick, Lady Rose. I'm Macfee.' Minn bobbed. This was her first task upstairs.

The voice shouted from behind the bed curtains. 'Fill a bath for me.'

Minn knew about hip baths and bringing up jugs of hot water to the outer door but had never had the honour of seeing to the whole palaver before. 'Straight away?' she queried.

'Of course, Brown, in front of the fire.'

Minn scuttled down to the kitchen to check with the cook. Mistress Lamont was too busy to fuss over her.

'Just make sure the bath is on the mat or you'll shoot her over the polish like a curling stone.'

Up and down Minn rushed, trying not to slop the water over the floor. The bath was dragged on to the mat and the fire stoked up to provide some warmth, the screen placed discreetly while Lady Rose flopped on her high bed in a silk peignoir reading a book.

How Minn wanted to soak in a warm tub herself after all her exertions. There wasn't even a hefty man about the house to help with the carrying.

Lady Rose did not lift her eyes as she wafted her away. 'That'll be all ... stay upstairs in case I need you.'

Minn hung at the top of the stairs watching how the rain spatters made patterns on the vaulted dome window above her head. Each pane was edged with blue and gold stripes of stained glass.

She could hear the sound of splashing and

a thin reedy voice attempting some tune. There were no warm towels airing on the fender. She dashed into the linen press and brought out a set of face, hand and bath towels, knocking gently once more. 'I'm just going to warm your towels, my lady.'

'Good girl ... while you're here see to the commode in the dressing room.'

Minn saw to her task and opened the dressing room door, trying not to retch as the stench of a full pan hit her nostrils. There was a slop bucket with a lid, tucked discreetly away, and scattered around the floor were pieces of dirty toilet paper left for the maid to pick up. Could a lady not dispose of her own dirt? Picking up each sheet she held her breath with disgust.

Lady Rose was not an invalid but a lazy lay-a-bed who seemed incapable of doing anything for herself. How could she expect someone else to... But I'm not someone else, I'm just invisible ... a nobody, a dogsbody servant at the beck and call of anyone who demands my services. It's no fair! Suddenly her cheeks were on fire with indignation and humiliation. I won't do this, she screamed inwardly. I can't... Is this going to be my life for ever, trapped on Phetray? There's got to be a better way than this drudgery, but what?

Minn stuffed the dirty papers into the pail and closed the lid sharp. She flung the scattered clothes back on to their hangers and wiped around the commode. Whatever I do, I shall need a good reference, and I need better English, better manners; so use what's here to better your chances, she thought.

She flung up the window sash to let the sweeter air scour the smells, and gazed out at the sea view.

'Shut that blasted window! Do you want me to catch my death, Brown?' She still hadn't noticed that there was a new maid.

'Sorry, ma'am,' she said, trying not to smile.

'Bring me a towel and you can rub me down,' came the order. 'Then lay out my clothes in the right order.'

Minn lifted the towel as the old lady rose out of the water, standing like a lump of wet plaster, her skin hanging from her bones like rolls of dough. Minn had never seen such ugly nakedness before, such old skin like cooked apples.

'I've not done this before,' she confessed.

'So I noticed. Just pat my back for me and fetch the powder. You can do my feet between my toes. And not so rough. You've a lot to learn.'

'Yes, Lady Rose,' she stammered, hardly daring to raise her eyes. Now she must collect the clothes from the closet drawers: underwear, chemise, corselet, silk stockings, drawers and petticoat. There were so many dresses in the wardrobe to choose from: day dresses, tea dresses, house coats and wraps, skirts and tweeds, woollens with a softness of lamb's wool. Everything was so beautifully lined and finished, so expensively tailored, laid down under the canopy of the four poster bed with its eiderdown pillows and satin counterpane.

Minn thought of her own mother's one Sunday dress, tough heavy wool woven coarsely into scratchy tweed the colour of the dark earth, her sackcloth apron, black skirts, peat-stained boots and coarse hand-knitted underwear with stockings to the knee.

This was a world away from their humble living by the seashore in stone houses smelling of stinky rotting fish bones and cow dung fires, with dampness creeping into every nook and cranny of their thick walls. They stood like grey tombstones on the edge of the machair facing east, backs to the wind.

'That'll do, leave me now. I can see to the rest,' the lady dismissed.

Now the bath must be emptied and the linen changed, the soiled clothes removed, the bed made, the fires stoked again, up and down all morning while Lady Rose breakfasted in the morning room. All this effort just to give one person a bath! Tomorrow it would have to be repeated if Effie Brown did not return to work. If this was life above stairs, sniffed Minn, you could keep it!

When Effie Brown left to get married Minn was promoted from tweeny to parlour maid. Lady Rose was ill and the nurse engaged to see to her nursing left after only a few months of the island winter. She found herself used as nurse companion and lady's maid to her frail employer. Lady Rose grew eccentric and dabbled in clairvoyance and other such 'devilments'; much to the minister's dismay, it was whispered.

On her good days the invalid would dress and be helped to the fireside where she sat gazing into the flames. She said she could read fortunes in the flames. Minn dared to ask her once for her own fortune, praying it would not be to marry some fisherman, raise six bairns and look like her mother before she was thirty.

Lady Rose pointed with a bony finger towards the fireplace, 'I see you are a water sprite, ruled by the tides, happiest close to the shore but never far from the sea.' This made no sense to the maid and she turned to draw the curtains. She had turned her back on the sea since Agnes drowned.

Sometimes Lady Rose would take herself slowly to the piano and finger out some tune. 'Do you know this one, Macfee? Sing it to me!' There were no wirelesses on Phetray just the fiddle music of the ceilidh bands so Minn knew nothing of the mainland music. She shook her head sadly.

Sometimes the old lady would smile and go to the gramophone and place the black circle on the turntable, her eyes far away dancing to 'The Peanut Vendor'.

Minn had to wind it up tight and gently lift the needle on to the surface. 'Don't scratch it, girl!'

From out of that box came the most wonderful sounds from far away places. Lady Rose would point them out on the round label and give her the names of the composers: Beethoven, Mozart, Bach, waltzes from Vienna and tangos from South America, ballet music from Russia and military two steps, highland reels and jigs.

'This is what you do...' Lady Rose would open her arms and hold her stick, tottering and swaying with an imaginary partner.

It was rumoured down the back stairs that Miss Struther once was engaged to some handsome viscount who died of cholera in India.

Minn pretended she was in the arms of Rudolph Valentino, whose picture appeared in the glossy magazines strewn about the guest bedrooms.

Once his image appeared on a sheet on the wall of the church hall in the moving picture show. His romantic antics had shocked the worthies of the kirk and the film had been quickly whisked away, replaced by a film on African elephants. Try as she might to recapture his picture, the only gentleman's face that danced before her was that of the dark-eyed son of the manse, Ewan *dubh*, who had grown tall and broad since he went away to college, who never passed her by without a nod.

They never spoke of Agnes Mackinnon's drowning. The two survivors exchanged only glances over the years. The minister was always curt in his greeting when he called at the house and she sensed she was still blamed for her friend's death. It was hard, for Minn could rake up no memory of the incident and wondered why it was she who was 'saved for a purpose' not Agnes. It was like an invisible yoke bending her back.

Sometimes she took wild flowers to Agnes's grave and sat on the grassy mound to tell her news of all the children in their class. Minn sensed she was just talking into thin air.

Agnes was lost as a little girl and knew nothing of the grown-up world Minn must inhabit, but it was the least she could do to keep her informed. Everyone said there was a war coming soon and that worried her.

Once she met Ewan Mackinnon standing by the headstone. He looked as if he was about to speak to her, hovering for a second and then moving on. Cook said that he was sweet on Johanna Macallum, who was training to be a teacher in Glasgow. He still spent most of his holidays in a canoe paddling across Loch Beag at great speed, like Hiawatha in the poem, or helping the fishermen at the harbour. Ewan was growing tall and straight and handsome in his cadet uniform, far too grand now to mix in Minn's humdrum world.

On bad days Lady Rose only wanted to hear sad ballads and Gaelic laments. Tears would roll down her crinkled face and she sniffed into a lace handkerchief when Minn sang for her the lament *'Griogal cridhe,'* about a widow weeping for her beheaded husband whilst singing to her baby.

'You've a fine voice, girl, and a good ear. A good song gives wings to the spirit. I shall have to teach you to accompany me.'

To cheer her up Minn would mimic the old waulking songs that the spinners and weavers would sing when waulking the cloth to shrink it. Often the words were lewd and suggestive but Lady Rose had no Gaelic and just tapped along with the rhythm. 'Do that again!' She clapped her hands like a simple child.

When Lady Rose smiled, it was like sunshine through the dark clouds, for she taught her servant to play cards and finger tunes.

Minn's own English was improving, too, for she was blessed with a parrot's ear for mimicking accent and vowel sounds. She was copying the educated voice of a high born lady. Her vowels were round and distinct. She had decided long ago if she was going to speak English in public then it must be the best sort without the usual Highland lilt to it.

In the record collection on the bookshelf was one with actors and actresses speaking plays and poems in perfect English, and she would sneak down when Lady Rose was asleep to listen and rehearse their sounds over and over again. She swallowed their sounds, projecting the words back in a perfect rendition of the original.

Some days Lady Rose grew restless and wanted all her porcelain figurines out of the glazed cabinets to be washed and dusted. Each one was lovingly inspected and the hallmarks underneath explained in detail. Soon Minn could recognize the Sèvres from the Rockingham, the Royal Worcester and the Chelsea from Meissen by their distinguishing marks and the colour of their glazes.

She absorbed the information as if she was back in the schoolroom, squirrelling it away into a drawer inside her head. To be a lady she must know all these things. How to select the right cutlery, how to play the piano and dance gracefully, how to wear jewellery and recognize good pearls or serve tea from a silver pot without spilling it everywhere. Lady Rose was an excellent instructor.

Then came those grim days when her mistress lost grip on reality screaming and lashing out at Minn and the household as if she did not know them. The doctor was summoned and she was put to bed out of harm's way until she slept off her thrashings in a drugged sleep.

'What's the matter with the mistress?' Minn asked her mother as they sat by the smoking dung fire carding sheep rovings into rolls of raw wool for their spinning.

'They say all the Struther family go that way in the end: too much high living and in-breeding on the brain, but I am saying it's an ancient curse on that place when the old laird sent his poor lover across the open sea to her death. No Struthers have prospered here.'

'Will she die?' asked Minn, fearful of her own prospects.

'Sure as death comes to all of us, so mind your own ways. No prancing to the devil's tunes. I'm after hearing what you get up to in the Big House. If I catch you warbling on the Sabbath again ... you're not too old for a skelping! Haven't we corncrakes enough to rattle us awake without you screeching to high heaven,' answered Eilidh, her eyes sharp as flints.

'I can play a tune on the piano now and make chords,' Minn boasted.

'How many times must I tell you, music is the curse of the Macfees. I will not have it in the house, do you hear? It is bad enough you pretending to be some milk white loaf when the whole island knows you're nothing but an oatmeal bannock. It'll all end in tears.'

51

The harsh years had wizened her mother's features and she looked more like a grand-mother in widow weeds than a woman not much above forty. I will never look like you, Minn thought. I am going to be a lady one day.

'What's so wrong in playing the piano? There's one in the church hall.' Minn argued. Why was music so wrong, she puzzled?

'It's no for the likes of you to be dabbling your fingers on gentry's finery, aping your betters. No good can come of it...'

'Lady Rose says I have a good voice, so she does.'

'There's more to music than just a tune. It is the devil's instrument of lust!' said mother looking into the fire, rubbing her hands.

'I don't care. I can sing in English if I want to!' Minn was brushing so hard on the card-ing boards trying not to argue.

'Haven't the English caused us enough grief? If you must open your mouth use your native tongue.'

'Lady Rose says it's a peasant's noise... "No more peasant noise, Macfee. Time to speak properly!"' Minn mimicked her lady so accurately that even Mother looked up with a half smile.

'Remember who you are Mairi-Minna Macfee.'

'I'm a Teuchtar, daughter of the tide, hewn from Phetray granite, Lady Rose says.'

'Aye, highland daughter of Phetray ... *a' Ghaidhealtachd.* Never forget the soil that nourished you. Think of our forefathers, forced to wander over the earth with no land to call their own because of the English lords. It's said to me only yesterday that this Mister Hitler is doing just such to other poor cottar folk over the water. It won't be long before we'll be getting a taste of his wickedness. I hope the good Lord calls me home before that day.'

'Is there really going to be another war?' said Minn eagerly, having missed all the excitement of the Great War.

'We must pray that He will spare us from that hour. Phetray men are all for the sea and who knows how many of them will find some watery grave in the King's service?' Mother warned.

'I shall be a soldier then and join up. I want to see the world one day, Mother.'

'I don't know where you get such notions. Come what may you'll be staying here to see to your elders, to grow food for our sustenance. Who will tend our patch with me so crippled in the joints? One wanderer in the family will be sufficient. Uncle Niall will do his duty if called upon,' Mother said.

'Then I'll be a nurse,' Minn argued.

'How will I be managing without your wage? No more words on the matter. Such a trial you are to me, sent on this earth to punish my wickedness. I thought here on Phetray you were safe from temptation but once already you have shamed us.'

'What temptation is this then?' Minn was curious.

'You'll know it when it comes along, *mo ghaoil*...You must be strong for you're fair of face. Never turn your back on a man. That's all I'll be saying. Mind and don't let me hear you blaspheming the Sabbath again!'

'No, Mother.' Minn bowed her head to hide her smile.

Over the next few months she often dreamt at her polishing, watching sunlight beaming down on the piano like a searchlight. Nothing of this servile time would be wasted. Its drudgery only spurred her forward towards a better life and learning the piano before it was too late. One day she would be a lady too.

Lady Rose grew strange and wouldn't eat. They took her away on the ferry to an institution and the house lay empty. There were only two of the staff left to clean up. The world was already changing for the threat of war brought builders to the island.

Suddenly concrete hangars and control towers sprang up like trees, and water pipes snaked across the fields, roads widened and electricity brought its magic to the aerodrome.

Then came the time to pack the Struthers' porcelain in tea chests: all the little friends put to bed. Minn loved the dancers and shepherdesses. She had given them all names, English names: Pamela, Clarissa, Arabella, looking so delicate in their finery. Not one of them was broken for her fingers were fine tuned to caress them with care. One day, she vowed, as she was packing them all in tissues into special boxes, I'll be having some of my very own. Then they took down all the portraits from the wall. The Royal Air Force was commandeering the Crannog as an officers' billet for the duration and Minn's services were no longer needed.

The piano stayed where it was. Sometimes she used to sneak back, open the shutters and climb through the window to practise in her spare time, to finger the keyboard and test out the chords and harmonies. The right blends came easily to her ears from some unknown source within, and with the music came a certainty that her life must change. She was not going to be chained by ignorance.

Sometimes she walked around the little loch along a boggy path, watching the moorhens scuttling among the reeds, listening to the distant rattle of a corncrake. Working at the Crannog had opened the doors into other worlds where music and china and paintings mattered.

She felt bereft of the porcelain, her dolls, her imaginary friends. They spoke of a world far away, full of other beautiful things, when she grasped them in her hands, feeling their cool textures, savouring their pastel colours, gold trimmings and their craftsmanship.

She stood by the water edge vowing that one day there would be a cabinet full of china dolls, just for herself. The thought of such ambition was scary. It would set her apart but she didn't care. Sometimes she felt like a lonely island set in a sea of busy people. No one cared for her wishes. She must make her own dreams come true.

Three

Kilphetrish Harbour, 1939

It was a summer of blue skies and sunshine. The island shimmered in the sun, as if to compensate for the gathering gloom of events unfolding in Europe. Everyone was on the move, making preparations, talking of air raid precautions and camouflage, but the kittiwakes still dived into a turquoise sea and seals sunned themselves on the rocks as the Local Defence Volunteers paraded up and down Kilphetrish Bay with pitchforks and scythes for their weaponry.

Nothing was going to stop the annual summer regatta when the islanders gathered in the harbour to watch the sailing boats racing, the dinghies and swimmers competing for the trophies and all the sideshows lined up on the grassy slopes with beach games and races for the children. It was time for the crofters and fishermen, tradesmen and kelpers to strip off their workaday clothes to row lobster faced and sweating for the honour of their township in time-honoured fashion; time to square old rivalries: Balenottar versus Kilphetrish, Ardnag against the clachan at Loch Beag.

The day dawned glorious to behold and the Ladies' Guild prepared the trestle tables with white linen cloths spun from the white bog cotton grass. The home baking was covered with voile shower cloths to keep the flies and thieving fingers of the toerags from the tray bakes, cakes, biscuits and lemonade in stone jars.

Even the sick and elderly wanted an airing on such a beautiful day, sitting in makeshift carts with moist eyes, recalling their own youth and fitness. Everyone wanted the day to go well, for who knew when there would be another such regatta?

Minn loved Phetray regatta. There was always this feeling that the whole island was gathering together, with crowds as far as the eye could see. She thought that this must be what it was like all the time on the mainland: hundreds of folk just milling around, thronging the streets of Oban in just such a bustle. How Minn yearned to board the SS *Hebrides* and sail away, but there was never any occasion to justify the expense.

Yet this was a gap in her education that never would be filled until she saw the mainland for herself. She wanted to see how people walked and talked and dressed there, and envied the lucky crofters' wives who went to visit relatives in Glasgow and Inverness, who came back full of boasting and fancy gadgets for their homes.

Here she was stuck with just her mother and herself as usual and Uncle Niall was now back in the Merchant Navy so Mother would not hear of her venturing abroad.

'Abroad's no all it's cracked up to be, believe me... I should know.' Eilidh was briefly in service in Glasgow but returned homesick and terrified of city ways. She would never talk of that time and when she did the events were recalled in hushed tones as a time of abomination in her life. It was making Minn all the more determined to leave the island.

'When I'm twenty-one I'll save up and go and see for myself,' she argued. 'No one will stop me then!'

Mother would purse her lips and knit

furiously, 'I'll no be stopping you then. You'll soon learn that they city streets are no paved with gold. You'll no have far to find yer sorrows there, *mo ghaoil!*'

Now that the Crannog was being cleared out waiting for military billeting orders, Minn foraged for jobs to fill the empty purse. The money that Uncle Niall sent home came in fits and starts and sometimes it seemed as if there was only the milk cow and egg money to keep them from starvation. Mother knitted rough wool boot stockings from sheep rovings and her share of the fleece, knitting up thick jerseys for the builders.

She helped out in the vegetable fields or gathering the kelp from the seashore to load on to carts for spreading over the crofters' fields. Sometimes she helped in the village stores, minding the schoolmaster's young children or running messages on a borrowed bicycle.

She looked with disgust at her coarsened skin and rough hands, her weather-beaten face, how the sun had streaked and bleached her fair hair and mottled her arms with freckles. It was hard to keep up old standards and look respectable. How she yearned for her days in service when food was plentiful and bathing regularly had made her feel like a lady. Her life had taken a step backwards to the shore again.

Today she was going to forget all her woes and enjoy the atmosphere of the regatta. She watched all the coloured sails bobbing on the water, the bunting fluttering overhead round the harbour, the flags waving in the soft breeze, all the women in their printed frocks and hats like rows of bright flowers. Even the fierce westerlies had calmed for the day. Later there would be a bonfire on the beach and a ceilidh with singing and dancing and she was not going to miss that for anything.

Yet she felt so dowdy in her faded blue Sunday frock. She loosened her braids, letting her white hair fall down her back, catching it up with the velvet blue Alice band found stuck behind the dressing table when she was clearing Lady Rose's belongings from her room.

Everyone was gathering in groups; families of fishermen lugging creels stuffed with food, the crofters with land standing in their tweed jackets, their wives in linen two-piece suits bought from the catalogue stores on the mainland. The fishermen stood in shirt-sleeves and cloth caps with bright neckerchiefs.

The families of the minister, the doctor, the schoolteacher and the factor had the best view, sitting in deck chairs watching the sailing boats with binoculars and sunshades. The ladies were dressed in silk dresses with white hats and the men in linen jackets and Panama hats. Here and there were the uniforms of officers and ratings from the Navy and Merchant fleet. It was then that Minn spotted the tall figure of Ewan *dubh* standing next to his father, pointing out the competitors. The sight of him made her heart thud with a strange apprehension.

'We're short!' yelled the skipper of the Balenottar boat pointing to the young naval officer. 'Come on, Ewan! You can take an oar!' There was a cheer as he tore off his jacket and shirt, rolled up his trousers, to his mother's consternation, and raced down to join the boat, but Minn was pleased to see that the college boy was still a Phetray man at heart.

He leapt aboard and grabbed an oar. The team rowed off unevenly, all the oars crashing and splattering, but after some practice and manoeuvres the crew began to row in unison, striking out with a rhythm to the starting line, where all the township boats were lining up.

The Kilphetrish boat was always the favourite to win and Minn by rights should have been shouting for them, but as the gun went off and the race began her eyes could not leave the Balenottar crew and the muscular shape of the minister's son, who strained on the oar.

They began slowly far behind the Kilphetrish men. Then as they gathered their timing together they began to edge towards the leading boat as it thrashed its way towards the marker buoy just out of the harbour where the boats must turn and head back for the finishing line. The yelling was deafening as the Balenottar boat began to ease its way forward, making the Kilphetrish crew strain on their oars pulling to a faster beat. Ewan's boat struck out in response even more strongly until they were neck and neck, red faced with the agony of the effort to take the lead. On either side of the harbour the crowds roared encouragement.

'Come on, Ewan! You can win!' Minn was jumping up and down.

Her mother tugged at her skirt. 'Whisht! It is shame you're bringing on us making an exhibition of yerself. It's not for you to be calling out for him... Miss Macallum is over there, quite capable of calling him in herself.'

Minn stopped, suddenly aware that Johanna Macallum in her striped pinafore dress and straw boater was waving her handkerchief and shouting to Ewan's boat, 'You can do it! Come on Balenottar!'

'It's only a wee race, Mother. I can shout for who so ever I like. Come on, Ewan!' she continued.

It was going to be a close call, neck and neck to the finishing line, but somehow the Balenottar crew managed to summon enough effort to take the line by a whisker. The township rose as one to cheer their heroes up the quay. The crew sat back exhausted, exhilarated, clapping each other's backs heartily while the Kilphetrish men sat slumped with bent heads, surprised by this unexpected defeat.

What a change in Ewan Mackinnon! He was so dark, so confident, grown into a man in that world across the water. As he strolled up the quayside being slapped on the back and congratulated, he looked so changed. Why had she never noticed just how handsome he was, with his black hair flopping over his bronzed face? Her first instinct was to run down to congratulate him herself, fling her arms around him, but she held back and turned away shyly. They were no longer children. It would not be proper.

Why should he recognize her in this crowd with all the other girls screaming and fussing over him? She was just another rough cottar girl in a shabby frock with nothing but their childhood friendship to recommend her. She would be only another tragic reminder of his lost sister, Agnes. Why should he acknowledge her presence with Johanna already standing by his side.

Something was sparking inside her like a tinderbox set alight. Had she caught a look or a smile of instant recognition? She had the sudden overpowering feeling that she and Ewan were joined for ever by the drowning of his sister and of him saving her own life, bound together like buoys tied with a rope. In that spark burst such a flame of love for him. In that flash of insight she knew that Ewan must be hers alone.

He must be mine ... he's always been mine. He saved my life. We were such friends before... Why should Agnes's grave always stand between them? They were bound by suffering, but she could still feel that terrible despairing doubt. Who are you, Minn Macfee, to stake a claim on him? You're just a field worker, a serving girl, a nobody. Suddenly she could feel again the chill like clouds overshadowing the harbour, darkening the skies as she wrestled with that strange sick feeling of yearning and jealousy, punching her hand with a gnarled fist. He's mine, he's mine but how can I make him notice me?

The dancing was held in the open air by the light of many flickering bonfires on the beach. The sand was still warm as bare feet stomped to the fiddle and the circling couples made patterns on the shore. The old piano from the Tulloch bar was dragged to the edge of the grass and a drummer made up the makeshift trio. Older couples sat on the benches and grass, children darted like horseflies in and out of the swirling dancers.

It was coming to the end of a summer's day

when the sun had burnt Ewan's forehead and shoulders and his limbs were aching from the races, while clegs feasted on sweaty arms and swollen ankles: a day to linger long in the Phetray memory. This might be the last day of summer 1939, the last dance before the world might come to an end, he thought. Hearts were heavy now as he looked around old school friends assembled who soon would be posted off like him to God knows where! How many of us will be returning for the next regatta, he wondered?

There was a lull in the dancing and Ewan's group drifted towards the harbour benches while the musicians had retired to the bar. Someone was fingering the keyboard, picking out a tune, a few quiet chords and then a traditional waltz. One or two couples got up to spin around the sand smiling. Ewan was punch drunk with sun and the pleasure of being home. It was the end of a perfect day.

'What'll I do when you ... are far away?' Catching the mood of the moment the singer in the distance was crooning softly. Johanna stopped to listen to the song and crooned along with the music but a little out of tune. There was a ripple of applause, which gave the pianist the encouragement to keep on playing.

'Who's singing?' he asked, curious. Johanna shrugged her shoulders.

The clapping grew stronger and the

impromptu entertainer stood for her finale, singing in Gaelic: a lament for a lost lover. It was a sad haunting tune calculated to bring a tear to any highlander's eye. There was something about the singing of the ballad that got him on his feet.

'Come and see the blonde piece, singing like a mermaid,' yelled Lachie Munn, one of the boat crew. 'You'll never guess who it is down there,' he laughed. 'I'm away to get a dance frae her.'

There was a stunned silence as she bowed and slid from the piano while the pianist patted her on the shoulder. 'Well done, Minnie Macfee, you're a wee siren. What a voice! Fit to make the angels in heaven weep. Why aren't you singing in the musical festival at the Mod?'

Ewan stood transfixed by the sight of her. Was it really Minn? How she had grown up, slender, taller, with white hair rippling down her back. For an instant he thought about his sister and how she would have looked now, but his eyes feasted on the girl in the blue dress.

The clapping was still ringing in his ears but it faded away when she looked up at him leaning on the door of the Tulloch bar, smoking his pipe and talking with his group. He turned in her direction and stared at her, the brass buttons of his dark naval uniform flickering in the bonfire light. He was glad he had dressed for the dance in his uniform. He found himself pulled slowly towards her, smiling.

'I thought it must be Dame Nellie Melba singing to her seals again. You took me back all those years ago... You know Johanna ... and Duncan and Ishbel...' he introduced his friends. They all nodded politely, looking at her with little interest.

Johanna was brushing the folds of her dancing frock, which rustled when she turned. Then she held on to his arm. He found himself edging away. Jo was pleasant enough, a good friend, a pen pal. It was not as if they were sweethearts or anything mushy, but she was edging him away.

'Come on everyone, the dancing's going to start again. You've a lovely voice, Minna, you ought to get it trained...'

Ewan paused for a second, hesitating as if to draw Minn along with the crowd into their circle of dancers, but the others strode ahead and called him once more. He ought to be polite but he wanted to talk to his old friend, to dance with her and touch her and it shocked him. It was as if he was seeing her for the first time. When did she become such a beauty? The pull of her was like the tide.

Minn's heart sank. Her moment of glory was over. It was a hopeless cause to set her sights on a naval officer who was practically engaged. She would return home, not wishing to be a wallflower at the dancing. Turning to go, her arm was grabbed by Lachie Munn, her neighbour's boy.

'We're short for the eightsome reel, Macfee ... gie us yer hand!' Reluctantly she was pushed into the formation of dancing groups and turned to face her partner with a heavy heart. Lachie Munn was about her stretch, she sighed, a fisherman from the same clachan of cottages on the shore. He was smiling at her hopefully but she ignored his grinning. There were better fish to fry than a laddie she could only recall at school with scabby knees and lugs like jug handles.

Swung this way and that as the band struck up the music, Minn soon found herself caught up by the beat and the swirling couples. It was a progressive reel and the moment moved ever closer when she would be swung in the arms of Ewan *dubh*. She could hardly breathe waiting as his circle drew closer and closer. Then they were laughing and swinging round together and the weary world spun away like a top.

She was dizzy with skipping and prancing, clasping Ewan' s firm hands as he spun her round so fast that she felt herself lifted off the floor into his arms. She gazed shamelessly into those dark eyes, drowning in the power of his undivided attention. He was smiling, responding to her signals and the rhythm of the dance, and suddenly there was no one on the beach but the two of them. Was there promise and admiration in his eyes or was she dreaming?

Minn wanted the dancing to go on for ever, but in an hour the Sabbath would dawn and everyone would away to their beds. Just for this moment there was magic in the air. Her prayer had been answered by the warmth of Ewan's firm arm around her waist and the look in his eye. Thank you. She winged a prayer heavenwards. He's mine for the moment. It's up to me now to make all other competition fade away.

In those furtive glances something strange and wonderful was happening between them. Buoyed up by such emotions that Minn could hardly express, she felt she was swimming in a sea without a shore, floating endlessly across the world.

How could one day in her life begin so quietly and end with such a roar?

She did not sleep a wink, listening to the crash of water on shingle. She felt like a restless tide, rising and falling, living those few precious moments of the dancing over and over again in her mind's eye. She felt like the sea just before a storm when it heaves and sighs, tossing and turning until it was dawn and another quiet Sabbath must be endured.

There was the long walk to church, the

droning sermon, the cracking and gossip at the kirk door, the walk home, and then it must be endured all over again. Why could she not go back to the old kirk and see if Ewan was sitting in his family pew?

This morning she wanted to sing and dance and shout her excitement to the world, but a Phetray Sunday was a day for walking sedately, reading spiritual books and praying. Her heart was racing with plans. Where can I go to meet him? Where can I go and not be noticed? I have to see him again, she prayed. Suddenly she knew: there was only one place possible safe from prying eyes.

Minn walked slowly along the coastal path gathering wild flowers as she had done as a child: blue harebells, golden vetchlings, honey-scented bedstraw, clover to make a posy for Agnes's grave.

At the crossroads close to Balenottar Point was the little cemetery set on a hillock where the weathered gravestones with backs to the sea looked out over the island eastwards. It was a peaceful spot to sit and mull over all that was happening in her heart.

It must have been some sixth sense that brought Ewan to the window of the manse from where he could see a girl in a faded cotton frock gathering flowers from the machair.

Months away from home had made him hungry for its timeless beauty, the brightness

70

of the sun on water, the white sands, shimmering waves frilled with white spume, the diving terns and the kittiwakes, the carpets of flowers. Phetray was all the colours of the rainbow. It was criss-crossed by just a few roads strung with white cottages streamlined for life against the gales, harsh in winter; but spring came early and now there was such beauty. Minn was part of his island and he must speak to her again.

He shot down the stairs of the manse through the back door that led to the wrought iron gate, on to the path. He knew where she was heading and this time he did not turn from the sight of her as he had once, years ago, but squatted down by her side as she placed the flowers in the little urn. He could hardly breathe for the nearness of her.

'I'm glad you've not forgotten her,' he whispered. 'It never goes away from you, does it ... what happened all those years ago? I'm glad I've caught you here, I do so want to explain... It troubled me that we never talked about the accident. When I saw you here all those years ago, I flunked it. I should never have taught you both to swim... I blame myself. I gather you were shunned in the school after I left... I'm sorry.'

'Say no more, Ewan... it is all past and we cannot hold the tide by the wishing of it,' she replied, her blue eyes staring into his.

'Aggie was your friend... I wanted to clear

the air... No one knows but us how it all happened. Agnes wouldn't want us to go on punishing ourselves, would she?' He must have looked so sad that Minn reached out to touch him but drew back blushing.

'To tell the honest truth, I've no memory of it still, just flashes and sounds,' she confessed and rose to brush down her skirt and make for the road.

'Don't go yet, Minn... I've not told you how much I enjoyed your singing last night. You looked like a mermaid in the moonlight singing a siren song to lonely sailors. Do you remember how you used to sing to the seals and we laughed and called you Dame Nellie Melba?' he smiled feeling his pulse racing.

'It was good of you to speak to me when you were with your friends. I thought you would've forgotten those days before Agnes...'

Ewan drew to his full height and gazed down at her.

'How could I forget my old sparring partner. There are good memories with the bad, Minn. I would have asked you to join us but you know how it is...' His voice trailed into an apologetic mutter.

'Is Johanna your sweetheart?' she blurted out, being still as blunt and direct as she was as a child.

'Not exactly... We've always been chums. We write to each other. Our families are friendly. I suppose one day they expect we'll ... but the war will change everyone's plans.' He was trying to be honest with her.

'I see,' Minn gulped, drawing back her gaze from him.

'Have you anyone special to be dancing with?' Ewan sounded casual but he was anxious to know the truth. Minn to his relief shook her head.

'I'm waiting for all the boys in blue to fill the island and then I'll take my pick,' she laughed.

'Be careful! Some of those chaps can be tricky. Here today, gone tomorrow.' Ewan's face grew stern. Now he had found her he didn't want to share her with anyone.

'Like you sailors with a girl in every port, then? Don't worry I can take care of myself. I have to go.' Minn turned for the path but he blocked her way.

'Do you fancy a walk later ... down to the cove, not down there where we ... but to the Singing Beach in the hidden valley? The flowers are still blooming fine.'

'I have to go to church again with mother but yes, later...' Minn answered, clearly surprised by this unexpected invitation.

'I'll wait for you after church by the finger post and we'll catch up on all you've been up to since I've been away. You can tell me all the gossip then! See you soon.' He made a mock salute and touched her arm. He could feel sparks shooting from where his fingers pressed on her sunburnt skin.

'Tonight it is,' she laughed, bounding down the path like a puppy.

It would not be long before the whole island knew where the minister's son was walking out and who with, but he didn't care.

The weeks sped by in a dreamlike trance for Minn as their paths crossed and re-crossed until they stopped making lame excuses and accepted that there was a serious attraction. She was packing messages into a box for the weekly orders in the grocery storeroom when Ewan appeared from nowhere with a bunch of garden roses.

'These are for your mother, and can you come to tea tomorrow after work? I want you to come to the manse and meet the folks. It's time we all got together; no more skulking in coves and corners. I'm going to ask your mother if you can come.'

When Minn got home from Kilphetrish her mother was in a flurry of consternation after this unexpected visitation. The roses were stuck in Keillor marmalade jars in pride of place.

'To think you are walking out with the minister's son! Susan Mackinnon will no like that, to be sure, her son cavorting with a cottar.' Eilidh sighed. 'Mind what you say ... say nothing but sit straight and don't shame yerself. I dare say you know how to behave in a parlour but you're going against the natural order o' things ... not that he's not a braw young man and kind with it. You could do far worse, but mind, he's a sailor and away soon to fight a war. Don't pin your hopes too much on it, *mo ghaoil.*'

For days before the visit she searched through the small case of clothes she had rescued from Lady Rose's cast-offs. Even though it was warm she chose a fine woollen jumper and a skirt that needed the hem letting down and patching. She brushed her hair into a modest coil. It was important to give the right impression that this cottar girl knew how to dress for company.

She found herself sitting in the manse parlour stiffly, trying to hold her cup and saucer with care, trying not to stare at the clutter of books and papers, prints and photographs, trying not to look at Agnes, who was staring out of a silver frame with her black ringlets and serious look, overseeing all the proceedings.

Susan Mackinnon sat like a ramrod, eyeing the visitor's every movement with disapproval, sapping Minn's confidence until she could only squeak when she was spoken to.

'Ewan tells me you visit Agnes's grave, Minna. That's good of you. It must be hard to live with such an event on your conscience,' said the minister's wife, making

Minn want to rush out of the stuffy room; but she bowed her head and said nothing.

'What Mother means is that none of us can forget such a terrible accident,' Ewan interrupted, staring at his mother with dismay. 'Minn is helping out at the stores and Mr Niven is teaching her to drive the van in case he's called up.'

'Do you intend to join the forces, then?' Mrs Mackinnon ignored his pleasantries, looking at her with expectation.

'I think I'll be needed here now that Uncle Niall has to go away.'

'Ah yes! Niall Macfee! We've not seen him in church for many a year. Do you think it wise for a woman to drive a vehicle? It may come to the wearing of breeks, I'm after thinking, and that is an indecent proposition, don't you think?'

Minn swallowed her tea feeling like a skivvy caught on her knees scrubbing the grand hall, out of place, out of her depth in this venomous atmosphere. Then she saw the figurine and smiled.

'What a lovely piece of porcelain, Mrs Mackinonn. Do you mind if I take a closer look?'

'Help yourself but don't drop it, it's Sèvres.'

Minn grasped the figurine firmly and looked at its mark with enthusiasm. 'Actually, I think it may be a Chelsea piece, look at the anchor mark.' She saw the glare on the minister's wife's face and knew she'd said the wrong thing.

'I see they taught you something then at the Crannog. It's only a trinket. Does it matter who made it?'

There was a deafening pause and Ewan passed round a plate of shortbread. Minn was in no doubt now that Susan Mackinnon was not happy with her son's choice of girl-friend. She was going through the motions for the sake of propriety. They were all relieved when the maid took out the tea tray and Ewan made excuses for them to escape into the sunshine to forget this grilling.

'I'm sorry. I thought she'd be pleased for us. I thought she would soften when she met you properly. It was a pity Father was out on a call. I'm sure he would have welcomed you more warmly.'

She was embarrassed by his apology. 'It doesn't matter, Ewan.' Minn shrugged her shoulders. It was only to be expected in this narrow little island that tongues would wag and fingers would point at this unexpected courtship.

Then suddenly the weeks of waiting were over and Ewan's call back to base was days away. They walked in silence knowing this was their last night together, strolling slowly towards their favourite beach only too aware of the power growing between them. Minn sensed that this glorious summer was coming to an end. The tide was turning and Ewan would leave and perhaps never return. She couldn't bear to think about not seeing his face every day. Since he had made her special, walked her around the island proudly, she felt as if the everyday world going on around them, crofters harvesting the fields, fishermen at their nets and children playing tag, faded into a grey mist. Even her own boring duties just drifted in this trance.

Only once did she think of Johanna Macallum waiting patiently for Ewan in her father's house, wondering why his visits had dried up so suddenly. How could she know that Ewan was always for her alone. Only when he was by her side could she see clearly, breathe deeply, but his days were numbered on the island and his leave was ending. She didn't dare count how many hours they had left.

Soon he would sail for the mainland or maybe overseas. She was digging into every moment, clinging to his strong body, afraid it would vanish like the morning mist.

They lay in the sand dunes in the hideaway cove named in Gaelic *Traigh gaodh nan seinn*, beach of the singing winds; a deserted beach where few locals ever bothered to fish.

Ewan was fingering her hair in wonderment. 'No one else has hair as white as yours. It's like spun gold, made from the sun and the moon. Your mother is dark, so is it your father we must thank for such mermaid's hair?'

'All of Phetray must know who my father was but me. My mother will not say, but your father must know of him,' she replied.

Ewan shook his head. 'You were born before we came here. I doubt if he knows anything.'

'They must think badly of me.' Minn sighed

'Don't care what they think. It's what we think that matters. Will you write to me every day and when we are old we can read our letters to each other again?' he said, staring out to sea. 'Think of this war as just an interruption.'

'If only it were... I'm afraid, Ewan. What'll happen to us? What if you don't return?' Those dreadful words were let loose out of her mouth into the air.

'Just remember we were meant for each other, you and I, sealed by the sea and the waves. When I first heard you singing and when I saw you dancing on the shore. I've not been a saint. There have been other girls, but I knew there'd never been anyone to match you. It's simple. Who cares who your father is or was or has been? We can make our own destiny, you and I. Write to me every day. Promise? I'll leave you lots of stamps. I'll buy up all the stamps at the post office and shock poor Miss Macfadyen with my need of them!' He lay back, fingering up her back, making her shiver.

'I'll join the navy and follow you to sea, so I will. Perhaps your mother will think better of me then.' Minn had no intention now of being left behind.

'No,' said Ewan firmly. 'You must stay here and support your mother. I want to know you are safe here for me to come home to one day. There will be much to do when the men leave. Women like you will have to see to the land and the boats. You'll be sorely needed here. Promise me you'll never leave the island. Stay safe for me. I couldn't bear anything to harm you now that we have found each other, *mo ghaoil*. Promise me?'

They knelt on the warm sand of *Traigh gaodh nan seinn* and held hands. She looked into those dark eyes, meaning every word of her vow.

'I, Minna Macfee promise to stay here and wait for your return. I swear on Agnes's grave that I will keep this promise, with the help of God,' she whispered.

Ewan held her face in his hands. 'And I, Ewan George Mackinnon, promise to return to you, all of a piece. Then I'll never leave you again. That's my solemn promise.' They kissed each other to seal this vow. 'If I had a ring I'd be giving it to you, here and now,' he said.

'I need no ring to know you mean every word you say.' Minn smiled into his eyes. They kissed each other shyly, tenderly, but then the kissing grew more urgent and deep as if they were melting into each other, harder and more passionate until Minn was dizzy and drunk with happiness, holding him ever closer into her body, feeling the fire of his response until all her mother's dire warnings exploded like a firework in her head and she drew back.

'No... No... Never turn your back on a man, do not let him near your body... Yield not to temptation.' Her mother's warning was shouting in her ear. Now she knew what temptation was all about. It was about lying in the sand under the stars. It was kissing the salt and sand from Ewan's lips and his neck and his chest. It was about strange stirrings between her legs and a longing to be joined together like a fierce magnetic force. It was begging time to stand still, feeling the warmth of his beating heart, drowning in his black eyes, drawing him ever closer into her body. No! NO! Minn was afraid.

'We'd better go.' Minn sat up brusquely, shaking the sand from her lap. Ewan grabbed her arm.

'Do we have to? I'm so comfortable here with you. The sun is still settling and the moon creeps slowly. Plenty of time yet to seal our vow.

'I won't harm you, Minn, don't be scared. There will be other nights than this when I come on leave. I'll take you to Oban to see the stores and the town and the trains. That's another promise,' he whispered, putting his arm around her, drawing her down again to his side.

'All these bright promises.' Minn shivered, feeling a sudden chill. 'Hold me, Ewan, hold me so tight. I'm afraid.'

'I'll hold you for ever, Minn Macfee, don't you be worrying over me.'

She cooried into his broad chest, watching the purple twilight between day and night, listening to the whish of the water on the gravel, begging the evening sun not to set over the horizon.

'I don't know why I'm after feeling this fear, but just hold me, Ewan, please,' she said, feeling the tears stinging her eyes.

Why was the world going mad around them? They were little more than children thrown into a whirlwind, powerless against the magnetic force of a world at war. Now she had found him how could she let him go?

Four

Normandy 1942

'Keep that bloody stern up, Mackinnon,' yelled a sergeant major's voice in his ears. Ten tired men in a dory with a conked-out engine rowed desperately away from the French shoreline: backs bent double in a frantic rhythm, hoping against hope they would make their rendezvous somewhere in the open sea. Ewan was fighting his exhaustion and fear as the dawn light was streaking to the east, exposing the raiders to the guns along the concrete coast.

From the start the mission had been a total cock-up. Two injured men, one having to be left behind to the mercy of the Boche. Nothing had gone right and now they were rowing for their lives with only fitness and anger fuelling the power of their strokes.

Ewan watched the sweat pouring from the back in front knowing he must distract his mind away from bursting lungs and the cramp in his legs. He must not let the others down. He looked at the grimaces on the faces around him streaked with black grease-paint, black hoods bobbing, eyes blinking with blank, fixed stares. Each man was fighting his own private battle to survive with only the discipline and months of training for just such an escape on their side.

Was this what it was all about: Those months at the White House on the Isle of Arran, based at the shooting lodge of the Duke of Montrose? One of a bunch of raw recruits, all scruffy Herberts and oddballs who wanted to be part of the new special boat squadron section of the Royal Marines: a secret force selected from volunteers mad enough to want more action behind enemy lines after the fall of Dunkirk. Now they were putting all those back-breaking exercises into practice.

Think about Arran, all those bloody exercises, the pain and cunning, Ewan was panting to himself. Think about that daft professor who cycled five hundred miles on his old tin bike to show them all the delights of seaweed. The grimaces of revulsion on some of their faces as they tasted hedge salads, seagull eggs and raw kelp for the first time made Ewan grin to himself. He recalled how in desperation they had paid a local fisherman to smuggle them sole and lobster and scallops for a secret feast over an open fire.

Then there was the old *cailleach* who cursed them for profaning the Sabbath as they skimmed up the cliffs and scared the sheep, creeping about under cover of darkness on the leeward side of paths to avoid sniffing farm dogs and insomniacs. They were a team of raiders, invisible, silent, a lethal bunch lurking in caves, under rocks, canoeing for miles, with a ton of demolition equipment in their backpacks; each individual with his own expertise, his own method of surprise and attack, his own way of disposing of the enemy.

The training was tough. It had to be. At every stage men fell by the wayside, disappearing back to former regiments. Only the fittest survived: the loners and the wiry nonconformists, and now his life depended on this motley crew of misfits from all ranks and none. They were being put to the ultimate test.

Ewan had earned his place as a canoe-cum-beach recce specialist, swimming offshore to test the depths and quality of the shoreline, plumbing the sea bed to test the graduations and shelving at twenty-yard intervals while his mate was on the beach taking sand samples. Each looking out for the other until they swam back to the rendezvous boat to put their information on the waiting chart.

On his last recce off the coast of Dieppe he had found no safe shelving beach but a jagged spit of rocks and was battered by waves ripping his canoe. It had been a struggle to complete the task, to avoid guards on the lookout. Only when the beach had been examined could they swim back to the waiting boat.

Now their skipper was flashing his torch, hoping to goodness the rendezvous boat would loom out of the darkness and haul them all aboard for mugs of hot coffee laced with navy rum.

Why do we keep putting ourselves in these crazy places? he thought, while spurring on his effort, not wanting to slacken the strike rate. He pretended he was a kid again, paddling like fury around the Phetray coast.

Had he not been risking his neck on the sea for as long as he could remember? The sea was his obsession. Ocean-going ships did nothing for him. He liked to be close to the restless water, to his kindred spirit, feeling the spray and the waves underneath him, testing his strength against the elements like some human seal swimming and sunbathing on the rocks. He could see the little tent he had made out of a sail, feel the rough surface and his nights under a stretch of sky and stars.

He discovered that the two-seater canoe was his second skin, light and transportable, silent and easy to conceal. Damn his long legs! They had nearly cost him his selection to the squadron, but his overall wiriness and sea legs were giving him a chance now to prove his worth. They were all rowing for their life.

No one on Phetray knew his true unit. He still wore his old naval uniform, fabricated manoeuvres and excuses why he was still on dry land. Administrative duties, mapping convoys were what his family thought he was doing. If his mother wondered at his weather-beaten muscular wiriness, his reticence about this office job and the bruises appearing after each bad parachute jump, she said nothing.

If only they would accept Minn as his unofficial fiancée, but they were still tight lipped about her and guarded in their opinion of her worth. How could it ever be after Agnes's death? He could see it strained their Christian duty to be pleasant when he brought her home for tea.

Minn tried her best to please, sitting so pale and shy, her manners impeccable as Mother tried to be polite. She was not blind, reading the 'not good enough for our son' plastered across Mother's furrowed brow.

She was working as a postal assistant helping Miss Macfadyen and driving a voluntary mobile canteen for the construction crews building the new aerodrome, serving teas and snacks around the island in the rickety van in all weathers. Her letters hinted at all the new concrete buildings and barracks that soon would bring thousands of airmen and crews to Phetray.

The very thought of Minn was spurring

him on, firing his aching arms with new resolve. She was his girl and he was proud of her. On his last leave he was the first person allowed to take her abroad, to Oban to stay with his aunt, chaperoned by a nervous Eilidh Macfee. He would never forget that look of pure astonishment on her face when she saw the tiers of houses rising up from Oban Harbour, the crowds bustling around the harbour watching their arrival, the fishing fleet and the car traffic. The streets were full of fine shops and the rows of terraced houses rising up the hill with such gracious splendour amazed her. 'When do all these people go away?' she had asked.

'They don't...' Ewan smiled recalling the look of incredulity on her face as she browsed in shop windows. That was what he loved about her: that look of delight in those blue eyes over the simplest of outings.

They dined in cafés and in the hotel. She watched the soldiers and servicemen with girls laughing on their arms going into the public bars. She practised her English slowly in the shops, and he was thrown by such a pukka accent. Each word slowly pronounced in an English accent with no trace of a highland lilt.

They found an antiques shop up a side street full of old furniture and ancient pictures. He wanted to buy her something special as a memento, clothing, a hat, but she turned her nose up at his suggestions, preferring to ferret amongst the old junk until she found an ornament, a china figurine.

'Look, Ewan, this is what I want.' It was a sentimental piece: a shepherdess and boy entwined round a tree. 'You can start off my collection for my hope chest,' she laughed.

He wanted to buy her the sun and the moon, but most of all an antique ring: an aquamarine to match her eyes clustered with seed pearls, but she had eyes only for the ornament and it cost hardly anything.

Then the visit came to an end in Oban station as he headed south and she went back home on the SS *Hebrides* with her mother, carrying her precious purchases as if they were the Crown jewels.

They clung together as Minn sobbed into his coat, great gulps of tears. Ewan could taste the salt tears in her kisses. This was why he was fighting, for Minn and Phetray and the goodness and beauty of all they stood for.

They rowed on in the darkness, faces grimacing with pain. It might be sentimental bosh but he believed in justice and that right would prevail.

His secret warfare was dirty and violent. Smash and grab raids were rush jobs with knives and grenades. However covert the mission it let Jerry know that Britain had not given up the fight. Cross Channel surprise attacks were a reminder that some day soon armed forces would be coming back to France for good. His chosen work was fraught with danger, chances of survival often slim, but what the hell! Someone had to do it!

Ewan wondered how many of his nine lives he had used up. He thought about his first raid on a radar station close to Cherbourg. The plan was to snatch enemy troops to see what calibre of man was guarding the coast. They stormed aboard the motor boat so confidently, squeezed in the hull, and were buffeted by the waves until they were reduced to retching into buckets, staggering ashore to scramble up cliffs with a Bren gun, all set to cut the telegraph wires.

That was the plan but reality was so different. There were too many guards and the coastal defences were too thick. They abseiled back down under cover of darkness empty handed and sped back over the Channel with frustration. Other recces along the Bay of the Seine had been more successful, but tonight's had been a bloody disaster.

The patrol had been parachuted low while two Whitley bombers took the flak above them. They were supposed to land in a stubble field near St Valery en Caux but somehow most of them had overshot the target. Precious time was wasted in gathering in stray parachutes and finding each other in the dark. They were camouflaged in combat jackets, netting hoods and grease-painted faces. A hidden dinghy with supplies had to be found and hidden under the rocks so that the men could begin the beach recce and take samples and measurements.

The routine descent down the cliff injured two men badly and then they realized they were some seven kilometres away from the rendezvous boat. There was little time left to do a decent job as they crept along the coast dragging their wounded. Eventually they made for the waiting dory but the damn engine cut out and there was nothing for it but to strip off and paddle her out.

Far in the distance blinked a flashlight from the motor transport. 'Hurry up,' came the signal for it was almost dawn.

Ewan lifted his gaze. Surely the boat was almost out of danger now? Then a searing flash of light was bearing down on them with a sickening splatter of gunfire from a patrol boat. The dory rose up into the air with the swell tipping the crew sideways into the water as bullets ripped the surface.

Ewan dived down for cover, his eardrums bursting with the roar and commotion. The rest was a blur of flashing lights and screeching voices. It was every man for himself now. He did not fancy spending the rest of the war 'in the bag' so he took another lungful of air and dived down into the darkness. He would head out to sea and take his chance.

There must be some hiding place from that cursed searchlight.

He was swimming offshore, drifting with the tide; the sea was still warm, buoying him gently back and forth into the inky blackness, but streaks of dawn light were rising higher in the east. His mind was spinning from panic to calm. He knew he was tiring but tiredness meant death and he wanted to stay alive. How he wanted to stay alive, but the sea was warm and oily drowsiness would soon overcome his strength of will.

In the darkness he could hear voices calling, Gaelic voices, as he floated helplessly now: the sea *cailleachs*, sirens of the deep calling him down to play with them.

'No!' Ewan spat the salt water from his lips. 'You canna have me. You've had Agnes, you're not having my bones!' Every stroke was an effort of will but the voices called out louder and he tried to struggle as the arm came up to drag him under.

'No! Ach away with you.' The arm was too strong and held him fast.

Five

RAF Phetray, 1942

When the postie volunteered for the army, Minn Macfee wasted no time in volunteering to drive his old van. Archie the blacksmith gave her extra lessons and soon she collected deliveries from the ferry and bumped her way around the island trying to eke out their meagre petrol ration. Driving came easily for she had the confidence of youth and the wings of love at her heels. All the wolf whistles and calls from the construction crews just rolled off her as she delivered mail to the civilian gangs and took orders for filled rolls and pastries.

It was hard to persuade her fearful mother to be a passenger for a tour of the island in the van. Eilidh surveyed all the concrete hangars and huts with horror. 'Yon's a very Sodom and Gomorrah breathing fire over our heads night and day … to be sure there'll be trouble for us. We'll no be safe in our beds!' she said.

At the same time she was proud of her daughter's connection to the minister's son. It gave her new purpose in rising from her bed to sweep the floor, milk the cow, collect the eggs for her basket and hold her head a little higher in the stores. Minn was going to marry above herself so she was.

The coming of an airbase to Phetray was bringing new life and prosperity to the islanders. There were billeting fees, extra provisions ordered, extra whisky for the bar. A city of grey concrete was erected in the middle of the island with its own piped water and electricity, tarmacadam roads replaced the dirt tracks, with look-out posts and Nissen hut barracks lined up alongside.

It was rumoured that there would be more airmen than civilians living on the island, and many more men than girls, news of which worried many a crofter husband and father alike.

'You must keep busy and your eyes forward and don't give temptation any encouragement,' warned Eilidh every time Minn left for work. 'Where men and maids meet, oft comes mischief and there's plenty wee Jezebels on this island with time on their hands to make plenty mischief. Mark my words.'

'Oh, Mother, why must you take the joy out of everything? Why is it so wrong to enjoy a crack or two with the airmen? They are such gentlemen,' Minn argued. The airbase was bringing life to this dull place with servicemen in jaunty caps whistling and waving.

'Get them on their own and you'll soon

find they're no Christian men, these gentlemen of yours, after only one thing, I'm after thinking, even from a girl who is spoken for! There is only joy in heaven after the work is done and sins are paid for, *mo ghaoil.* Don't go looking for pleasure in this life. I have never found any.'

'That's because you don't open your eyes and see the beauty all around you, the flowers and music and the dancing. Why don't you mix more with your neighbours?' Minn pleaded, sensing her mother was lonely with only her spinning wheel and knitting for company.

'I live as my Church says I must live, separated from the world's wicked ways. It is the only true preparation for the life ahead when we, the chosen ones, shall be as new creatures in the eyes of the Lord, not frail sinners at his mercy every hour of the day! Get you to your work and mind what I say.'

There was no talking sense to Mother when she was in this mood and Minn was glad to leave the gloom of their four walls for the brightness of the day.

She lived for Ewan's letters, savouring each page, reading them over and over again until she knew them by heart. She always called into the Manse when they arrived to share his news, sensing that his letters to them were shorter and more dutiful. She dusted the little figurine with care each morning until it sparkled in the sunshine from the tiny window of her boxroom. With each rub she made a wish for his safe return.

Driving the mobile canteen van grew from the island's first haphazard catering effort to supplying teams of builders each day. Then it was formalized into a special post by representatives of the Women's Rural Institute. They thought a single girl far too young and flighty to be let loose on her own among airmen, but everyone knew of Minn's unofficial engagement and felt she could be trusted not to seduce the workers and jeopardize the war effort.

Minn took this job seriously, checking her engine, her supplies and the dates on her pass on to the site as if she was on a mission. Hers was the neatest, cleanest canteen. All her old training at the Crannog stood her in good stead. She collected fresh supplies of home baking when rations would allow: Forfar bridies, sausage rolls, jam tarts and shortbread. Everything was labelled up and stacked neatly in her own military operation.

Once the flap was lowered for a shelf, the urn brought to boil and the cakes and snacks displayed under lacy cloths to shield them from the dust there was just room for a slim whippet of a girl to stand behind and take orders.

Sometimes Minn's own daily trip around the island was held up by lines of supply vehicles jamming the tracks just off the ferry transport. She would park up in a passing place until the sand settled down. Then there were grouses and grumbles if her van was late for a shift. In all weathers she wore sensible overalls and a turban round her hair, even when her feet were frozen and the van was rocking in the westerly gale. Standards were kept up and nothing was stored away until it was washed up, polished, 'Mirro'ed until sparkling and all her surfaces spotless. Then the crockery was boxed and strapped up, the shelf raised and the van locked for another morning.

She was getting to know all her regular customers' likes and dislikes. She tried to provide a variety of biscuits but supplies were erratic especially when the boat could not land. Then an SOS call went out to the island bakers to do their bit. She never let the men down even if all that was left on the shelf was a cheery smile and fresh gossip as they warmed cold hands on a hot mug of Bovril.

This was the safe little cocoon she was building around her promise to Ewan; being useful in her own sphere was valuable war work and worthy of respect. She saw herself in the service of her country. Does not an army march on its stomach? Phetray was far removed from the horrors of bombings and blitz on the Clyde and the terrible carnage among the convoys crossing the Atlantic, but familiar names were appearing in the casualty lists in the *Oban Times* nevertheless.

Then came that terrible accident when a Halifax doing its routine training of circuits and bumps stalled when coming in to land. She had been serving teas and watched in horror as it crashed in flames on the beach. The smoke could be seen across the island and people came running thinking Hitler had landed.

Eight good men were incinerated in a tin coffin. Such a waste. She had worked through the night to keep the investigators plied with warm tea, feeling sick at the thought that the young men would be buried in coffins filled with sand.

Minn polished her porcelain each night like a talisman, safe in the knowledge that Ewan was protected by her daily rituals, until the night when the minister stood in the doorway of the cottage, dripping with rain from his oilskin cape. She was hoping for a letter in his pocket until she saw his face drained of all expression. 'Minna, *mo ghaoil* ... bad news I'm afraid.'

Minn led him to the fireside to Uncle Niall's empty chair and Mother poked the fire nervously at this unexpected visit.

'What's happened? It's Ewan, isn't it?' Minn's voice quivered. His silence was frightening her.

Reverend Mackinnon nodded sadly, his

cheeks sunken and his mouth tight with controlled emotion. He looked an old man in the firelight trying to hold back his tears. 'You'll have to be brave. Ewan is missing, presumed drowned in some action at sea. I have few details. The telegram said nothing more.'

'What ship was he on? Was it sunk?' Minn's voice seemed to come from far away. She was standing rooted to the rug like a wooden post, unable to move.

'I don't think he was sunk. It is something to do with the Marine Units ... some hush-hush encounter. We knew he was doing undercover work. He never said much, only hinted, but obviously no one will tell us.'

'Then he could have been taken prisoner,' Minn insisted stunned by the discovery of Ewan's secret war work.

'The boat was hit, child. No one survived. This much I was told when I rang.' At this bleak news Eilidh started to wail, rocking and moaning, in the old way, back and forth, distracting them with little moans.

'Whisht! Mother let's hear him out.' Minn was cold with fury. 'How can they be sure? He could have been picked up in a lifeboat? Where did it happen?' She knew all about the air sea rescue units scattered around the islands that went out in search of pilots and crews ditched in the Atlantic and the aeroplanes that skimmed the surface of the water to spot life rafts. There had been some spectacular rescues.

'It was not that sort of operation, child. I fear we'll never know the truth of the matter,' he whispered, trying to hold back his tears.

'And poor Mistress Mackinnon to be losing her two bairns. How is she the now?' Eilidh shook her head in disbelief.

'We've put her to bed with a draught from the doctor. It was seemly to be telling you before the rest of the parish. I'm so sorry, child.'

Minn stood rigid, stabbing her chest with her fists. 'He's not feeling dead ... not here in my heart. I would be knowing in here if he was gone. Until there's proof I shall go on hoping. The sea shan't have him!' she cried.

'Don't build on false hopes, *mo ghaoil*. The fall is always the harder to bear. Better to accept now and move forward slowly,' replied the minister shaking his head.

'But we don't know for certain. Until I know for sure... Thank you for telling me. I know I was never your first choice for a daughter-in-law.'

'Minna! Remember who it is you're speaking to!' snapped her mother, bowing her head with embarrassment.

'The truth is told and the devil shamed. I speak as I find. We loved each other from the start, Ewan and I. Don't make me give him up for dead yet. Hope is all I have to cling to. I shall call on Mistress Mackinnon when she feels able to receive me. You do understand?'

'Yes, of course. Believe what you must but the Lord will guide you in due course. We shall be praying that you are right and we are wrong.' The minister rose and made for the door.

It is a pity that the Good Lord could not have guided Ewan's boat to safety in the first place, Minn thought as she bowed her head, but bit her lip. 'Thank you for coming Minister.'

He paused at the door looking her straight in the eye. 'This is not an occasion for thanksgiving, I'm after thinking.' The man stooped under the lintel out into the rain.

Minn marched out next day to *Traigh gaodh nan seinn*, to their special beach, where memories of Ewan were strong. She scoured the grey-green sea for comfort, watching the tide racing over the sands throwing seaweed and flotsam over the shingle. She stood like a finger of rock battered by the wind, unbending in her anger. If his spirit was waiting for her there she would know. There was no one there.

'Listen to me. The sea shan't have him!' she cried into the wind clutching on to their love token, polishing it with a cloth like Aladdin's lamp. Ewan can't be dead. His name must never be scratched on the war memorial. He's just missing. No news was good news. How could such a strong swimmer, a human seal, and such a survivor not find his way out of the sea to return home again? He must come back. Her whole happiness depended on it.

Then she thought of his sister, Agnes. She must take flowers to the grave and beg his sister to help them bring Ewan back to Phetray once more.

Word soon flew around the island of the fate of the minister's son and the gossips clacked and turned to eye Minn with pity and not a little relief. It did not do for cottar girls to get above themselves in marriage. Minn stood behind her counter stoically refusing to be comforted. He was still alive. She could feel his pulse in her heart.

She rattled along the dirt track planning all sorts of crazy schemes to rescue him. First she would join the Wrens or the Waafs and go in search of him, but no one was going to tell her where to look. He had lied to her about the nature of his posting. She had thought as had the islanders that he was in the navy. Now she was told he was in the Marines.

There was news of daring raids on French shipping ports. Was it in one of these escapades that he had been lost? Perhaps he was wandering alone, dazed and in danger. One of these days he would roll off the *Hebrides* with his knapsack over his shoulder like jolly jack tar, his cap stuck at the back of his head, laughing and grinning... She was too busy dreaming to take much notice of the long grey road misted by sea haar.

There was a slide and a bump and a crunch as her van veered off the track into the watery ditch among the bog grass and the horsetails. In her daydreaming her concentration had lapsed and her precious van was stuck fast in a rut. She banged on the steering wheel in frustration and burst into tears, tears long overdue

'You stupid *cailleach!* Silly stupid bitch! Half your crockery will be broken, pastries reduced to crumbs, the back axle probably snapped, the whole van in ruins and no one will get their elevenses!'

Rivers of tears poured down her face soaking her handkerchief. She was sobbing as if her heart would break.

A face appeared at the window, a worried leathery face. 'Are you all right, miss?'

'It's gone off the road. It's all my fault, Ogh...' Minn babbled in Gaelic and the face looked puzzled.

'She's in a right state, speaking double dutch. Have we a *Teuchtar* to translate?'

Minn heard his comment and looked up through her tears. 'I can speak the King's English when I have to. Can you please get me out of here?'

The young man smiled and touched his cap. 'In two shakes of lamb's tail, miss. Just let's be having you out of there.'

There was a convoy of canvas trucks lined up, with blue berets poking out and men jumping down with ropes. The rope was attached and the van lifted back up on to the straight and narrow track none the worse for its accident.

Minn stood there snivelling, feeling foolish, red faced, mouthing her thanks to anyone in earshot.

The young sergeant smiled and showed her the few bumps that would need knocking out. 'Just a bash on the wing. You were lucky it didn't turn over. Let's open her up and see if there's any damage inside. I suggest we make a cup of tea and wave these lads on. You look as if you've had a nasty shock, miss.'

Minn could feel herself shivering with shock and relief as she opened the van door and saw that nothing had shifted from its secure shelf. She soon had the water on the boil and the collapsible stool took the weight of her trembling knees. 'How can I thank you? My mind wasn't on the job, I'm afraid.'

'Just let's get some sweet tea down you, miss. That's the stuff to give the troops as've had a bad turn. Sergeant Broddick at your service.' He smiled, holding out his hand and she clasped it, looking up into a square face with a neat moustache over the lip and warm brown eyes; not a handsome visage but open and weathered, creased up like corrugated paper.

'I'm Minn Macfee.' She was still shaking from the shock.

'Come out in the fresh air and sit down. We'll soon fix you a cuppa. The cup that cheers but don't inebriate as my old mother keeps telling me, but she's never tasted Naafi tea. That strong it could fuel a Spitfire!' he paused, seeing the smile on her face.

'That's better, a smile on yer face, at last. Don't look so worried. Get that down the hatch.'

Minn sipped the piping hot tea and surveyed her team of rescuers rolling onwards toward the camp. 'Just arrived?'

'We have that, a right rum do on the boat, rocking from side to side, worse than the Big Dipper at Blackpool. My giddy aunt! My stomach was wrapped round me throat. It's a bit of a bleak hole, if you don't mind me saying so, just sheep, cows and a few stone cottages,' answered Sergeant Broddick, looking around him with disappointment.

'You were lucky to land at all, these September tides are rough,' she replied.

'Well now I'm here I intend to make the most of it, miss, and things is looking up already, don't you think, lads?' Sergeant Ken Broddick winked at his driver and crewmates.

Minn ignored his flirty manner, anxious to be on her way to the far end of the island. 'Thank you but I think I'll manage fine the now, Sergeant Broddick.'

'Any time, any place, at your service. It was a pleasure to be of assistance. Hope to meet you again but not in a ditch. Byesy-bye, toodle pip.' He waved.

She climbed back into her van to clean up their mess. Thinking about Ewan was dangerous when she was driving. From now on she must concentrate on one thing at a time and wait for his return. He was not dead, of that she was certain.

Six

France, 1943

Ewan awoke on a mattress of straw covered by a horse blanket. He could hear rustling in the hayloft, suddenly alert to strange surroundings and the sounds of the night stable. Where was he? Everything was a blur of images, thrashing in the water, salt in his mouth. Then the arm was grabbing him, pulling him into the boat.

He was alive, but where? A stab of pain in his knee jolted him. He could just about finger a rag bandage round his leg; its throbbing worried him. In the half-light he saw the enamel jug and glugged down its water with relief. He was feeling hot. His stomach stirred to life.

Lying back to assess his predicament he tried to piece together the raid, the explosion and his rescue. Hellfire! He must be still in France behind enemy lines. The odds against evading capture were stacked against him.

In the heat of the escape he'd had only his life vest and combat trousers and his plimsolls. Where were his belt and his escape equipment? At the bottom of the Channel or waiting at some police station? He heard someone climbing the stairs, panting with the effort.

An old woman in long black skirt and apron appeared. '*N'avez pas peur, mon ami, vous êtes avec amis.*' She smiled a toothless grin.

'*Vous parlez français?*'

'*Pas beaucoup...*'Ewan answered in his best schoolboy French, struggling to lift himself. How long had he been here? Days, by the smell of him.

'*Vous êtes soldat?*'

He nodded.

'*Mon mari était soldat aussi... Verdun...*'The widow gave him a chunk of black bread and some cheese smelling as ripe as his armpits.

'*Merci beaucoup, madame.*'The pain in his leg made him wince and fall back.

'Eh la!' She examined the bloody bandage, shaking her head. '*Vous restez là ...*

bientôt Monsieur le Curé ... arriverai.'

He lay back. There was nothing he could do with a festering wound. How on earth had he managed to gash it so badly? It was enough to know the old woman was risking her life in hiding him here. How many others were shielding him? His leg needed attention. Perhaps the priest would bring a doctor and he could be on his way, but how the hell could he move on when he had not the faintest idea where he was heading?

The priest came when the sun was high bringing more bread and cheese and a bottle of good wine. He had a little English and between them they were able to understand each other. He examined Ewan's wound carefully. The priest called himself André and told him that he would be addressed only as Etienne.

'You were rescued by fishermen on the coast and passed down the line to us. A bullet went through your leg. It is safer you stay here a while longer until all is prepared. I'm afraid there is no one to see to your leg. Monsieur le Docteur was arrested a month ago. It does not look good for him. Things are rough here in Ste Eulalie. Many are taken prisoner. The defences are strong. We wait for the coming of allies but after the raid on Dieppe...' The curé shrugged his shoulders. 'Ah well, patience. God alone knows... I will speak to the committee now

108

that you are able to talk.'

'Committee?' Ewan looked puzzled.

'We have to take care. They will ask you questions. They have to be sure before they send you down the line. Let me see the leg.' The stench was bad. 'We'll have to deal with this the old way. I will come back later when I can.'

He returned when it was dark with hot water and some strips of clean linen. There was a pot of foul-smelling green paste. The priest smiled sadly and apologized. *Pardon, Etienne,* but there is something we must do first.' He produced a jar of writhing maggots.

Ewan turned his eyes from the sight of them, trying not to squirm. All his tough special training, eating insects and other unmentionables, but the thought of those creatures on his leg made him feel faint. The curé placed the maggots in the open wound and covered them with the jar. 'It is primitive but some of the old ways are best. They will feed off the pus wound so we can dress it afresh.'

Ewan was in no position to protest. He did not want to saw off his own gangrenous leg without anaesthetic!

The next day, under cover of darkness and curfew, the room was filled with a bunch of tough-looking men from the village. One of them held a lantern into his face. 'Your name, rank and number.'

Ewan produced his dog tag out of his boot heel. He could not tell them his real commando unit but his naval cover was sound.

'We will check that you are who you say you are. Spies are planted on us to break the groups and evasion lines. If we find you are Boche... You will never leave this barn alive.'

Ewan nodded weakly, feeling the fever kicking into his system again. *'Je comprends.'*

A man delved into his pocket for a slip of paper that he shoved under Ewan's nose. *'Vous dites?'*

The words wobbled before his eyes but he smiled as he repeated, 'She sells seashells on the seashore... And the shells she sells are seashells I'm sure!' adding the extra line for good measure. They seemed to visibly relax at this, but Ewan sensed there were more tests to follow. He was putting all their lives at risk. They had to be sure of him.

'Why are you here in the Pas de Calais?' asked their leader.

Ewan was on guard. Perhaps they were the traitors, waiting to trick him.

'It was a training exercise. There were difficulties and the engine broke down ... a fiasco!'

'How did you get the wound?' Suddenly one of the men crept round behind him and blasted some insult in his ear.

'Pardon? What the fucking hell was that all about?' They all laughed.

'Just another little test, *mon ami*. You are definitely English.'

'*Non, je suis écossais... D'Ecosse, compris?*' They smiled, not caring about the difference.

'Welcome, monsieur. Now we can move you to somewhere more comfortable and try to mend your leg. You cannot go on your way with such a leg ballooning out of your trousers.'

He was laid on an old door and carried through woods to the edge of the village where he was rested in the attic of the curé's presbytery under the widow Eugénie's watchful eye. The room was sparsely furnished: a bed, a skylight window with shutters, a candle and an old armoire with space for him to crouch in if there was a raid. He was ordered to make no sound night or day. There were those only too willing to report unusual movement in an empty house. For his comfort there was a marble washstand with a cupboard for his potty.

He would have to stay immobile until his wound healed and try to keep up his strength and muscle tone with silent exercises. If his bed-ridden legs grew weak escape might prove difficult. It was going to be a long and boring convalescence.

André brought him tomes of ancient books to read and a dictionary for translation. There were some wonderful old illustrations that in desperation he began to

111

copy on the bare walls to distract himself. He had loved drawing at school but no one had ever encouraged his talent, thinking it too girlish a hobby for a minister's son. Here he began to fill the walls with pictures of stone cottages and boats, the rigging of sails in Kilphetrish harbour and the faces of his friends and his beloved Minn.

The curé was amused at this initiative, pointing in admiration to Minn.

'*Votre femme?*'

Ewan smiled, putting his hands together in prayer. 'Not yet but soon ... when I go home.'

The curé himself took his own sketch pad and pencil when he travelled over his parish hamlets close to the coast. He tried to memorize any coastal defence systems and gun enforcements visible from his parish round. These he drew carefully, stuffing the paper down the spine of his missal, which was passed under the noses of guards and Milice down the line of known Resistance workers.

They were trying to accrue as much useful information as possible to help in the final assault on the coast of the Pas de Calais.

Ewan was impatient to get stronger and fitter and he began to exercise in his room, pacing the floor, bending and squatting, standing on his head and hands to strengthen his shoulders and arms. How had Eugénie managed to find such food for him? There was fruit and ham, bread and hot nourishing broths that lined his stomach and brought colour back to sunken cheeks.

How could he ever repay his hosts for such generosity? Only by getting fit and leaving them quickly to distemper over the evidence of his stay in the attic.

Sometimes he was allowed to roam the woods at night, silently tracing the secret poacher's path that twisted around the village to avoid patrols and guards. The comité met in the isolated farmhouse of Monsieur 'Didier'. Here the group planned their offensives: one small link in a larger chain of resistance and Maquis operating around the towns and cities in the forests and villages.

If only Ewan had found another canoeist from the squadron on the run, another survivor, they could have attempted to paddle back across the Channel. Others had made such attempts when the tides and weather were favourable. Weakened and alone it was unthinkable. Soon he would be passed along the secret escape line, putting so many other lives at risk. Yet Ewan was tempted to delay his escape and pit his wits alongside the Maquis using his training to teach them demolition tricks. It was the least he could do. He begged the curé to let him stay.

'It's not safe for you to stay. There is already suspicion in the village. It is enough for us to know we have helped one more soldier to return to fight once more. That is our reward. Tomorrow you will leave. Take care, trust no one. Use your instinct, if something feels wrong avoid it. At dusk I will take you through the forest where someone will come out to meet you with the password. You have no papers or identity. You must not go near an open road. It will be a long walk for you. God be with you.'

'How can I thank you?' Ewan was almost in tears.

'Get yourself back safely to your island and return one day to see us when victory is ours. May the cross of Lorraine be your guide.' The priest raised his hand in a blessing.

As Ewan dressed in his thick trousers and pullover and borrowed boots like a farm labourer, his black beret pulled over his eye, he knew he was dark enough to pass as a Frenchman, except that his accent would let him down.

Someone surely had transmitted his position by now to Britain. Once his family and Minn knew he was safe perhaps he could make himself useful to the next Resistance group and earn his rescue. His folks in Phetray would understand this delay.

He was passed slowly from village to village, hidden under sacking in vans, walking kilometres on his gammy leg through dense forests. His papers were basic. He was posing as a wounded soldier now doing agricultural labour. The documents claimed that he was deaf in one ear and not very bright. They would not pass tight scrutiny.

It was a time of despair and betrayal in the countryside. Only in villages was he protected from discovery. In a small village the Resistance knew who was for them and who was a possible informer. He was tested and checked over many times. Sometimes he was allowed to go out on the reception committee to torch in a Lysander dropping supplies or a secret agent. He taught young boys how to make fuses and detonators, to lay explosives on the railway track, to swim under bridges and place charges. There were hit and run raids on isolated guard patrols but the consequences of such offensives were appalling for the local village. Hostages were shot in reprisal.

His schoolboy French quickly became rough and fluent but his accent was unfit to be spoken in public without arousing suspicion. He lived rough in the woods where his survival training made him an excellent scout.

Sometimes they holed up in shepherds' huts, roasted birds over fires, sleeping by day, moving by night. Sometimes when there was paper he found himself sketching the black weary faces of his *amis*, firelight drawings to amuse that were thrown on the fire just in case. He played with scenes of home in his head, the colours of the island, the textures of pebbles on the shore so different from this world of the green wood and darkness.

Rules were strict and punishments harsh. There could be no risks. If the signs outside a house were wrong, the curtains closed instead of open, the bottles on the wrong step, they would make long detours, criss-crossing their tracks to see if they had been trailed.

Their small raids would not alter the course of world action but cutting telegraph wires and sabotaging points and track slowed down the enemy in their region. Making a nuisance of themselves spelt out that there were those whose day would soon come again.

Many months after his rescue, when winter had set into the forest, Ewan awoke to hear the repeated hooting of some imitation owl from the loft of the farmhouse hideout. He was up and dressed in seconds, shinning up on to the roof, his eyes straining to see a line of grey uniforms snaking up the path towards the ruined farmhouse. His companions were down the back of the roof and into the forest along a trail before the searchlight would beam out on their escape.

Ewan could feel himself sweating but strangely clear headed. If he was caught he would be shot. His progress through France had been untroubled so far. Now came the day of reckoning and he had a head start. It was planned that he should race on alone towards the river and, should anything happen, get himself out of the region as quickly as he could and make for the south-west coast of France. At least he knew this present terrain.

Ewan always felt safer close to water and he knew where there was a small dinghy hidden, but to his dismay the boat was not in its usual place. Had they been betrayed by one of their group? Was someone now screaming out in agony the names of their cell?

There was nothing for it but to swim across the chilly water, strip off his clothes and, tying them in a bundle around his neck, lie them on his back. Ewan sensed sniffer dogs making their way through the wood. He hoped the others had managed to make their way to prearranged rendezvous for just such an emergency. Nothing had been left to chance, but he wondered why the Jerries were on a manhunt.

Had some aeroplane ditched and they were hunting for a crew of airmen? Had some sabotage plan gone wrong? Thank God no one used real names. Real names meant death and torture. You couldn't reveal what you didn't know, could you? He prayed he'd never find out.

The chill of the water numbed him for a second, but it was fast flowing and he struggled to ford a straight line. The current was forcing him forward and he thought of Agnes and his own fear of drowning. This was the third time he had been at the mercy of water. Would his luck hold? He must find a branch, an overhanging branch...

Ewan forced his neck high to catch a glimpse of the riverbank and saw in the distance a clump of trees. This was his only chance to snatch at a branch and haul himself up from the current. He could feel himself tiring with the effort of keeping his clothes on his back.

When he saw the arm of the branch reaching out he lurched with his hand to grab it and cling on long enough to bring up his other arm like a trapeze artist. He pulled himself forward until he could feel the rocks beneath his plimsolls. He shivered in the moonlight as he spread out his sodden clothes.

He lay in silence listening for telltale signs but there were only the night sounds of the forest to comfort him. Then he cut swathes of leafy shrubbery to pleat into a makeshift shelter, piled dried leaves from the forest floor on to himself and rubbed himself back to life. Perhaps he might tickle some trout for breakfast, he mused wryly. This was no joking matter. He was back at square one, alone behind enemy lines. He was far from the coast with no proper papers. All that was going for him was a cursory map in his head, animal cunning and a better grasp of the lingo than before. Then there was his nose for open sea. Not much to go on but it would have to suffice if he wanted to see Phetray once more.

Seven

Phetray

As the bleak winter months dragged on with still no news of Ewan's fate, Minn relied more and more on the cheery presence of Sergeant Broddick and his transport crew to brighten the dullness of her routine. They would often meet at the harbour or pass each other on the roads round the island. The boys would stop the trucks for a quick cup of tea, inviting her to watch their football matches and camp concerts.

Life was going on around her as if Ewan no longer existed. It was hard to cling to the belief that somewhere he was alive. The temptation was to go out, especially when there were weekly cinema screenings on offer at the base, but if Ewan was a captive now she would not be shaming him by going out to enjoy herself. She would stay indoors and knit scarves and balaclavas, boot socks and gloves for the sailors' comfort fund; anything to keep her hands from trembling.

There was no news from the Red Cross, and his commanding officer wrote a letter of condolence to Ewan's parents that duly found its way to the stone cottage at Kilphetrish Bay.

Minn's spirits sank to their lowest at his words but that stubborny streak inside her could not believe that Ewan would not return. She withdrew into herself, finding it harder to put on a brisk business-as-usual mask for the troops and took to taking long walks along the shoreline, no longer able to smile to customers behind the post office counter when people asked if there was any news of the minister's son.

Even her mother was deserting her now. 'You have to face the truth after nine months, *mo ghaoil*. Since those sad words came to the manse there's been not one word that he lives. It's time to be putting away your hopes and getting on with your life. There's plenty of handsome blue fish in these waters only waiting to jump into your net. I want to see you provided for like I never was. Don't waste your looks in tears over what can never be. Grief has made me an old woman before my time. Anyone can see yon young sergeant has taken a shine to you.'

'You've changed your tune,' was all she

could reply. Her sadness weighed heavy. How could she even look at another man?

Sometimes it felt as if the whole island was watching to see what she would do next. The coming of the handsome pilots and their bombers, the madcap Polish crews and all the staff needed to run such a huge operation was giving Phetray a ringside seat in the Atlantic theatre of war.

Yet Minn felt only frustrated and trapped by the restrictions imposed by her work and her mother's needs. She had so little to offer the war effort. Working in a factory did not appeal but she desperately wanted to get off the island away from her sad memories. Had she not promised Ewan to stay put and help in the fields with the harvest, support the community and do her bit in this small world? She was trained for little else but service. Staying on was a way of showing faith that one day he would return.

By early 1944 doubt was creeping into her mind that Ewan could still be alive. Why was there no news? She walked along the beach, taking comfort from the roar of the crashing tide

'How can I keep loving a man who is no longer alive? How can I mourn the loss of a love that won't go away? Where are you now?' she cried into the wind as memories flooded over her. John Mackinnon's words about accepting loss were ringing in her ears. Fear of being without Ewan had blinded her to the reality, shielded her from the pain of facing the truth. He was not coming back, not ever.

If he was gone then all their promises were null and void too. Perhaps with this New Year coming it was time to take the plunge and begin a new life after all. She was earning enough to go to the mainland, to see the world across the water that once she had glimpsed so briefly in Oban a lifetime ago.

How can you live by yourself? she wondered. Who will you turn to in a big city? A fear flooded over her, crushing any resolve to leave. Perhaps it was better to stay put in case Ewan did return.

Then there was always Sergeant Ken, her ever-present shadow. He was good company. He brought her parcels back from his leave. He wrote to his mother and brought photos of his family and postcards of a place called the Black Pool, with its sandy beaches and seaside fun. He would sit round the fire with Mother or walk with Minn across the machair in search of duck eggs. He mended her tyre punctures and taught her how to maintain the van.

'Good old Ken.' When he was on leave she missed his honking horn at the passing places on the new tarmac road. He wrote to her and his mother added her own invitation.

'Do come and visit us. We have heard all

about your lovely island. We'll make you welcome. A friend of Ken's is a friend of ours. He is such a good son to his mother...'

Minn was tempted and Mother sensed she was weakening.

'You could do far worse for yoursel'. I know he can never be a minister's son but he has a good position and a steady way with him. His eyes mist with longing when he looks on your face.'

'I can't think of him like Ewan. I hardly know the heart of him,' Minn argued, puzzled at her mother's eagerness to see her settled with a man.

'Don't waste yer chances dreaming about what you canny have. Use what the Good Lord has given you,' Eilidh offered.

'How can you say that after all those dire warnings about men only being after one thing?' she argued.

'Aye, but once a girl's wed then no one can shame her if she lets him have his way. A bonny lassie like you needs a ring on her finger against temptation, I'm after thinking.'

They were sitting in the darkness of the cottage, and Minn looked around at the sooty walls and pressed earth floor, the humble furniture, longing for the space of the Crannog.

'When I look at Ken Broddick, I see a square honest face, muddy hair and hazel eyes. Nothing more do I feel inside but gratitude that he helps me out.' She was trying to be honest.

'He'll be the sort of man to shower you with presents and kindness, with a pair of strong arms to protect you from the icy blast of loneliness. Do not live as I've done at the beck and call of ungrateful men. Ken's a good man. You could do far worse,' Mother replied.

'But I don't love him!'

'Ach away! What's love got to do with the price of beef? Just some silly notion of our betters to make our drudgery more appetizing, I'm thinking. Look to your future, *mo ghaoil*. I won't always be here to guide you. Perhaps it's time you made provision for our old age.'

'Mother!' she was shocked at her mother's bluntness, but how easy was the temptation to find a safe haven in a stormy sea. Once the idea lodged in her mind, it was hard to ignore. Perhaps a future with Ken in some romantic place called the Black Pool sands would warm these cold years of loneliness.

If Ewan was lost, then she didn't care much what happened. How could she ever love twice in the same way? This first love would always be the deepest and the best but she had to be practical. Better to grab what was on hand, said her angry heart. You might as well make the best of things and live for today not tomorrow if you want to

124

get rid of this pain.

She looked up at the little china shepherd-ess and boy shining on the mantelpiece. It was just an ornament, a silly romantic orna-ment. It was time to put it away in a box. It looked out of place in this poor shabby room.

She must put away her mourning drab-ness and find some colourful stuff to wear. It was time to smarten up and get out of this dark house to make a future for herself.

The courtship was brief. Ken was ardent and Minn was too numb to care. Once she flashed her sparkling blue eyes in his direc-tion, stunning him with rays of undivided attention, dancing to his tune flirtatiously, singing duets around the piano at the ceilidhs, Ken was easy pickings, caught in the spidery web of love.

They kissed and cuddled in the van but she would never take Ken near any place where she had lain with Ewan. That was sacred ground, out of bounds.

'Now you're my girl, I want to take you home to show you off to my family. We can have a right good holiday. I'll take you to Blackpool and we'll go dancing in the Tower Ballroom.'

She nodded without much enthusiasm. He was a distraction and she was lonely and mis-erable, wanting only the comfort of another man's arms around her, any man would have done but it just happened to be Ken.

He was going to take her away from the island and that was just what she needed to hear, but Mother had other plans.

'No girl of mine goes abroad on her own. It's an invitation to sin! The tongues of Phetray will clang like kirk bells at such a disgrace, if you catch my meaning, Sergeant Broddick,' she whispered.

'Then we'll make an honest woman of her before we go and it can be our honeymoon. What do you think, Minn love?'

She was speechless at this sudden proposal, mother's cunning, shocked by the speed of things. It was easy to drift into the planning of a modest highland wedding with a high tea in the sergeants' mess. There was a tweed suit to be sewn, a veil to be borrowed, a trousseau to be found from the last of Lady Rose's oddments, the minister to be visited and Ken's leave to be sorted.

Yet sometimes, as she lay in the box bed wide awake listening to the wind howling over the roof, it was as if it was all happening to someone else, as if she no longer inhabited her own body, as if she was borrowing someone else's dream. It was too soon, warnings whispered, but she was past caring. Half a cake was better than none.

She sensed that the Mackinnons were relieved to see her married and away from their door. Ken got permission to marry and they made their vows before a packed kirk with Uncle Niall home long enough to give her away one Saturday afternoon in March 1944.

Clothing coupons for a two-piece tweed suit and new shoes bought from a postal catalogue meant there was little left over for any fancy underwear. The mess put on a spread and the islanders provided a faith supper to augment the celebrations. There was going to be another celebration when they got to Ken's house in Lancashire for all his relatives to meet his new bride.

All the doubtings melted in the warmth of everyone's kindness, but still in a corner of her mind the yearning for Ewan never went away. She should be marrying a sailor in navy not some airman in air force blue.

Yet deep in her heart, in that part that never fails to see through the fog of grief, she heard warning voices; but Minn didn't want to listen within when it contradicted what was going on without.

The wedding night was spent chastely in a haze of whisky fumes sleeping in Mother's brass bed lying shyly side by side, Ken not wanting to disturb her snoring.

The boat journey ferrying them south to Oban Station and on to Glasgow was rough. Minn's heart went out to the darkened city so bomb blasted and blackened by war. The smoke from the steam engines made Minn sneeze. She had no eyes for her husband when there was so much to see out of the carriage window.

On the second night of the honeymoon Minn lay wide awake listening to strange city sounds, afraid of the crowds and the darkness. They were staying overnight in a boarding house in a street of tall tenement houses where the roar of trams and motor-bikes, drunks shouting and singing underneath their window kept them awake all night. Ken dozed fitfully, bitten by fleas, and Minn was covered with red lumps.

Her husband woke and stretched his arm across her breast.

'Come on let's be having you...' He put his hand between her thighs and Minn froze as he heaved himself on top of her and began to fumble between her legs. He moaned and muttered, 'Come on love, open up ... it's alright, yer married now...'

'Open up what?' Minn struggled, having no idea what she was supposed to do. She was tired and exhausted by the journey. She wanted to turn over and go to sleep.

'Come on ... it's not difficult, let me put it inside and Bob's your uncle...' Ken was trying to cajole her into relaxing as his hand was groping ever deeper into her groin, forcing her to let him inside. A spasm of terror and pain shot through her stomach like a fierce cramp and Minn screamed out, terrified, in agony as all the muscles tightened their hold.

'Stop! I can't, it's killing me ... not yet.'

The sound of her crying had an instant effect on Ken's passion and he rolled off her with a grunt. 'What's the matter? Nerves... A few gins'll see you right tomorrow. We'll try again tomorrow, no sweat.' He rolled over on to his side and began to snore.

Minn lay rigid until the pain subsided, afraid to move in case he woke and tried again. What have I done? She cried into the pillow. So this was the big ... it. There was something ridiculous in all this humping and bumping. She felt nothing for the stranger beside her who was trying so hard to be patient. Would it have been like this with Ewan? The more she had tried to do her duty the more her insides had clenched themselves tightly in a spasm of fear. Perhaps she was just tired and needed to get used to the feel of such a swollen rod of a thing poking its way inside her body. They had a whole lifetime to get used to each other, she mused, drifting off to sleep as the agony subsided.

The journey south on the long black train from Central Station was exciting, crammed with troops in kilts and sailors in their jaunty uniform, all crowding along corridors as they rattled down to the Borders over mountains and fells with glimpses of the sea to the right. Then Carlisle, Lancaster, Preston and the smoky town called Wigan, where a line of giggling girls fell on Ken with delight.

He had four sisters and a mother hanging on his every word. It was not the welcome she had expected. There were no black pools or sands only rows and rows of brick houses belching smoke from the chimneys, cobbled streets with lines of sooty washing hanging across the road. And they were all expected to crowd into two rooms.

The tablecloth was covered with pies and cakes and strange cooked meats soaked in vinegar. She had made such an effort to be polite but Minn's stomach was still churning from the long journey and she couldn't eat her share, only pick at the tripe and the pickles. She had tasted nothing like this food before and she wanted to be sick.

'Waste not want not in this house, my girl. There's a war on. Food is hard to come by, but your eggs are always welcome even if half of them's cracked.' His mother smiled wanly at her gift to the family.

It had been hard to keep the present from being bumped and jostled in the crush and Minn was quickly aware that she herself was found wanting. Ken was waited on hand, foot and finger by his family like some Arabian prince: their hero returned from the war with his new bride in her Harris tweed suit, which they thought quaint and old fashioned.

Minn was ushered into the scullery to do the chores while Ken went out to visit school friends home on leave. He disappeared for hours leaving her alone to face the teasing of his sisters, Ivy, Rene, Beryl and Pat. It was hard to understand their chatter. It was quick and thick and made no sense. Her English was slow and deliberate and they roared when they heard her pronunciation.

'Ooh, La-di-dah! Where did you learn to talk posh?' They curtsied and bowed in mock salute so Minn retreated into silence, getting on with her dish-drying, swallowing back the tears. The next day Ken went out fishing and she was trudged around the town and the market stalls.

Where were the open fields with hidden eggs? Their meals came from stalls and tins and boxes. Their milk came from a churn not the udder of a soft brown cow. It was all so strange and confusing. The noise of mill hooters, siren bells and clanging trams on rails and the rattle of mill machinery through open windows startled her.

Ken's sisters were doing war work in ammunitions at the local ordnance factory and it was assumed Minn would bring her ration book and join the family to add to the general wage packet. Minn looked up in horror at this assumption. No one had said anything about staying here in Wigan. Ken had omitted to mention that he expected her to live with his family while he returned to Phetray. Minn began to shake at the very thought of being trapped in this town with strangers who were happy enough in this grey sooty world. She could no longer hear the beat of the waves in her ear or the sound of the sea birds calling.

It was hard to breathe in this acrid air. 'What have I done?' she screamed inside. How would she survive in a foreign land with no sand and sea and salt tangle? She would suffocate in this tiny house. At least Uncle Niall's stone cottage had thick walls and room for two or three. You could run straight out on to the grass or the shore and be alone with your thoughts.

Minn yearned for the smells of home: the peat fire, the crisp smoky tang of fluchties and ling, the tangle of seaweed and salt. She was panic stricken by the thought of being forced to stay behind with folk who didn't understand her.

This panic seemed to make Ken's love-making all the more futile, for try as they might she would not open up to him, and he banged at her until she was sore and he spilled himself over her nightdress. She felt the wetness and was repulsed by the smell of him sweating over her. Why hadn't she been warned of this nightly shame? What if she so

132

displeased him that he left her behind? She must take no chances and keep him interested in her body enough to want to keep her by his side.

All the arguments she rehearsed in her mind like a prayer. 'You know I have a mother to support. She needs me to see to the vegetable plot until Uncle Niall returns from sea. I still have my canteen work and there are jobs even for married women until the men return. I must go back with you.'

In desperation she found that if she shut her eyes and stimulated Ken by hand he found release and pleasure. It was the best she could offer but it made her feel soiled and left out.

Strangely no mention of her staying on in Wigan came up for discussion. To her relief his family were just as silent on the matter once they had examined her closely and found her wanting.

She overheard Ken's mother discussing her with a neighbour over the backyard wall while smoking a cigarette. 'She may be a looker but believe me, Elsie, she's a queer thing. Live like peasants they do up there, Ken tells me. She's no idea how to use the mangle, the dolly. They must throw their washing over the hedges like tinkers, and all her clothes are hand stitched and so old fashioned. I think Ken's wondering what he's taken on, to be honest. He's only taken her out the once to the pictures. I'll be glad when his leave is up and she's out of my hair. And ... she looks down her nose at us. Have you heard her speak? You'd think she was the Queen herself! I'm disappointed, to be honest, I thought she'd be bringing in a wage packet, but she's that thick she'd never catch on in the mill.'

Minn found herself smiling with relief at his mother's words. I'm safe! Ken went to book the tickets north as she packed up their belongings. She bought gifts to take home for Mother, material from the cotton market. If this was the mainland she never wanted to set foot on it again. Where were the corncrakes and the seagulls, the wild flowers? How she was longing for her little boxed bed and the sound of the gales whistling through the marram grass roof. She would never turn her nose up at Phetray again.

Then she looked at the band on her wedding finger with a sickening heart. 'You've made a big mistake,' she thought as the back of Ken's head popped up from the bolster, and shuddered. He's just an ordinary working man in uniform; a man who expected his wife to behave like his mother and sisters.

In Phetray he'd seemed dashing and full of promises. Here he was just like all the others. The two of them had nothing in common. You don't love this man, she croaked, you never did, but you're stuck with him now,

134

Minn, *mo ghaoil.* You made this bed of nails now you must lie on it. Thank goodness Ewan was not alive to see her stupidity.

She blamed the war for their difficulties. It had brought men like Ken and his crew to the island. Without the war their paths would never have crossed, and deep down she knew it was never going to work, never, ever. They came from two separate worlds.

On the boat home she was gripping the hand rail eagerly for a first sight of the long island. How could she pretend that this was not some living nightmare?

It was wrong to have encouraged him, let alone married him. Was their marriage over before the honeymoon was ended? Doomed to death in the houses of women: my dour house full of ignorance and his full of giggling women who laughed at my country ignorance. They had looked at her as if she'd come up river on a biscuit tin.

If only she'd been left to grieve for Ewan in peace. If only she'd trusted her instincts and held firm, but in weakness she'd married the first man who'd looked at her twice. Even she knew enough to know that love on the rebound was a dangerous liaison. Perhaps on Phetray it will be different. I must play my part and be a good wife. For better or worse I have made a promise, she resolved. I owe it to Ewan's memory to let go of things and welcome Ken into my arms.

Eight

Kilphetrish Harbour, October 1944

The SS *Hebrides* left Oban harbour early in the morning, steaming up the Sound of Mull and the rocky islands laden with seals and their pups with wet skins glinting in the sunshine, past the stern outline of Duart Castle and up the channel flanked by familiar purple hills, sailing towards Tobermory and Ardnamurchan Point.

The airmen unfamiliar with the Western Highlands hung overboard watching the shearwaters skim over the waves, throwing their rations to seagulls. Ewan watched them with amusement.

It would be a long crossing for them, smooth at first then the poor sods would be retching over the side. Some of the airmen sat smoking, playing cards, while officers sat below drinking cocoa and reading the *Oban Times*.

He sat in the fresh cool air half nodding with exhaustion, jerked awake by the excitement of giving everyone in Phetray a surprise at his sudden return. One minute he was in mortal danger, the next he had been scooped up from France, debriefed and offered a pass for three weeks' leave.

He had almost made it a year earlier when he had taken the escape route down to the Brittany coast, down the line to the Gulf of Morbihan where there was a Resistance group of gendarmes at Vannes who could get him out to the Scilly Isles. But the group had been smashed long before he'd got within sniffing distance of the port. There was no choice but to head back and take his chance with the Maquis.

It was his duty to fight on until news of liberation was no longer a rumour, and he linked up with the regular army, which screened him and sent him on his way back to report for duty.

It all happened so quickly and now he was going home. He couldn't wait to see their faces when he strolled off the ship. He had so much to tell them about his escape and the brave men and women who had kept him alive; how in the bitterness and grimness of war he had discovered his artistic talent, developed his eye for detail and clinical observation and honed his drawing technique. Once the war was over he knew what he would be doing with his life.

As long as he lived he would owe a debt of gratitude to France, its landscape and the brave people who had sustained his wounded spirit and given him hope. It would take many lifetimes to repay this debt of honour.

So many images were racing through his mind, but the face of Minn Macfee was foremost, imprinted like a sign post calling him home, his muse when holed up in shacks and caves. He couldn't wait to hold her in his arms.

Now the ship was swinging round into the open waters of the Atlantic where the familiar dark outlines of the island known as the Dutchman's cap came into view. The sea was rougher and the engines switched gear, puffing smoke like signals into the sky. Nearly home, he sighed to himself suddenly wide awake. This was the last lap ploughing headlong into the autumn swell before his beloved island came into view.

Phetray was flat and long, a brilliant emerald and silver in the summer light, now it would be grey and windswept. It hadn't the hilly grandeur of Skye or the ruggedness of some of the inner isles, but far out on the horizon these other islands shimmered as a backdrop.

As they chugged ever closer, hugging the coast, he saw some of the men rolling from side to side. One poor chap was spilling his guts over the side.

'You okay?' said Ewan, picking up his slithering kit bag.

'I shall never get used to this bloody hell hole,' said the sergeant. 'You on leave?' He was looking at Ewan's battered naval uniform. 'You'll be used to this then.'

'You could say that,' Ewan smiled. 'Back to the base for you?'

'Back to visit the wife,' came the reply. Ewan was going to ask if he knew the family, but the ship juddered, sending everyone flying. It was going to be touch and go if they managed to land in Kilphetrish harbour.

To be so near and yet so far. It was almost worth the risk of jumping overboard and taking a chance in the waves but that would be stupid. They would ride the waves until the sea calmed and edge their way into the little port. He must be patient.

Already the groups were gathering by the jetty, Sandy, the polis, Dan the *buth*, transport for the base and the post. Was Minn still delivering mail around the crofts? It was so good to be home.

'What's up with you now? That man of yours is not coming back for long... You should be away down to meet the ferry like the hammers of hell.' Mother was watching over Minn's marriage like a hawk, sensing the wind of discontent, chunnering into her knitting. There was not enough yarn to knit another pair of the socks to line airmen's boots that they sold alongside their eggs from under the counter of the mobile canteen.

Minn shrugged her shoulders. How could

she explain to her own unwed mother just how miserable marriage was turning out to be? How trapped she felt to be saddled with a man she had never really loved. How guilty she felt to have let everyone down by her physical revulsion for his body.

Ken was fast losing patience with her inability to make love properly, jeering at her reluctance with disgust.

'Are you a witch? Taking away my manhood with your *Teuchtar* spells.' There was a bitter edge to his voice now when he spoke to her.

She was glad when he was transferred back to the mainland transport depot now that there was a build-up of troops going south. Ken wanted to be sent over to France but his bouts of asthmatic wheezing spoilt any chance of an overseas posting. Phetray was as abroad as he was going to get. As their marriage failed so his wheezing seemed to be getting worse.

The gaps between his leave visits grew from cracks into chasms. Each time he returned hoping for some miracle when he stormed her fortress, but it was as if her whole body froze and tightened against him; her teeth were clenched as he tried to approach her with a kiss even, his breath reeking of whisky and desperation. If only there was someone whom she could confide in, but any whisper of physical contact between a man and woman however married was not a subject even to be discussed with the doctor.

There was no one at the canteen whom she felt she could talk to. The girls were cheery conscripts out for a good time and a laugh. She was not part of their gang. It was such a terrible shame and she felt such a failure.

Sometimes after another night of arguments she rose early in the darkness and took herself to Ardnag Point, to the rocks that had dashed out Agnes's life. If only she had the courage to throw herself into the sea. They said that drowning was quick. What was there to live for here?

She cried out to the moon and the water. Is this my punishment for a hasty marriage to a man who I cannot love? What am I to do? There was never any answer but sighs from the sea.

Ken never took her back to Wigan on leave. The very thought of that house and those sisters with their prying eyes made her shiver.

Sometimes he would sneer at her, 'I think you wanted out of this dreary place. That's why you married me, isn't it? You just wanted some poor sucker to whisk you away on a white horse to his palace, but you were too posh for Wigan. My mam was right about you. All you're after is a meal ticket! Well you and your mother can rot here for eternity for all I care. I've had about enough of this mullarky. Believe me there are plenty of lassies willing and able to dance on my arm. We should never have wed.'

His last letter had stung her to the core, for in some ways every one of his words was bruising and honest.

Ken Broddick was a comforting arm at first, a kind young man now turned bitter by her coldness. If only she was stronger. There must be something dreadfully wrong with her. Perhaps the Macfees were cursed indeed. It was all her fault that their lovemaking was a disaster, and she deserved his anger.

Now in the exciting aftermath of D-Day and the slow crawl of the Allies across Europe, the war was at last on the turn. The forces of the Coastal Command were already deployed elsewhere and winding down the aerodrome's operations. The sorties still went out each day to record the Atlantic weather but the whole base was contracting.

Soon Phetray would return to its sleepy ways and Minn would find herself washed up on the shore, out of work and only half married. Even Uncle Niall against all the odds had survived. He would return to his armchair by the fireside. The future was looking bleak. Perhaps she should make one more effort to revive their marriage, seek help from the doctor and try to make the best of her lot.

Ken had tried his best after all, now it was her turn. Divorce was out of the question.

Minn wrote one last conciliatory letter

pleading with him to come back one more time and promised to talk over her difficulty with old Doctor Murray, however embarrassing she would find it.

She promised to try to please him and be a good wife. There must be a future for them on the mainland away from sad memories, she argued. His reply was prompt and more hopeful. He gave her the date for his next leave.

Minn dressed carefully in her tweed suit and best hat on that fine October morning when she would go down to the harbour and wave the ship such a welcome home.

At first the SS *Hebrides* bobbed over the horizon like a puff of smoke. Soon it was looming larger, lurching over the rough water, and the usual crowd gathered with trucks and carts while the seagulls screeched and the wind howled and tore at her skirt, whipping her hat up and away across the harbour. The troops were hanging over the side, air force blue with a sprinkling of khaki and navy waving at anything that moved and laughing as she chased her hat right into a puddle.

Minn's heart was thudding at the thought of Ken's arrival. She must be warm and generous. He had gone out of his way to return to her. He hated the sea and would be queasy with the motion of the steamer ploughing through the waves. The men were coming down the gangplank and then she saw him and her heart stopped in horror.

He was walking down the gangplank, tall and suntanned. Time stood still as he strode nearer and nearer, grinning; her heart was bursting at the sight of him. She had forgotten how tall Ewan was, how dark and how handsome. He was coming towards her, his cap plonked jauntily on the back of his head. How many times had she dreamt of this moment, cried in her dreams for this moment, prayed for this moment.

Ewan had come back from the dead. Minn's eyes were wide with terror, as if she had seen a ghost.

'Minn, my darling Minn... How could you be waiting for me? I've dreamt of this day for so long!' Ewan flung down his kit bag and raced towards her, lifting her up and flinging her around and round again.

'Dearest heart, I'm home at long last... I wanted to surprise you all but the news had flown before me... Minn! Let me look at you. You've no idea how good it is to see you ... dear heart.'

Minn stepped back dizzy. 'Ewan! Ewan *dubh*... Oh, Ewan, we thought you were dead but you're alive. Oh God, you're alive! They wrote to your parents. I saw the letter. It's nearly two years since we heard from you. Oh, Ewan, why have you come back now and not a word from you for two years?' Minn edged away from him with tears streaming down her face, bumping right into Ken, who was hurrying to rescue her from the unwanted attentions of some randy sailor.

'Is this chap bothering you, love?' Ken had seen all the action from the gangplank.

'No, This is Ewan ... my old friend Ewan *dubh*, returned from the dead. I'm sorry, Ewan Mackinnon ... this is Sergeant Kenneth Broddick, my husband,' she said, spitting out each syllable slowly.

The two men eyed each other up warily. 'Not Mackinnon, the dead fiancé?' said Ken, and Minn nodded, not able to look either of them in the face. 'Oh dearie me, sorry old chap, tough luck! You may have been the old boyfriend, Lieutenant, but she's my wife now so kindly keep your mitts off her in future. I'm the one that does the handling of her.'

Ken was staking his claim and Minn saw Ewan blanch as his words struck home, his dark eyes flitting to hers for confirmation.

'It's true,' said Minn wearily. 'We've been married over a year. I was told you drowned at sea and there was no hope. I'm sorry. Ask your father, or did they know all along of your coming?'

'It was a rush jobbie.' Ewan shook his head, spluttering, hardly able to take in her words. 'I thought I'd give you all a surprise.

I thought you all knew I was holed up in France behind enemy lines. The resistance said a message would get through. It obviously didn't. I'm so sorry.' There was an awkward silence.

Minn spoke softly seeing his distress. 'I don't know what to say. You've been hidden all this time? How could you be so cruel not to send word and put us out of our misery? Do you expect us to believe that no one knew you were alive? Oh, Ewan ... there's nothing to be done, is there? What can I say? You'll have to excuse us now, Ken's on short leave. We've a lot to catch up on too. I'm sorry, Ewan but two years is too long for silence.'

Minn dared not look up at him, sensing the shock and hurt in his voice. This was all too much for her mind to take in and she felt faint. All the old feelings were roaring through her body like a flood tide. He was so close but so utterly out of reach now.

'We're glad that you are safe, of course. It's a pity no one thought to inform your folks...' she muttered, holding on to Ken's arm to stop her legs from collapsing beneath her. He grabbed her round the waist, steering her away from the crowds who were gathering to congratulate the minister's son on his safe return.

She dared not look back, sickened by the cruel fate that had torn them apart, stumbling across the harbour grass towards the welcome waiting at the cottage door, feeling sick to the stomach. You didn't wait for him and it serves you right, cried her heart!

'The whole of Kilphetrish is cracking with the news o' the minister's son. There's to be a service of thanksgiving. 'Tis a pity sure it is ... and you not able to welcome him,' said her mother with a shrug. 'You canna milk the coo and sup its milk, that's for sure... Still what's done is done.'

Minn could not concentrate on anything now for Ewan's accusing eyes kept flashing into her mind. All she knew was that they must speak again in private. She had to explain her actions to him in private.

It was all so unfair, she cried. If only she hadn't written to Ken begging him to come one more time.

Ken was infuriating, trying to pretend that nothing momentous had happened, that Minn had no feelings for the sailor and could carry on as if she hadn't been swung in his arms. To him it was simple, she had promised to be his proper wife. But now it was worse than ever.

There was no hiding the joy when the maid from the manse brought a letter requesting that Ewan should have a private meeting with Minn, but Ken was furious.

'I'm not letting my wife be seen out alone with another man. It's not on, our Minn. I know he was your fella and him being a prisoner an all, but Lord love a duck! It's just not cricket. He just can't take up where he left off!' Ken was studying the note brought by the minister's maid.

For once Mother stepped in to defend this unusual action. 'Now, laddie, the poor man was away at the war. It's no his fault his messages got all twixted up, now is it? The ways o' the Almighty is strange in our eyes! They two have things to be explaining to each other. It is said he's to away abroad again and the minister has organized this meeting so there's no saying against it. I shall take ma knitting and walk with them so none of you can say they were up to no good, now can they?'

Ken shook his head, unconvinced. 'I suppose so, but we're not wasting another precious leave in argy-bargy. An hour … it can all be said in an hour, surely, and then I want you home!' he ordered as if his wife was his corporal.

Ewan and Minn stood side by side at the end of the harbour jetty looking out to sea while Eilidh Macfee sat on the wooden memorial bench knitting socks on number three needles, in sight but out of earshot of the couple.

'I had to see you, one more time, to know you're happy in your new life.' Ewan spoke formally as if he was talking to a stranger.

Minn was searching for an honest reply but the words were choking in her throat. 'I waited for a year. I knew in my heart that you weren't dead. I was the only one who wouldn't give up hope, but your father... I wouldn't believe what I was told, not for many months.

'Life goes on, your father preached to me over and over again, so I took a chance with Ken.'

'Has he made you happy? Your eyes look lifeless and sad to me.' Ewan was peering into them closely so Minn lowered her gaze.

'Things could be better. This surprise hasn't helped either of us. Ken is jealous.'

'I'll no be hanging around for long. I'm going overseas again. Now that... Oh, Minn! If only my message had got through. What a mess! All those broken promises, how I've let you all down.' He was trying to explain about his escapes but she was not taking any of it in.

Minn stayed silent then whispered, 'At least your mother must be dancing with joy at the sight of you. She has not been a well woman since you were gone.'

'Not that you'd notice. She can't believe it's me. She holds back from the touching of me. And while I thought we'd be standing at the pulpit together, you and I, my own father married you off to a Sassenach! If only...' Ewan punched the air with his fist.

'If only doesn't help any of us, Ewan. I don't know what to say. This is agony for me too.'

'Why?'

'You know why. To have you so close and know we'll have to part soon, never to kiss or touch as we used to do. I'm going to have to walk away from you back to Mother, but I just can't bear the thought of it.' She was trying not to cry.

'I asked if you were happy. I know now you're not. You don't love that Ken and I can't bear to think of his hands over you in the bed. It's not right,' he said.

'No it's not right and it's never been right between us, not ever. I hate it but I'm married now and that's that. We'll just have to make the best of it somehow. The sooner you're away from Phetray, the sooner both of us can start afresh and leave these yearnings behind us. Our time's nearly up. Mother is waving.'

'Let her wait! I'm so sorry, *mo ghaoil.*' Ewan turned again and stared her full in the face. 'I've not given up hope yet. If you need me, you know where you'll be finding me. There must be something we can do to ease this hurting.'

'There's nothing, Ewan, not now, not ever. It's all too late, my dear heart. How can I be walking away from you, but I must. Wherever you go you'll never be out of my heart, I promise. It's the only promise I can keep for you. Bye the now.' Minn turned from his face to speed back to the Tulloch Bar and the bench where her mother rose up to greet her.

'Well?'

'Well what? All that's needed to be said has been said. Time to go before Ken is champing at the bit, thinking we've eloped to Gretna Green on the high tide. Come on, there's nothing here now.' Minn turned her face into the wind, trying not to cry. In truth she didn't care a jot what her husband was thinking, her heart was dead and she would never care for anyone again.

Nine

Beach of the singing winds

'So what did you say to the sailor? Told him he'd missed the boat?' Ken whispered, leaning over Minn in the iron bed that creaked with every move.

Minn turned her back on him. 'I told him that I was married and what's past is past. What else do you expect me to say?' She hunched the thin blankets over her head but Ken was restless.

'Did he tell you he loved you? Do you still

love him? I have to know!'

'What's the point?' Minn muttered, wanting to blot out his face and his smell and his gloating. Ken yanked back the bed covers.

'I'm sick of you turning your back on me. Look at me when I'm talking to you!'

Minn could smell the whisky on his stale breath. 'There's nothing left to say, is there?'

Ken pulled her roughly. 'Oh yes there is. I'm not putting up with this state of affairs any longer. There's more than one way to skin a rabbit. On your back... Open your legs. I'll show you whose head of this household. No more delay tactics, I'm sick of your tricks,' he threatened, pushing her hard into the mattress.

'Shush! Mother will hear! I can't, you know I can't...'

'Shut yer bleeding mouth! I don't care if the whole of bloody Phetray hears what's happening in this bed. Open your legs or do I have to prise them open with my fists, you whore! I'm sick of rubbing off on you like some tuppenny tart. You're my wife, for God's sake. How will we ever get a kiddie with this palaver?'

'I don't want a bairn,' she whispered, struggling against him in the darkness.

Ken slapped her head. 'I'm sick of what you want and don't want. Shut up, open your legs or I'll ram it up your backside good and proper.' He was pinning her down underneath him, shoving his hand on her face, twisting it into the pillow until she could hardly breathe.

She bit his fingers and he yelled. 'You bitch! If it's a fight you want... You've asked for it now. There's more than one hole down there and you can scream for your mammy all you like. She won't interfere if she knows what's good for her...'

'No, please,' whispered Minn limp with exhaustion. 'I'll try. Be gentle with me, but it hurts so, Ken.'

This time he held her fast forcing himself inside, thrusting himself over and over as she struggled against the burning pain and humiliation. 'Think about lover boy ... if it makes you feel any better. I'm giving you one for him!' Ken was panting, excited by his power.

'No! Stop! It really hurts!' Minn could not move from the agony as he finally broke into her, spilling himself with relief.

'There! That's what you've wanted all along, a bit of force. That's what you ladies like. We'll have to do that again to teach you a lesson.'

Minn turned her face from him, weeping into the bolster. The pain was like a burning fire. Only over her dead body would she let him do that to her again. Soon he was snoring evenly and she slipped from the covers to wipe off the blood and the mess.

Never in her life had she felt so dirty and

used, so shocked by this side of her husband. Her stomach wanted to throw up at the thought of what he had just done to her. For a second she was numbed and unbelieving but as the shock subsided a cold fury fired her resolve.

For a second she saw the heavy fire irons by the hearth and wondered if she could smash them over his head, but her surge of rage was tempered with reality. That would be a hanging offence. Ken was not worth dying for.

She raked the fire for a glimmer of warmth and searched for a thick plaid shawl, gumboots and an old mackintosh. She must get out of the house away from the smell of him and cleanse away the dirt of the night. He had raped her like an animal and she hated him now. Her tormented spirit needed fresh air and pure water to wash away his soiling.

How she wished she had the courage to throw stones at Ewan's window at the manse and call him to her defence, but this was her secret shame and punishment. 'How can I live after this? What did I do to deserve this?' she sobbed.

Only thoughts of Ewan kept her sane as she walked through grass in the early light, her nightdress soaked in the dew. 'I have to see him again. I can't sleep for the want of him,' she whispered to herself.

Nothing had changed. After that first

wondrous sighting of her old love coming off the ferry her heart could not lie. Alongside Ewan, Ken would never exist. He was a mere shadow of her first love but she had clutched at his shadow when the real substance had vanished. Then the full sun had returned and the shadow was all she was left with.

I need to clear my head and think again, she said to herself. I can't let Ewan go away again. He's my love and my life. We made a promise. There's no turning back now. Ken has no hold on me ... not after this, she was thinking. There was only one place to go for peace and cleansing if she was ever to love again.

She strode across the coastal path in the moonlight with her head into the wind, the early morning scents like an infusion of herbs; she crept past the silent thatched cottages and crofts, waking sleeping dogs, past the boats moored on beaches and the Martello watch tower towards the creaking iron gate leading to the velvet grassy slopes of the secret gully of streams: a valley opening out into the secret cove of the Beach of the singing winds.

The sun was rising on the horizon over the rolling waves as she raced into the white sands to bathe her broken spirits, shedding her clothing. She lay in the tidal path letting the cold chill of the water roll over her bruised body, numbing the pain, the salt soothing the soreness in her thighs, washing away the shame, sifting the grains of sand through her fingers for solace.

Then she remembered the old Colonel, her friendly seal, who used to come when she sang to him round the bay and bob in the waves, curious and kindly. Was he still alive?

If only she was a child again not a confused frightened woman at the mercy of so many conflicting emotions. For so long her voice had been silent, her throat parched and strained. There had been no songs in her heart for years, but now the chords loosened and she began to sing an old lullaby, more to rock herself to sleep than attract an audience, hugging herself for comfort, sounds halting at first and then soothing in their sadness.

Here there was only sea and sand and sky and the pain gritting her mind. She lay amongst them like some fragile plant soaking up the morning light, watching the sea birds dancing, wishing she were dead.

The music of the waves washed over her painful memories and calmed her fear. Who would understand what it was like to be at the mercy of a violent man? What was worse was that Ken was made violent by her own frailty; but to be forced into submission against her will? How could she ever forgive an act of such unspeakable humiliation? Oceans of time would never wash that first filthy act from her soul.

'You're no going out in this weather, Ewan!' Susan Mackinnon was clinging to her son as he waved from the doorway.

'Just a stretch at the oars on the lake to blow the cobwebs away. I'm not used to a soft bed,' he replied.

The atmosphere in the manse was cloying in its intensity. His unexpected presence on the doorstep had brought floods of tears and recriminations. 'My son is restored to me! Praise the Lord!' his mother kept touching his arm, afraid he might disappear.

'We put your obituary in the *Oban Times* and your name is carved on Agnes's headstone. Oh, son, why did you not send us a telegram or give us warning to make our preparations, and me with not a crumb in the house to give you? All the joy of preparing a welcome is taken from me,' his mother's voice kept whining accusingly.

There was no way of explaining away this gross error of judgement. His father's silence was worse, for he sensed some deep crisis of faith in this turn of fortune.

'The Macfee girl showed more faith in you being alive than I did. She clung to her resolve until I told her it was unhealthy and suggested she looked elsewhere. I'm sorry but perhaps it is for the best.' This was the only comfort John Mackinnon could offer.

Ewan was in no mood for all this, but his mother shoved a letter in front of his face.

'It's from Johanna Macallum and she's still teaching in Glasgow. She'll be thrilled to know our good news. You must write to her for she's been a faithful friend to us over the years.'

Not home five minutes and his mother was matchmaking, thinking he could throw off his desire for Minn as easily as they had believed him dead.

He spent that first restless night back on Phetray out of doors, camping on the tip of Skerrin in his old haunt. It was better to be alone with his torment under the stars. What a fool he'd been to make the assumption that his own rescue was worth risking radio detection. He was not important enough for a special mention on the underground wireless network.

He tried to explain to them why he had delayed his rescue and stayed undercover with the Resistance for so long. Once the Brittany route was closed he had simply melted back into the high ground with the rest of the group and fought on. That was what he had been trained for after all.

Nothing was turning out as he had expected. The welcome at the manse, Minn's anguish at his return; all those dreams of home conjured up in hours of boredom hiding in the woods faded into this grey dismal reunion and the shock of Minn's marriage.

How many times had he sketched her face in chalks on plaster walls? Yet he was stunned once more by the beauty of those piercing sea-blue eyes, the gentle wave of her fair hair coiled discreetly in a victory roll. His fingers ached to unpin the tresses and let them splay out over her bare shoulders. She was his silver mermaid.

Now another man had the honour and the right to make love to her. He wondered how she could give herself to that puny sergeant.

'Why didn't you wait for me? What have we done to each other?' he yelled into the crashing waves, but his words were blown back into his face.

At dawn, his eyes heavy with soul searching, he decided to stride out over the marshy machair to the only place where he could feel her presence. He needed to be near her in spirit before he left Phetray never to return. His eyes scanned across empty beach and then he spied a speck by the shore, the outline of a shape, and raced in fear thinking it was a body thrown from the sea, his heart pounding with relief, his prayers answered when the body stirred and rose slowly.

You've come to me! You knew where you'd be finding me if you needed me, sang his thudding heart.

Minn was singing, unaware of his presence. He listened and spoke softly so as not to startle her. 'Such a sad song you are singing to the winds? I was so hoping that you'd come. No one can chaperone us here with an egg timer. This is our place.'

She looked up startled and he saw the tears and red eyes. 'What am I going to do?' she cried.

He sat down beside her. 'I don't know but just hold me...' He ached to gather her up close to feel the warmth of her to himself, but she hung back.

'I can't... There's something I have to tell you.' Minn's voice broke into sobs as she spilled out gulps of her unhappiness. 'And I can't bear him near me. I can't be physical with him ... but tonight he forced me to... What's the matter with me? I'm not normal...'

He sat in silence, shocked by her words, putting his arms round her shoulders gently. 'I'm no doctor but I'm sure it takes time and the right feelings. It's not your fault... How could he force you? I'll kill him for that! So you've never actually...'

It was hard to speak the words in his shyness. She was shaking her head.

'Not once properly until...'

He felt his heart leap for joy. 'So you're still a virgin? There is no marriage if there's been no lovemaking.' She had never made love to the sergeant in all this time. It was wonderful news quickly crushed by her reply.

'Not any more. It's not that simple.' She was sobbing but he had to know the truth. There were some advantages to being a minister's son when it came to marriage law.

'In the eyes of the church and the law, if there's no consummation there's no marriage. You are safe from him. The marriage is null and void. You are free!' he replied, not grasping her full meaning in his anxiety.

Minn looked up puzzled. 'Even if other things happen but not that? We are not married until we sleep together?' Ewan nodded. Then she burst into sobs.

'But tonight he forced me... That's what happened. He was angry because I do not love him and he lost patience. Tonight he broke down my defences. I'm not a virgin anymore so I must be his legal wife.' Minn was flushing with embarrassment. 'I shouldn't be talking like this. I'll not be staying with him now ... not after this. Oh Ewan! What a mess I've made!'

'You must tell the lawyer, the minister, the doctor. If there was no marriage and he forced you, you should be free to walk away from him,' he argued, hoping that there might still be a way out of this terrible dilemma.

'How can it be that simple when we've lived as man and wife and made our vows? Who would believe me? It's all changed now.'

'Doctor Murray can examine you,' he

pleaded. 'He could give evidence for you!'

'And have my shame over all the *Oban Times* for all the old *bodachs* to read? No, Ewan, it would shame us all. This is my fault. I'm not normal. I should never have been married. I drove him to this by my refusals.' Minn was staring across the water lost in her own thoughts.

'Nonsense, Minn! Of course you're normal, the most normal person I know. When we kissed and hugged we both had to hold back our feelings. There's nothing wrong with you that the right man and a tender moment couldn't sort out. That man is the monster and he should be punished. I shall deal with him.'

'No, don't make matters worse, I beg you! Deal with me, Ewan, prove to me that I'm normal: that my instincts are natural. There's no one else I can trust to prove such a thing.'

He could see she was in earnest as she reached out to hold him. This time it must be right.

'But if we do make love together we undo the proof of Ken's attack. This is getting more and more complicated. It's as if we're in some crazy dream.'

He was hesitating, knowing that, technically, if there was any adultery her case was lost. But how could he refuse her?

Minn was grabbing hold of him desperately. 'Love me, Ewan, show me I'm not some freak. I have to know. I have to wipe his dirt from me. Please help me. It's you that I want. I saw your face in my darkness. It has been my only comfort.'

'I'll not be doing it to order. This is a shock to me too. It's all too soon for you. I cannot fail you in this. The time has to be right, special, relaxed. We need time to find each other again. I'll no be rushed like some bullock on heat,' he said, shaking her off gently, smiling, though, at her eagerness. 'If I'm going to be taking this road then let's choose the time carefully. There must be nothing to spoil our concentration. Do you know what you're asking of me and yourself? What if it fails and I hurt you even more?'

'How can you fail me? I've loved only you and we should have come together long ago. See, the sand is warming with the sun, lie with me now and let us seal the bargain.' Minn was lying on the sand with her arms open, her hair down her back like a mermaid sunning herself on the rocks, and he was afraid.

He stood up. 'NO! I'm not a stud horse. Wait until tonight. We'll meet by the creaking gate at dusk. Then I promise you I'll no be so quick to refuse. All day I want you to think about the pleasure it will be for us. You and I joined together, one flesh. Think of our skins touching and let your mouth water at the thought. Can you think of my touch without wincing?'

'I'll try.' Minn smiled shyly.

Minn walked home slowly knowing she must face her husband again. Her mother did not look her in the face when she arrived back covered in sand and dishevelled. Mother must have heard all that had gone on last night but would say nothing.

'I've been chasing the cows off the vegetables again.' She was lying but she didn't care. 'It's such a lovely morning.'

'You're in a good mood all of a sudden,' said Mother, eyeing her as she peeled the potatoes. Ken had done the morning chores and Minn could see he was trying to make up for last night.

'A man can only take so much, love,' he whispered. 'We all have our breaking point. No hard feelings?' She stared at him but said nothing. 'I told you it would be all right in the end.'

It was easy to ignore him. Nothing was going to spoil her daydreams today. Tonight she would be a real woman at long last, loving the only man she had ever desired; she would lie in Ewan's arms and feel his strength around her. But first she must find a cover story. She would lull Ken along with her supposed change of heart and find a way to escape from his clutches. It was not going to be easy.

164

'We can go to the Naafi to see the latest Ronald Colman film, if you like,' she suggested. 'You can go and have a pint with your old mates and I'll join you later,' she lied. 'I have to sort my stock out and do the books for the canteen. Have a few jars and a chinwag. I won't be long,' she offered, taking him off guard with her friendliness. She was shocked how easy it was to lie with a straight face.

Since last night her world had shifted on its axis. Now it was as if Ken was just a stranger to her. The terrible knowledge that they had not even been married in law was too awful to contemplate. In bringing him back to Phetray she had only made her situation much worse. Yet strangely she felt calm and cold, as if the slate was wiped clean. If there was no marriage then there could be no adultery. She had taken no part in his rape of her body. In her mind there was still no marriage.

Yet she could feel the jitters in her stomach. No one suspected that she was taking the canteen van out to the valley under cover of darkness, using precious petrol. Having transport would quicken the journey there and back to give them more time together. She would wear her overalls and her work clothes over her jumper and tweed skirt in case she was spotted en route.

How the hours ticked by so slowly and it

still wasn't dark. She prepared Mother and Ken their favourite meal of mince and tatties cooked with carrots from the vegetable patch, but she was too nervous to eat a spoonful. She pushed them both out of the door early with a smile. Mother was off to her Guild meeting at the kirk, to another of their 'make do and mend' sessions. Tonight would come sooner if she kept busy sorting the eggs into trays.

Ewan was waiting by the wrought iron gate that led to the hidden valley of *Traigh gaodh nan seinn*, and they strolled slowly by torch-light, hand in hand, watching the last of the crimson clouds fade into purple and the moon rising in the east.

She told him about the day's deceptions. 'I can't believe I'm doing this... I hope one of us knows what's going to happen. What if it doesn't work?'

'Who needs lessons, my silver mermaid. This is not some biology experiment,' he laughed, feeling nervous, and quickened their pace. He tried not to think about Ken Broddick waiting for his wife in the canteen. That man had forfeited all his rights when he raped his wife. She belonged only to him, sealed by Agnes's death, both bound together in her loving memory.

'It's hardly the weather for rolling in the sand, is it?' said Minn, her hands cold in his grasp. He could feel the wind flapping through his trousers.

'Have patience, all is prepared. Have faith, young lady! Anyone would think you were impatient to get going.' He hugged her tightly. 'I want it to be right for us, this first time.'

He led her towards the side of the *Traigh gaodh nan seinn*, where during the afternoon he had constructed a little bothy of greenery over two large boulders: a hidden cave lined with a ground sheet and a tartan rug with even a pillow. There was a flask and glasses and a small lantern waiting.

'Your bower awaits, my lady. It's not exactly the Crannog...' he paused hoping she would see the funny little snug and relax.

'It's lovely... All my world's in this beach. It's better than any four poster bed in Oban. The laird himself couldn't find a better trysting place, so sheltered with a lovely view and a friend who's the best company in the world to me. It's lovely! Where shall I sit?' she said, plonking herself down eagerly.

'First you sip the cognac brought by my own fair hand from the perils of France. We must toast all the good allies who sheltered me there. Then you nibble a petticoat tail biscuit in memory of the "auld alliance" between Scotland and France. I'm sorry there's no music,' he laughed, 'but we'll make do with the lap of the waves and the whistle of the winds.'

'That'll do me fine,' she replied, lying back on her elbow.

He could see Minn was shivering as she sat down, her courage beginning to fail her. As if reading her thoughts he sat down, wrapping them both together in an old blanket. He held her close.

'When I was holed up in the forests, I used to dream of this place ... of this moment. The wind would be singing and the waves lapping... Next I'm after telling how I've always loved you from that first day when I was teaching you to swim. The walls of all my hiding places in France were covered with sketches of your face. You were my inspiration.'

He told her how in hiding he had rediscovered his love of drawing. 'You're the only woman I shall ever want, and just how much I love you I'll be showing you. Don't cry... Enjoy this time, the first of many, I hope. Have another sip of brandy, it'll calm your fears. We shall learn together what our loving is all about. I'm going to lie down with you and let my hands run over you gently. If you're afraid tell me and I'll stop. And you can touch me slowly, slowly... Gently Bentley. Let's see how far we can travel. Let me take away the pain and the bad memory of last night. Let's heal the wounds together.'

He kissed her softly and whispered in her

ear, making her smile and relax, feeling himself roused by the trust in her eyes as they flickered in the lantern light. 'Let's take the first steps on our path ... taking our time. There's no rushing our journey...'

For Minn it was like a gentle ache in her loins as she pulled Ewan closer into her. A gush of warm feelings flooded over her as if she was a child dancing on the beach, dipping in and out of the warm sea. For a second she felt that old familiar tensing of muscles, but by looking deep into Ewan's eyes, seeing the trust and gentleness of his concern, she found the courage to let go of the fear, move to the rhythm of his love-making until she was rolling down, down, letting the waters flood over her, soaking her. There was no fear. 'My love!' she cried, the tears pouring. It was so simple, so effortless, so wonderful, and he was inside her. There was no pain and no resistance from her body.

'Now I'm really yours.' She was weeping with relief. 'I'm normal... Thank you, I'll love you for always and for ever for this. No more broken promises... Ewan, my dear, dear love.' They lay in the moonlight content and at one.

Ewan stared up at the sky, counting the stars. Now they belonged together and no man on this earth would tear them apart.

She was no longer another man's wife but sealed and bound only to his tender care. They were meant to be together in this life. She was the face that had kept him alive all those months ago. Now she was part of him, part of the wind and stars and the magic of this island. 'You are my light, my sunrise and sunset. None can separate us now, but ourselves.'

Minn put her fingers on his lips. 'Don't say that. I know we must part and I must face Ken and my mother, but he'll never sleep in my bed again, I promise you. I'll find a way.'

'We must find a way to be together. You know my leave will end and I must go abroad but there's no reason why we both can't go south and leave all this behind.'

He was talking with his heart not his head. It would not be simple to run away and shame all who were left behind.

'Your parents will be heartbroken, there will be shame for all of them.' Minn was reading his very thoughts before him.

'We can be discreet. There must be a way to do this so no one gets hurt. If that man goes back to his base on the mainland you can promise to follow him this time but come south with me. No one need suspect until it is all done and too late to alter. We can't be separated again.' This had to be the safest bet.

'If you're sure.' There was hesitation in her voice. 'Nothing has ever gone right for us before...'

'Until tonight. This'll be the first of a hundred nights of loving. We have the rest of our lives to be together and share our future. All our old promises are coming true, at last! It's all going to be different from now on.'

When he looked at his wrist watch it was after eleven o'clock. 'Hell fire! You're going to be late. Straighten yourself, darling. If we take the old track we might just get to the barracks in time for the end of the picture show.'

'But I've hidden my van on the roadside outside Balenottar. There's no need to panic. This is the most wonderful night of my life and I don't want it ever to end. When can we do it again?' Minn sighed.

'Minn, if you run away with me now we can go hammer and tongs at it for the rest of out lives! First, let's be getting you home without arousing suspicion. Everything must be thought through. Will you come away with me when my leave ends? You know what I'm asking of you?' He kissed her on the lips to seal their promise and the wind whipped the grasses from the shelter. It was time to head for home.

There was nothing like the first time with a woman, he sighed. Together the two of them had wiped all the past loathing and fear from her mind by their tender lovemaking. No other lover had ever ignited such a force within him. They were brief drunken couplings, but here on Phetray under the stars there was magic in the air.

Ten

Minn returned quietly to Kilphetrish and slept in the chair by the fire. She did not want to disturb Ken as he lay prostrate over the bed in a drunken sleep. She sat in the flickering firelight looking at the lines etched on his puffy face, the wavy line of his moustache, the middle parting of his slicked-down hair. His mouth was gaping. He had been waiting to challenge her late return but a drunken stupor had overtaken him. Minn felt no guilt, no remorse, no shame only a sad emptiness inside. How could she have ever found him attractive?

Their reconciliation had been ruined by Ewan's return. The whole episode seemed a disastrous mistake and the sooner she ended his misery the better. When both men were off the island she would sort out how to leave discreetly and for ever. First she must pretend to resume her old life while preparing for a new life with Ewan, scrub away the dirt of this sorry relationship as if it had never happened. How easy to say but how hard it would be to accomplish.

No one need know the circumstances of their separation. If necessary she would seek work on the mainland away from prying eyes and gossip. She could disappear into a big city where Ken would never find her.

On their journey back to Kilphetrish Ewan had talked of art college, of training as a teacher, of developing the side of him that had lain dormant so many years, now stirred by his experiences in France. He talked briefly of his escapades and she was enthralled. She sensed he was censoring all the bits that would disturb her.

Dear kind Ewan, always trying to protect her. Now it was time for her to support him in his chosen career. There must be domestic work somewhere close to the college that would bring in some money. As long as they were together she would scrub stairs and wash sheets. They would take on the world and win.

Now she was courting sleep but it would not come to her, too many schemes were dancing around her head. She cooried under the scratchy blanket and dozed fitfully, rising at first light to see to her chores, feeding the hens and ducks, pumping water from the well.

With luck Ken would be making his way

back to the ferry. His leave was over and she couldn't wait to see the back of him. If only she hadn't begged him to come back and start again. Why was her timing always so out of kilter? It was as if there was a curse on ever doing anything at the proper time, but she pushed this morbid thought to the back of her mind. There was enough to think about just getting Ken out of the house and out of her life. He must leave without a fuss.

He was grumpy when he woke half dressed with a hangover, half recalling she had not been at home when he returned. 'Where were you last night?' he accused.

'I came back by the shore path with a headache. I was feeling tired and I knew you'd be enjoying yourself. There you were half seas over the bed. I didna have the heart to wake you,' she explained, half believing her own words.

He was looking at her with one eyebrow raised as if to ask a question. 'You said you'd come to meet me. Where were you?'

'Ach, it all took longer than I thought and then the van was playing up so I tinkered with it and took it for a test run. I knew I'd miss the main picture and I felt so awful I thought some fresh air would clear my head,' she said, turning from him to hide her flushed cheeks; lies did not sit easily upon her this morning. 'Come on or you'll miss the boat. I'll walk you down.'

'There's no need to wave me off today, I know it upsets you. I'll write to you. You see to your own work. I'm sorry this was not the leave we'd planned,' he said, not looking at her as he laced his boots.

She was busy brushing his jacket. It smelled of the mess and smoke.

'Thank your mam when she comes in for another cheery visit,' he said and she knew it was his turn to lie now. Mother had not spoken a word to him since that terrible night. He nodded in the direction of the door and pecked her on the cheek. 'Be seeing you, love, and think on. I only did it for the best. Now it's all sorted we can get down to married life like a couple of lovey doves!'

How could he pretend that nothing had happened between them? How could he think that all was well between them? She gave him a perfunctory kiss on the cheek and gathered up his clothes into his kit bag. She wanted nothing left of him in the cottage. There were no loving feelings left for him in her heart, only this eagerness to see him away from the island for good. How could she have married this little man?

Only the heart sees clearly, she thought, and my heart was blinded by grief and fear, snatching at affection and calling it love. Now she was free of him she would never make that mistake again.

They walked down the machair towards

the harbour along the coastal path and she waved him towards the waiting ferry until he was out of sight. She turned back skipping across the grass to the stone house, slamming the door with relief.

Thank God he was gone! Tonight she could meet Ewan in peace with no fear of intrusion. Nothing would stop their love-making now.

Yet some vague uneasiness haunted her all day. It started when she found her van disturbed and dirty footprints on her clean floor. Her cash box and accounts had been shifted around. Someone had been in her mobile but nothing was missing, the cash float was correct enough, the cigarettes still tallied and the sweets on the tray untouched. Who was checking up on her work? That feeling of unease lifted but she kept peering up and down the road to see if she was being observed.

Perhaps the authorities had reason to believe she was not doing her rounds efficiently but the roads were just full of the usual carts and transport trucks. She stopped at the corners of farm tracks and the airbase as usual, laughing away her jitters, chattering to her customers.

The tracks were bare with few bends and boulders but she sensed a presence lurking just behind them, a shadow that was unnerving her. This was her own guilty conscience stalking her. Her love for Ewan was making her devious and shifty. She would have to learn to live with it from now on.

It was a relief to see Ewan waiting patiently at dusk. All those silly misgivings were pushed to the back of her mind. There was no one left on Phetray now who would wish them ill. It was stupid to think their loving might not be discovered, but tonight was for them alone.

Ewan had been helping with the kelp harvest, gathering the seaweed from the shore at low tide, loading it on to carts and barrows to be spread to dry under a shower of black flies. He had always liked to lend a hand and make himself useful on leave. Now he was sweaty and ready for a swim.

'You smell like a midden!' she laughed as she hugged him. Nothing could harm her when Ewan was by her side.

'Come and swim with me then...' He was racing her down the gully to the secret cove.

'It'll be freezing!' she replied.

'I'll soon warm you up...' They flung off their shoes and dipped into the icy water but it was too full and rough for anything more than a quick exit.

Ewan dunked himself head first and Minn rubbed him down with his towel, chittering with cold and excitement. They chased each other over the grass like wild children playing tag yelling into the moonlight. No one ever came here at night.

They lay on the soft grass in a hollow counting the shooting stars as they streaked across the night sky, picking out the constellations on this clear autumn night. It was a perfect night for lovemaking, slow and tender, fast and furious; there was so much lost time to make up.

How could she ever have thought herself frigid and unfeeling when lovemaking was so natural with Ewan? Locked in each other's arms they rolled down the slope, lost in a world of their own until a voice yelled out and a torch speared them with its bright light.

'Stop that mullarkey! Get off my wife! You fucking slut... You thought you could fool me but I knew you were up to something behind my back. Like a randy bitch on heat!' The voice was croaking, rasping, struggling to spit out the words as if the emotions were taking the very breath away.

Minn went rigid at the sound of Ken's voice. He was standing above them staring down at their nakedness, gasping for breath. So her instinct was right. 'It's you who's been following me? It was you in the shadows... I never thought you'd be a spy... Oh, Ken, why didn't you go?' she was screeching into the darkness.

'I had to know. I'm not stupid. You lied to me last night. I went to meet you but the van was missing and you were nowhere to be seen. You weren't doing no bookkeeping. This was what you was up to ... with lover boy. So I set a trap and you fell right in, you bitch!' He was striding down the grass waving his torch

Ewan stood, pulling up his trousers, calling into the light, shocked, but his voice was threatening. 'Calm down, Sergeant Broddick! Your marriage is over. It was over before and after what you put her through... It's over. You have to understand. I'm sorry. Minn is mine. She always was!'

Minn's eyes were straining to make out the outline of Ken clutching his chest, gasping out his words. 'You'll be bloody sorry when I've finished with you both. It's my wife you're shagging. She'll cheat you like she cheated me... All those phony excuses. "I can't do it, it hurts!" She's been shagging half the airbase behind my back. Can't get enough of it! Stringing me along with a pack o' lies.' He was wheezing badly now, struggling for breath. Minn wrapped the towel round herself anxious to go to his aid, but he was stepping back from her.

'I'm not standing for it.' He was gasping out his words. 'You're my wife so you'd better come back with me to Wigan, right now. My mam'll sort you out, good and proper. You'll do as you're told. I'm your husband for God's sake! No one makes a fool out of Ken Broddick!'

'You're making a fool of yourself right now if you think I'm going anywhere with you,' she was screaming at him. 'I hate you! You shamed me. I was never your wife legally. We never were physical enough. It was never a proper marriage ... not ever and I never loved you. Go away and leave us be. It's over between us.'

'Rubbish! If Lazarus here hadn't come back from the bleeding dead you'd be glad enough to take my wages and call yerself my wife! You just want some sucker to provide for you, you lazy slut! Pull the other one... Whiter than white? My Aunt Fanny. You're no virgin and that's for sure! Don't talk so daft!' Ken was still gasping for breath but as he stepped in closer to pull at Minn's arm Ewan stood between them.

'Don't touch her. I don't want anyone hurt, Sergeant. This has to be sorted out calmly. Now's not the time to do it. We can go back and talk this all through.' Ewan's voice was hard.

'Don't you give me orders as when's the right time to talk. I've got you by the short and curlies, Lieutenant, shagging my wife silly! She deserves a slapping, the little whore!' Ken shouted, lunging forward again, but Ewan grabbed him.

'Don't you lay a finger on her again, you bully! I'm warning you. This is between you

180

and me,' Ewan replied.

Ken was struggling for his breath. 'She's trouble, that one, trouble all the way, a bitch who looks like butter wouldn't... I came back to give her a second chance and I've now gone AWOL to save my marriage, but she's not worth the bother, is she? She's trouble. You stay out of my business, mate, if you know what's good for you.' With one lurch Ken threw himself at Minn, blinding her with his torchlight

She stepped back but he lurched again so, instinctively, she pushed him from her. Ken slipped sideways, tottering for a second with a look of surprise on his stricken face as his torch launched itself from his hand and he fell backwards into the air down the slope hard on to the rocky outcrop below.

They could hear him in the darkness as he lay stunned, gasping and wheezing for breath. The choking and wheezing bubbled in the darkness as the lovers scrambled down blindly to find him.

'He's having a wheezing fit! We've got to help him or he'll stop breathing. Where's he fallen? I can't hear him!' yelled Minn in panic, knowing the sides of the cove were slippery and treacherous.

They searched with the thin torch beam until they found him on the rocks, his head gashed and bleeding, but the choking rasps were faint and bubbling now.

'Raise his head and feel for a pulse!' ordered Ewan, and Minn shone the torch in Ken's face to see his eyes staring unblinking at her. 'What shall we do?'

Ewan was thrashing through his survival knowledge. 'We've got to get him air but he's not breathing now... Oh God! I think he's choked...'

'We can't let him die... We've got to do something. I'll run and get help but I've no shoes on. Where are my shoes?' Minn was panicking now. She was floundering in some terrible nightmare of her own making. She heard Ewan's cold voice and knew it was useless.

'It's no use. He's dead, Minn. There's no pulse. There's nothing anyone can do for him now.' Ewan was sitting back on his knees with his head bowed as she crouched beside him.

'But he can't be dead! Do something! Carry him back to the van. Call the constable. We have to save him!'

'No. We'll let the sea take him,' he whispered. 'It's the kindest way out for all of us.'

'But we can't do that... His mother, his sisters, they're expecting him back,' Minn heard her voice squeaking feebly. 'They will raise the alarm.'

'I don't think he was planning to leave until tomorrow, do you? Let the sea have him, it can sort out all this mess better than we can ever do, *mo ghaoil.*'

'But I pushed him and he fell. I killed him. Oh, Ewan, what have we done?' She felt so weary, exhausted, stunned into inertia. 'This is Agnes all over again! Are we never to be allowed our happiness? Is it to be blighted by death and the vengeance of the sea? I can't bear this. I didn't want this to happen to him,' she sobbed. 'It's all my doing.'

'Look! It was an accident. Nobody's to blame. He was wheezing and he slipped; he was already too breathless and unfit to clamber over rocks in the dark. It was a tragic accident.'

'But it was all our fault!' she cried. 'We killed him!'

'No, we didn't. You mustn't say that, do you hear me? He followed you and saw something that he didn't want to see. It triggered off a breathing attack. He should have left you alone. That was his choice. It was an accident and we can report it later, if you like.' Ewan was shaking her.

'How can you be so cold? We've killed him. He saw us together and it killed him!' Her voice was shrill and hysterical and he slapped her cheek.

'Shut up! Calm down. That man raped you, or have you forgotten? You wanted rid of him and so did I. He brought this upon himself. No one knows he came here. As far as you knew he left today on the steam ferry back to his depot. That's all there is to it. If we push him off the rocks he'll float away. The sea will see to him. Then no one gets hurt. Then you are free from his clutches for good. Don't you see? This is for the best. What's the point of dragging others into this mess? This way it's clean and finished. I'll go away as I planned. You can stay here and see what happens later. No one will suspect. It was an accident. Come and help me drag him down to the sea.'

They dragged his body out of the wedge where it lay and pulled him to the edge of the rocks. Ewan threw the broken torch into the sea. Minn was shaking as she watched him ruthlessly straighten Ken's uniform.

'Don't do that, I'll see to him,' she whispered. 'What are we doing but acting as if we murdered him, disposing of his body like this? How can you be so cold and calm? I don't know you, Ewan *dubh*,' she turned from him but he spat his words in her face.

'I've seen far worse things than this in war. I've seen executions and killings. Don't ask what else I've seen. This time, I tell you, no one was to blame. He's dead and nothing changes that. I won't let him spoil our chance of a future together. Give him to the sea. Trust the sea. It knows best. Three things it will do for us. It will throw him on the rocks or drag him down under the waves or carry him far out into the ocean to feed the fishes. Let the sea decide for us. Come on, there's no time to waste now while we have darkness to cover us.'

'But he's my husband. I can't just leave him on the cold rocks.' Minn was weeping, trying to button up Ken's uniform, straighten out his limbs and wash the blood from his face.

'Then we'll lower him on to the water when the tide turns. We'll say some proper words and you can sing a hymn and give him an honest sea burial, if it makes you feel any better. That's all that we can do for him now,' Ewan answered coldly.

She was stunned into silence by the hardness of her hero's words. There was a steel edge to this man she had never seen before. From this rock-like strength must have come the will to evade captivity. He had seen battle and death before and it had changed him, separating him from her. She was not sure of this hard Ewan but he was strong now for both of them and she was crumbling fast.

Yet her heart was sad as they prepared Ken for his watery burial. A surge of raw pity washed over Minn as she bent over and kissed his forehead, closing his eyes in a silent farewell. She stroked his brown hair back how he liked it, buttoning up his pockets, taking nothing from his uniform. She wanted nothing more from him but his name for a while.

Then they stood as Minn clung to Ken one last time, waiting for the turn of the tide, the moonlight catching his body as it rose and swelled ready to be launched out on the water

Ewan stood with bowed head and repeated the only bits of the burial service he could remember in Gaelic.

'We commit this body to the deep to be turned into corruption, looking for the resurrection of the body when the sea shall give up its dead...' Both of them were praying that this was one corpse that would sink down to the bottom of the sea never to return.

Minn clasped hold of Ken's cold hand in a lingering gesture of both guilt and kindness, holding it like a mother grasping the hand of her wandering child. She sang two verses of the sad widow's lament: *'Griogal cridhe'*. Her voice crumbled into a sob as Ewan pushed him out into the sea of everlasting sleep, into the sea without a shore, on the final journey to *Tir nan og*, land of the ever young. They watched silently as he floated away like a buoy bobbing on the surface.

There was a crumb of comfort in the dignity of this departure, the softness of the gentle waves as they caressed their charge. It was the best they could do and she knew many a poor fisherman had never even had such a burial as this. 'If only you'd taken the ferry,' she wept. How different things would have been then.

They returned to their lair, dressing slowly, and sat watching long into the darkness. 'We mustn't meet again, Ewan, not on Phetray. Not until all this has died down. I cannot take it in,' she said.

'I suppose you're right,' he whispered. 'Better not to tempt fate now. The sooner we both forget what happened here the sooner we can begin our life again. You're free now to marry where you will. You must go home and prepare to play the abandoned wife or the grieving widow as the case may be. There's no need to rush now. I'll return to my unit and see out my commission. I'll be sent overseas but there's nothing to stop us sending postcards and letters to each other as friends.

'There must be no other collusion between us. When the time is right I'll come for you, dear heart. I'm so sorry. Why is the time always out of joint for us? Someday soon it must come right.'

His voice sounded far away but she felt so exhausted she could hardly move her aching limbs. This separation now would be a just punishment for all that had happened. She would never come here to the beach of the singing winds again unless Ewan was by her side. She was afraid that Ken's ghost would always be lying in wait to accuse her of a terrible treachery.

In the weeks following Ken's death she was physically sick with worry. It was hard to eat or sleep. Minn went about her duties like an automaton. There was no show of emotion, no crying fits when Ken's mother wrote asking why her son had gone AWOL and the military police were at her door. Her mother was watching her like a hawk but she did everything as planned.

She wrote to his family saying she had heard nothing from her husband since he took the SS *Hebrides* back to Oban. The only lie was about his visit being like a second honeymoon and he had left smiling. She insisted that there could be no suggestion of desertion and put the thought in their minds to contact the hospitals in case there was some bomb incident or some such accident on his way home. She even contacted the constable and he made a note that her husband was reported missing.

Then she waited in a terror of guilt and anguish, not daring to reply to Ewan when he sent a brief postcard with a BFPO address abroad. Hours went by scouring the coastline and the tides waiting for a sighting of Ken's body washed up in some crevice but the sea held its secret.

Dreams were punctuated with his staring eyes, flashing before her eyelids: those frightened eyes, wide open, so full of accusation. The sound of his last wheezing breaths rang in her ears making her dizzy until she vomited with disgust on to the grass.

Mother rallied from her usual lethargy as news of his disappearance began to register. There were military policemen and the local constable making enquiries, and Eilidh was able to confirm that she had been one of the last people to see her son-in-law, the night before he left for the ferry.

To her credit she said nothing of the quarrel or the terrible events of Minn's struggling marriage. Only her amber eyes flickered questioningly in her direction now and then as they sat knitting socks by the fire, as if she was half wondering if Ken's disappearance could be laid at her daughter's feet.

In truth Minn needed no script to play the grieving wife for she was racked with guilt and fear. Gradually it was dawning that without Ken's body there would be no widowhood, not for many years. The court demanded years of waiting before declaring him dead. She would not be free to marry Ewan for a long time. Phetray would have to be both prison and refuge from the coming storms ahead.

The love of her life was gone and the pain was unbearable. Her only true friend and she had sent him away. It had seemed the best option at the time. They were living in a world where convention mattered and she didn't want to harm his reputation or her own, what little there was of it. The island was so hidebound by respectability. They must each keep to their silent pact and no one would be the wiser.

Weeks passed and she took to watching the tide hoping Ken would be returned and she would be free at last, but the sea still held its secret. Sometimes she thought she could hear Ewan's voice on the wind calling to her but it was just the scream of a sea bird. He was gone from view and she must wait until the faintness and the aching passed over, until she could breathe again.

Eleven

Phetray 1945

'Is that you puking up again, *mo ghaoil?*' Eilidh caught Minn retching into a bucket.

'It must be the scallops ... too rich for my stomach.' She turned, seeing a strange look on her mother's face.

'It's a gey funny fish that has you puking every morn and night and me without a bust of wind in ma innards. Give it a few more months and it'll be swimming in yer stomach ready to make its way in the world, I'm after thinking.' Mother was laughing and shaking her head.

'What do you mean?' she gasped.

'What goes up has to come down in its own good time, lassie. Did you no reckon you could be with child?'

'I thought it was all the upset with not hearing from Ken for weeks that had upset my system.' She blushed. 'I don't know what to think. Surely not?' Her heart was sinking at the thought. There was no joy in knowing she was carrying a child and with it the awful thought that only God alone knew whose child it might be. It made her retch with fear. Surely not?

In the confines of a small cottage nothing could hide her growing condition from her mother's eagle eye as quietly she took up knitting needles and prepared for her daughter's confinement. 'Poor fatherless bairn it may be, not the first or the last, but the Lord has softened your grief, child,' whispered her mother. This was going to be a piece of good news to blow in the wind.

Minn went about her daily work with a heavy heart. No one on the island would begrudge a grieving widow this gift of life but an adulteress giving birth to a bastard was a different matter. She felt sick with apprehension and guilt.

Then Ewan's mother, Susan, died suddenly of a stroke and his father took another post on the mainland, unaware of Minn's condition. All her connections with Ewan were being severed. He was unable to return for the funeral now that he was serving in the Far East so Minn paid her respects and showed the minister postcards from Ewan.

'Still no news of your husband?' he said. 'It's a sad business and no mistake. He seemed such a decent young man. His family must be sore distressed. We know that feeling only too well do we not, lass?'

This only made her feel worse. She had only written once to his family, to tell them of his sudden disappearance but not of her pregnancy. She wanted none of them staking a claim on this baby whatever the outcome. As far as she was concerned that part of her life was over.

The hardness of her resolve shook her. She was becoming like this island, remote, inaccessible, with few harbours to shelter in, with a heart hewn from Phetray rock.

The months that followed Ewan's departure were dreich winter months of storms and gales when the island was pounded by swollen waves and gales. She made preparations for the birth but her nightmares were filled with visions of Ken's body rising from the deep, walking over the water, screaming out, 'Adulterer!' to haunt her, invading her body with a sweating terror.

'You've a beautiful daughter, Mrs Brod-dick... Hold her close.' The midwife smiled and the exhausted mother, sweating, turned her face from her child at first. 'Come now! Think yourself lucky you've got such a bonnie bairn!'

The screaming infant was shoved on to her breast to suckle and Minn cried with the pain of her efforts. In the last month she had left for the mainland to stay with a distant cousin until she went into the small nursing home in Oban, using the last of her savings to pay for her care.

The baby wailed but still Minn daren't look down at her face. She wanted no permanent reminder of Ken's treachery, but instinct made her curious. The baby's head was covered in dark soft down, and when her eyes opened they were navy blue, fringed with dark lashes so unlike her own fairness.

Her heart leapt with emotion at the sight of such a beauty. She unfurled the fronds of her long fingers, examined each toe. The little face was screwed up with rage at being torn from the comfort and warmth of a womb into this cold world.

A flood of love poured into Minn for this tiny creature, born of passion or shame, she knew not which. How she wished she could share this joy with someone, but the only man who mattered was halfway across the world. How could she tell him about this daughter if she was not his child?

In the afternoon after the birth she sat up in bed to write him a long letter.

I have called her Mor-Anna. Don't ask me why but I like the sound of it and it being the better half of my own given name. She is so beautiful, so different to myself, a delight to behold for I imagine I'm holding you in my arms...

The letter lay by her bedside and was never sent. What purpose would there be in misleading him? There had been enough deceit already. It was better that the child was accepted just as Anna Broddick. It kept them all safer that way. There was no turning back from what was done that night to Ken and she must protect this bairn from the truth of her parentage.

She didn't want Ewan to catch the first boat back from the Far East to claim this child and stir up a scandal of suspicion on Phetray. It would be better if their reunion was delayed to take place out of sight of local gossips. Only time would tell if Anna was a Mackinnon or not.

It was going to be a struggle to make ends meet now that Ken's pay was stopped on the presumption that he was a deserter, but

Minn had already calculated how much they would need to survive and there was now a small allowance for single mothers. The sparkle in her eyes vanished with tiredness and sleepless nights to be replaced by a flintier gaze.

The war was over at long last. There was a new feeling of optimism in the air and hopes for a better future for children but restrictions were worse than ever. She could not help herself dreaming dreams for her daughter as she rocked her in her arms.

I want more for you than a shabby cottage next to a byre and a shawl to carry you around like some tinker's child, she thought. It was time to leave the island, time for them both to leave all the terrible events of the past months behind here. You are my responsibility now and we can do better for ourselves on the mainland, I'm sure. It's not fair to rely on Ewan to bail us out of trouble. It's better to do this by ourselves. Macfee women have relied on men's promises for far too long. Time now to seek employment somewhere where we'll be just a war widow and her child, doing the only work I'm trained for, hard though it'll be.

She gazed up to the mantelpiece to her one precious porcelain figurine. 'I want you to be dressed in silks, with leather shoes that fit on your feet and books to read.' She pointed the baby to the little china doll. 'I want you to have all the things I never had and the opportunities you'll not be getting in this out-of-the-way place. We can't wait for Ewan to return. What if he's injured or worse? Time for your mammy to go back into service.' She sighed. 'Time for us to move away from Phetray and make a new life, just the two of us.'

'So you're going then?' Eilidh watched Minn scouring the *Oban Times* for positions vacant. 'Now your Uncle Niall's got hisself a Glasgow wife and seat by her fire he'll be in no hurry to return. What's to become of me, poor abandoned soul that I am? How can a daughter not do her duty and take me with her to mind the bairn?' she was pleading.

Minn stood firm, not wanting Anna's head filled with her mother's Highland nonsense. This must be a fresh start for both of them. 'You're strong enough when it suits you, Mother. Now there'll be only your own mouth to feed and the hens and the garden will fill your pot. I'll send what I can, but there's nothing for me here on Phetray now. I've counted six situations vacant in the *Oban Times*. I'm writing to register with the domestic agency in Edinburgh. There must be plenty of country homes wanting a housekeeper, willing to offer accommodation to a widow. Anna must be brought up on the mainland. It's all decided.'

Eilidh looked up from her knitting, her round spectacles at the end of her nose. 'You've grown mighty cold this past year. Grief's not softened the mouth on you, but the black becomes your colouring, I have to admit. It's a hard world out there for a servant. Mark my words, I know only too well that you're not safe off this island, *mo ghaoil*. It'll all end in tears.'

'What are you talking about? It's hardly been safe for me here!' she snapped impatiently. It was always the same old story of doom and gloom and wicked masters and poor helpless serving girls. 'This is nineteen forty-five, Mother. Things are different now after all we've been fighting for. The future is ours for the taking. No more of your warnings... Wish us well. We'll come back whenever we can. I have to think of the bairn.'

'And here's me thinking you'd settle with Ewan *dubh*, but he's vanished like poor Ken Broddick over the water to goodness knows where. You frighten all your suitors away... I don't understand you.' Eilidh was rocking the baby as she spoke. 'You have a hard mother.'

'Ewan will return when he's good and ready. Who knows what might happen for us both then? Better not to lose a tide or make plans too far ahead. That's one thing I'm learning in this life. Take your chances when they come. Live for today and not tomorrow. Tomorrow may never come.' Minn patted her mother's leathery hand.

'Aye, you're right enough there. Who knows what's round the next corner for you? Better not to know, I'm thinking. Only the Good Lord knows what's in store, and he makes the back for the burden.'

When the letter arrived from Pitlandry House in the autumn of 1945 inviting Mrs Broddick to take up a post as live-in maid, with accommodation provided in house, she did not hesitate to accept the position. She had asked her old dominie for a reference and borrowed the school atlas to find just where Pitlandry was to be found in the Borders of Scotland. It was close to the town of Peebles and the River Tweed in the Lowlands; far enough away to make a clean break from all the sadness of the past year.

Only then did she write to Ewan telling him of her change of circumstances, but of Anna she said not a word. What he didn't know wouldn't harm him, she reasoned. It was all turning out for the best. She would write to him when she was settled and when she knew for certain that Mor-Anna was his child.

PART TWO

Blow the wind southerly, southerly, southerly,
Blow bonnie breeze o'er the bonnie blue sea;
Blow the wind southerly, southerly, southerly,
Blow bonnie wind and bring him to me.

One

Pitlandry House, 1945–46

'Look, Anna, see the sheep and the horses in the fields! We're on our way at last, away from the rough sea on a puffer train.' Minn was dangling her baby on her knee, looking out of the carriage window, her heart racing with excitement at the thought they would have a new home in the Borders. She was sitting opposite a young sailor who snored all the way to Glasgow. The train was packed with troops, sitting in the corridors, smoking and playing cards and eyeing her up with interest.

They could stare all they liked for she was finished with romance. From now on her head would rule her heart in the same way it dictated that she still wouldn't tell Ewan about her baby. It was better to rely only on herself to provide for them both. This was to be a fresh start and no looking back. She would always love Ewan but they were not free to be together yet. She must prove worthy of his love and trust in her.

Her eyes flitted to the sailor's kit bag dangling precariously from the shelf above with a tag which read 'HMS' and nothing else. No one showed the name of their ship. Minn kept glancing back at the label. What was the missing name?

She was never called by her Sunday name, Mairi. Why had she stuck with Minn all these years? Who wanted to own up to a name that sounded like a well-known household polish? Now she was back in service she could be any name she liked. Perhaps a new name would distance her from Phetray, from island gossip, adding a touch of mystique … perhaps not. For Anna's sake she would certainly stay Broddick. She sat daydreaming out of the carriage window recalling that first dreadful journey south on her honeymoon. Just thinking about Ken made her shiver with guilt and fear. This journey must be a fresh start. The past was the past and there was no going back.

Anna slept fitfully in her arms as the train chugged on through the grandeur of lochs and glens towards the outskirts of Glasgow. Soon it was time to alert the guard and go in search of her case and battered pushchair. As Minn alighted from the train with the help of many pairs of hands, she sniffed the soot and the smoke and saw the bustle of passengers rushing for connections. She took a deep breath.

You've done it, *mo ghaoil!* You've put all the bad luck behind you. From now on it can only get better. A new start deserves a new name, so onwards and upwards Mairi Broddick!

Minn stopped to gaze out of the window of the bus to the Christmas card beauty of the fir trees dripping with fresh snow as they stepped down in Pitlandry to walk the last few yards to the house.

A robin hopped on the dripping branches flicking them with wet snow and Anna screamed with delight as they walked through the wrought iron gate down the slushy path between the lawns, gazing at a soft rise of hills and fir trees frosted with icing. She crossed her fingers as she took that first look at Pitlandry House for luck. She still could not believe her good fortune in finding a position in such lovely countryside.

The house nestled in a hollow beside a rolling tributary of the river Tweed: a fine stone house built in the eighteenth century for a family of merchants, secluded, set back from a minor road by an avenue of tall poplars. She was coming as domestic help to Colonel Hubert Lennox and his ailing wife, Dorinda, who were renting this rambling old mansion with only a local cook and gardener and some sporadic daily help.

It was obvious as soon as she arrived that this place was far too big for the couple. It was proving hard to cling on to pre-war standards without adequate heating and with all the restrictions of post-war rationing and little help. Her appointment was made through the agency by their son without even giving Minn an interview. Her job was to make sure that the house did not freeze his parents with the chill.

Young Mr Lennox had written explaining that his parents were too frail now to adapt to change, and while he was away on business he wanted to be sure they did not neglect themselves. His sister lived in London and would visit when she could.

Minn's experience with Lady Rose so many years ago had swung the position in her favour. 'This is not a post for some old trout. I want someone young and energetic who will not mind the draughts and the chills. You may burn as many logs as is necessary to keep them safe and your young child too. It will do the folks good to hear a baby around the place.'

She suspected that no other applicant wanted to be stuck out so far from buses and comforts in such inhospitable surroundings but this hideaway was going to suit them both fine.

The Lennoxes were a charming couple who staggered up and down the dusty staircase among dingy, dog-haired sofas trying to keep up Edwardian standards with virtually no staff. Minn drew a deep breath and set about spring cleaning all their living rooms, beating carpets and rugs choking in the dust of years. She found the old nursery bucket pram and Anna was sat up to supervise all the sponging-downs and vacuuming with Edie Lawrie, her devoted slave, who came twice a week from the village to do the rough work.

Minn was so busy those first weeks after her arrival that there was no time to dwell on the past year's tragic events. Her job was to organize the household, see to the deliveries and the everyday running of Pitlandry until such time as the colonel's army son, Henry, returned from his regiment.

She was given a small cottage attached to the old stables. For the first time in her life Minn had her own space, and was told to furnish it from some of the rooms in the old servants' quarters in the house. She distempered the walls and polished up the stone floors, found rugs and a table and chairs, a bed and washstand and even a wooden cot for Anna. It was like being given the key to a treasure trove of riches. In the evening she had her own kitchen fireplace to hug and the choice of any books from the colonel's library.

Sometimes she kept pinching herself to see if all this was not some dream that they had wandered into by mistake. One of the first things she did was to set her figurine proudly on the mantelpiece. It had survived the journey intact wrapped in woollen baby clothes. She wanted everyone to see she knew the genuine article.

There was no electricity, no modern conveniences, but then this was no different to conditions on Phetray; here, though, there was privacy to wander through the woods and by the river and feed the horses in the fields, and she could jump on carts to get lifts to town.

She found the colonel's motor sitting on bricks in the garage so she hinted to them that she had driven vans for years, and Mrs Lennox suggested they might license their car again. This would enable her to chauffeur them into town for appointments and fling herself round the stores while they took afternoon tea in the Pitlandry Hotel.

Minn began to enjoy a freedom from worry and shame for the first time in years. So much so that she was even reluctant to boast in her infrequent letters to Ewan the dramatic change in her fortunes. It was too soon for them to meet up. Much as she loved him, the birth of a child and Ken's death on those rocks had shattered something precious between them: something she was finding it hard to define.

In the silence of the night, in her heart of hearts she knew Ken's disappearance must have caused his family such grief and puzzlement. She alone could have put them out of their misery but it was too late now without raising suspicion of them both.

Ewan was part of the Phetray conspiracy and Phetray had no place here in Pitlandry. There were no reminders here of her secret past. Here there was peace and beauty to share with Anna. All that had delighted her in the Crannog was here in abundance: the fine porcelain in glass cabinets, beautiful furniture to polish and examine closely, the gracious proportions of each room with walls lined with portraits and hunting scenes.

It would be her joy to restore it all to its former glory, to fill the bowls with evergreens and flowers, to repair the soft furnishings and draperies and make the old couple as warm and comfortable as possible in this draughty barn.

She suggested they decamp into the sunny morning room, which could be freshened up and well heated. Here they could sit with their papers. A writing bureau was moved for their correspondence and sometimes meals were taken in the old kitchen so there was constant warmth and less upheaval.

Now that Christmas was coming round again and all the family were returning for the holidays Minn took delight in preparing the drawing room, dining room and bedrooms for the coming celebrations, and there was always somewhere safe for young Anna to toddle.

For her sake alone she had placed her wedding portrait prominently in her little sitting room so that no tongues would crack about whether she was one of the many dubious 'widows' with posthumous children. Here she was Mrs Broddick: Mrs Mairi Broddick. This fresh start was honoured with her best name.

As Minn went about her Christmas preparations one winter morning, she stamped her feet in the snow sniffing the air with a strange excitement. There were trees and hills all around Pitlandry; afternoons off were spent wandering through the parkland with Anna in the pram trying to identify an oak from an ash, a rowan from a beech, kicking the leaves into crunchy piles. There were no howling gales and salt spray to stunt the growth of a forest. Shrubs were sturdy and full of berries.

It was the lushness of this border country that stunned her senses. Pitlandry was like living in a woodland paradise, with no sea lapping at the door whispering, reminding her of their treachery.

Not that paradise did not have its own noisy side. Minn smiled, staring into the old stables, which were piled high with boxes, wheels and spare parts for motor engines. Strange vehicles came and went in the night leaving drifts of weird tarpaulin shapes by the stable door. She never knew what might be parked up each morning outside her cottage door, but one thing was for certain, Captain Henry Lennox and his band of merry men would trough the last of the bacon rations at the kitchen table.

The captain appeared one morning in the October after her arrival blocking her in.

'Do you mind not parking that crane outside my door. I can't get out!' she yelled out of the bedroom window forgetting that the neat plaits she coiled round her head were dangling down like a schoolgirl's braids. 'How am I expected to get a pram under that?' She was addressing a tweed cap thinking it was workmen.

The cap was raised and a pair of eyes appraised the vision in the window from under bushy eyebrows the colour of a foxtail. That was when she recognized him from the photograph on the mantelpiece, which had the pride of place above all others.

'Sorry... You must be the new housekeeper. Didn't Pa explain? I run my business from the back of the house.' He raised his eyebrow in a question. Minn flushed with embarrassment but he just laughed and waved. 'Give me two shakes and it'll be shifted.'

Captain Harry came and went like the tide. A week would go by and then a convoy of assorted vehicles would trundle up the rutted back lane scattering mud in all directions. Sometimes the whole driveway to the main entrance was littered with army surplus equipment and the lanes outside Pitlandry would be lined with vans and lorries with strange number plates. Men in brown felt trilby hats would exchange wads of bank-notes as if in some horse-dealing auction.

Colonel Hubert explained that his son was running a haulage business transporting goods and ex-army supplies now redundant because of the demobilization of troops. Minn wondered why he chose such an out-of-the-way base when it would be easier to find central premises in the nearby towns closer to the main routes south out of Scotland.

Occasionally he stayed overnight but mostly he came and went in one day. 'Now you see me now you don't,' he would wink and raise his cap. He certainly brightened up his parents by his visits, never arriving at the house empty handed. Sometimes there were chocolates with foreign labels or a box of stockings for his mother, which she pushed aside.

'What do I want with these at my age? Here, Mistress Broddick, you share them with Cook. They'll look better on your slen-der legs. When my son comes bearing gifts I start to worry... What's he up to now, Hubert?' The colonel was deaf and smiled benignly. Minn was grateful for such bounty, keeping the stockings safe in a glass jam jar.

Harry was the Benjamin of the family, born

when his mother was 'on the turn', Cook whispered. He was a beloved indulged only son, for his elder brother, Roderick, had fallen in the Great War. His handsome face peered from behind an ornate silver frame on the grand piano. Daisy, their daughter, was married and had a line of daughters with her on the piano. The portraits were colour tinted and each child and grandchild shared that same sandy gold hair.

Harry was the joy of their old age, and Minn sensed the warmth and affection between them all. How different from the stiffness between her meagre family. A child should know it is loved, she sighed, and I never was, but Anna must have love in abundance.

A mother, a father and a child, that was what she wished for Anna, but Ewan was still abroad unable to give them the security that clung like ivy to the walls of Pitlandry House. His letters were often delayed and forwarded from Phetray. They were few and far between these days. Anna's first birthday had long past and Minn still withheld knowledge of her child. She feared she was leaving it too long but what could she do?

Sometimes when she heard car wheels in the night, and the torches flashed under her window, Minn worried just what caper the captain was really up to. Sometimes he disappeared for weeks and the house settled down to its old routine until the vehicles lumbered down the lane roaring their arrival again.

Harry was a born tease. He took delight in teasing her about her accent. 'Where's the Highland lilt? Where's the whiff of the dark isles? You could give Princess Elizabeth lessons!' He picked up her child with enthusiasm. 'Little Anna gets more stunning by the day, a real Shirley Temple! Now her hair is black as a raven's wing and you with hair of flax. Such a mysterious combination, Mrs Broddick.' He did not question her background and she was grateful.

Minn tried to stay unruffled and not rise to his baiting but she was unused to such teasing and didn't know how to react. One afternoon he returned from the town with a handmade wooden trike with three sturdy wheels that Anna could trundle across the cobbled yard and pretend to ride. From that moment he was hers and she ran to him, the minx, like a puppy waiting for a dog biscuit, tugging at his pockets.

It was the oldest trick in the book to get to the woman through the bairn. Minn stepped back on guard from this charming young employer. All her mother's dire warnings were ringing in her ears. He was not particularly good looking: rugged, foxy, with bright blue eyes and creases on his cheeks from grinning a lot. He wore tweeds and outrageous shirts, gaudy ties that didn't quite match. There was no mistaking his accent, his breeding, his affluent generous manner, and she was suspicious of his obvious charm.

Men like him could take this Pitlandry paradise for granted, the land, the house, the elegant surroundings, driving an open-topped sports car with a foreign name. He was everything Ewan was not: worldly with a shrewd business sense, more English than Scottish and no sailor. Yet she sensed he was fishing for a response from her, flirting with an ease that unsettled her. This was new territory and she was afraid.

All the troubles in her life came from the men around her. A storm of rekindled passion for Ewan had thrown her marriage off course and nothing would be in its expected place ever again. It was safer to be wary and polite, until Harry laughed and called her 'Mrs Danvers', a gibe that meant nothing to her until she took Daphne Du Maurier's *Rebecca* off the shelf.

Anna had no such qualms about the man who bounced her on his knee and brought her pop-up picture books and sang nursery rhymes, to her delight. Minn felt so guilty that this might have been Ewan's privilege not Harry Lennox's role. She was robbing him of the pleasure of knowing all about her antics.

Then, out of the blue, Ewan wrote saying

he was soon to be demobbed and wanted to study art in London, of all places. He wrote to say he had won a travel scholarship and would she go abroad with him? Minn panicked that he might call on them unexpectedly. He was from the past with all its secrets. She wanted no reminder of her perfidy, however much Ewan was a part of her heart.

How could she contemplate dragging a child round war-torn Europe: a child he didn't even know existed? Minn agonized whether to reply. Perhaps he was trying to forget the past as much as she was. Going abroad was his way of dealing with it all. How could he now afford to support a woman and child? Was the strain of this enforced separation beginning to tell on him too? They were out of touch with each other. Better to let things slide for a while longer, she reasoned long into the night.

How she longed to feel his arms around her again, to be loved and warmed by his body, but here in Pitlandry House she felt safe from the pressure to face the future. Here she spoke only her refined English like a foreign language. Here there was beauty and security and no one was interested in her history.

Harry Lennox was another matter. What was he up to? Was he amassing a fortune on the black market? If so, good luck to him, she mused. He was taking his chance as she was taking hers. Is this why he had dumped his parents in this country hidey-hole? Was some of the stuff on secret display not exactly surplus to army requirements but gently removed from the stockpiles by stealth? What the eye does not see, the heart does not miss? Was that how she was treating Ewan?

Lately she kept watching her daughter, her fierce stubborn tantrums, the way her hair curled tightly and those dark eyes. Whose eyes were those? Was it possible after all that she was Ewan's child? How could she deny him knowledge of her?

Minn shuddered at the thought of all her deception and wrote a Christmas letter at once to Ewan begging him to come up north for Hogmanay before he made any further decisions. There was so much she needed to explain to him in person.

For once she let Harry drive her into Pitlandry village for the bus to Peebles where she could buy a few small gifts for Christmas. Knowing Ewan would be arriving soon kept all her nagging doubts at bay. This deception had gone on too long. It was ridiculous not to share her news with him.

Christmas celebrations were still something new for Minn, so different from their puritanical Highland celebrations. On Phetray there had been no Christmas, only a New Year ceilidh and some black bun. There was never any money for lavish presents and fancy food. She hardly knew how to make lavish preparations that first winter and had to ask Cook what was the done thing in a household. It was Edie Lawrie, the cleaner, who came to her rescue, telling her which greenery to bring in and hang up, where all the Christmas decorations were packed away. There was to be a party for Daisy's children and someone would dress up as Father Christmas on Christmas Eve.

Soon Daisy Lennox would be arriving with her girls from London. Gil Chisholm, the gardener, brought in a large spruce in a barrel for their Christmas tree and it started to snow again.

Harry arrived bearing boxes of candles and wine and dried fruit, dates and walnuts, tiny oranges and a fruit called a banana, not seen since before the war. No one asked how he had acquired such luxuries. It was Christmas after all, and Christmas was a time for indulgence, Minn was learning.

Anna reached out to grab the candles from the tree, her eyes sparkling in wonder at the lights and tinsel. Minn had never seen anything so beautiful. There were even presents under the tree for Anna and Minn: a pretty dolly with a porcelain face and a cashmere scarf for the housekeeper. It was like watching one of those wonderful Hollywood film scenes coming to life before her eyes with log fires and tinsel, clinking crystal and the exotic spicy smells of the season. Nothing had prepared Minn for the pleasure of it all.

Daisy's girls, Bella and Poppy, latched on to Anna as if she was their own toy doll. They fought over who was to push her along the paths and play with her until she was thoroughly spoilt and fractious. Minn wrote to her mother with all their news and promised to visit in the summer when the seas were not rough.

On Boxing Day she was even invited to the family charades party and stood back discreetly whilst everyone made complete fools of themselves, drinking wine until they were quite silly. When it came to the clearing up everyone suddenly disappeared leaving Minn to sort out the debris with Harry hovering behind her back, the scent of his cigar wafting around the room.

'Black becomes you, Mrs Broddick. Although it's a pity you have to wear it so often. I should love to see you in midnight blue satin and silver. I know someone in the trade who could kit you out perfectly.'

'Mr Lennox, please, I'm the housekeeper not some fly by night. What would I be doing with midnight satin?' Her words shot out like a bullet from a gun.

'I'm sorry, I've touched a nerve. Just because we employ you doesn't mean I can't make a suggestion, does it?' he said.

'It depends what sort of suggestion, Mr

Lennox. I find that work and personal comments don't mix in my experience. I can finish all this myself, if you don't mind,' Minn replied with a frostiness intended to warn him off, but he didn't budge.

Harry stood by the fireplace puffing his cigar, his foot on the fender rail observing her busyness. 'I've been watching you... You're just too perfect, too correct. You never let down your guard. If I didn't know your references were impeccable I'd say you had something to hide.'

'Oh, please!' Minn bent her head to hide her red cheeks.

'No! Hear me out, Mrs Broddick. It takes one to know one. I like the way you keep your own counsel so discreetly. You see in business you sometimes need a partner who knows when to speak and when to be silent. Your daughter does you credit. It must be hard bringing her up alone. I can see you are ambitious for her. If you and I were partners, in the strictest sense, of course, she would want for nothing: ponies, clothes, the right connections...' he smiled, looking pleased with himself.

Minn put the tray of glasses down with a clatter to steady herself. 'Why are you saying all this to me? What can you possibly want with a domestic except the oldest promise in the book? I may be an islander straight off the boat but I've seen enough in life there to know what's what!'

'Steady, old girl! Nothing like that, I promise you, but I do need a partner to take around to certain occasions, a bit of a decoy, decorative and discreet, who can help with my work, entertaining clients, putting them at ease...' Harry was watching her reaction.

Minn looked him straight in the eye. 'Do you mean as a spy? What are you up to on the black market? Is it something not exactly legitimate?'

'Nothing terribly dodgy ... let's say just a few shades of grey: a few deals here and there that need a careful, delicate touch, a few palms greased along the way. Somebody wants a favour and I oblige with no middlemen to rake off half the profit. All strictly legit but on the QT...' Harry pointed to his nose with a smirk.

'I'm not sure what you're getting at,' she replied. 'I don't want to hurt my employers. They've been good to me and I like this position.'

'Who do you think picked you up from the pile? Who do you think pays for all this, heating, rent, transport? Did you think it was done on my father's war pension? Come on, Brodie. I chose the house and I want my parents to have every comfort. Do you think I'd risk their reputation? There's so much business out there for the taking but it all takes time and delicate negotiations at dinners and soirées. All I'm asking of you is to dress up and be my guest. No strings, I promise. I gather there's some Highland laddie waiting in the wings.'

Minn smiled with relief. 'Yes, there is ... someone I knew on Phetray, we were engaged once before the war. He'll be coming up for Hogmanay. If I do help you it will be only for a short time. I'm not in the market for any other arrangement.'

'No, of course not, I wouldn't dream of suggesting such an outrageous arrangement. Strictly business. What could be better, Mistress Brodie?' He smirked

'Mrs Broddick, please, in working hours.'

'Give me your measurements and I'll see to the midnight satin.' Harry continued to press his request unabashed.

Minn shook her head. 'Thank you, I'll see to my own wardrobe if you can find the coupons and the cash.' If this was going to be the arrangement the sooner Ewan was in the picture the better.

The snow fell gently at first like plump feathers blanketing out the gardens and the paths, but Ewan did not arrive. She had arranged digs for him in the village in Edie Lawrie's box bed. Minn waited for the post but there was no reply. She had found out all the connecting train timetables from the south just in case he needed transport. She waited first with impatience and then with desperation. Hogmanay came and went and still there was no word from him.

How could he not come when she'd called? Why had he not answered her letter? She wrote again in fury and her letter bounced back unopened and re-addressed: 'Not known at this address'. She wrote to her mother to see if he had written there but there was no reply.

The snow kept falling steadily, blocking the roads and the rail tracks and cutting off Pitlandry House from its village and suppliers. Now came the battle to survive against ice and snow on a scale not seen in the district for a hundred years. There was no time to mourn Ewan's desertion when there was a household to feed and keep warm. The drive was blocked and they shovelled a rough pathway until Harry's equipment supply came in the nick of time with a metal snow plough attachment that could be stuck to the old tractor. Every day Minn drove it up and down from the cottage through the courtyard to the back of the house to clear a path to the fuel store and the coal house, and watched with despair as their food supplies began to dwindle.

On bad days no supplies reached the house and Minn was forced to scour the larders and pantries for something to make warming broths and stews. All Mistress

Lamont's strict training came back into use as she gutted frozen poultry, pheasants and rabbits for the pot.

Mrs Lennox caught a chest cold and had to be laid abed downstairs by the fire. The doctor came out with snowshoes on his feet. Harry fought his way through the blizzards to relieve the siege with fresh supplies in an army jeep towing a trailer. Anna danced through the tunnels of snow to greet him and flung herself into his arms, fishing in his pockets for a lollipop. 'Sweetie, Dada!'

Minn blushed at the child's words. Oh, Ewan, where are you? What have I done? Have I left it too late? All those months I ignored your letters. Are you punishing me now? Have you given up on our passion, given up on our promises? Why shouldn't you forget me when it's all of my own doing!

Anna was growing too fond of Harry and Minn was wary of letting him too close to her. As the weeks expanded into months and years Ewan's image was fading like a photo in the sun, blurring into a shadowy outline, and sometimes she could no longer hear the sound of his deep voice booming in her head.

Harry's presence now disturbed the calm of their retreat. He was always there waiting patiently in the wings ready to pounce. Oh, Ewan, come back soon!

Two

In the spring of 1947 Ewan Mackinnon returned to London. He had not meant to stay in France for so long but when his bursary ran out he took himself down to the vineyards to help with the grape harvest. He had drifted through the autumn and terrible winter of early '47 visiting all those who had helped him evade capture in '43. Now as a free man he visited the forest haunts, paying homage to old friends in the Maquis who had been captured, tortured or shot, calling on those families who had risked their lives in making sure that he survived. Wherever he went he was pressed to dine and stay to talk over old times.

That first stay in France had altered the direction of his own career away from destroying bridges, rail tracks, gun turrets and killing men and towards creating pictures. He toured old haunts, sketching the broken fragments of warfare, bullet-strafed houses, execution posts, bloodstains and bomb sites, capturing the sorrow and the pity of war with his paintbrush. Now that the truth of the real Resistance had come out from the shadows he was able to verify and honour those brave souls mistaken for collaborators in the heady days after June '44.

That first return to Phetray had been overshadowed by news of Minn's marriage and the tragic events that followed their lovemaking. He'd vowed to stay away from the island for her sake to protect her from gossip and calumny.

Once his commission was finished, his tour of duty over he attempted to settle down into a training course, but formal teaching did not sit easily on this ex-commando, nor did the constraints of civilian life. It was not the way he wanted to learn his craft.

In truth he no longer knew exactly what he wanted to do. Only the thought of Minn eventually by his side kept him plodding at his formal studies but she was proving elusive and difficult to contact.

Why did she not write regularly or come to visit him? He was glad that she had broken free from the confines of Phetray for a temporary position in the Scottish Borders. Yet why was she so vague about her exact location and seemingly disinterested in the news that he had been awarded a minor bursary to help with tuition and the rent of a Paris studio? Did she no longer care about their reunion? Nothing was turning out how he had hoped. The chance to study abroad seemed the only answer to his restlessness and disappointment.

His mother had died while he was abroad and his father was now settled in a parish close to Inverness. There were few ties left on Phetray, just the occasional cheery letter from his old school chum Johanna Macallum, who was teaching in Glasgow. Johanna knew nothing of Minn's departure and seemed surprised that his old sweetheart had left the island.

Ewan wrote one last letter to her last address telling Minn of his decision to go abroad and suggesting that she might like to join him. No one would care if they were lovers. Why did she not reply? He waited and waited and then left for France without a backward glance.

Two could play at that game, and he was far too wary to query her silence. Only when he returned to his London digs the following spring to collect his battered trunk from a student friend was he given a pile of mislaid letters; among them was Minn's desperate letter written in Christmas 1946 begging him to come north for Hogmanay to Peebles by train.

His first instinct was to find a call box and make a trunk call but for the life of him he didn't know the name of her employers. He sent a telegram to the post office at Pitlandry to be forwarded to 'Mrs Broddick, Housekeeper at the Big House' saying he was on his way. He bought a ticket at King's Cross Station and sat on the platform dreaming of this long overdue reunion. Now there would be no one to hinder them being together.

Months of travelling had hardened his features, coarsened his skin, fleshed out his lean frame. Living on cheese and wine and good bread once more suited him. Only his clothes were worn to tatters; his corduroys baggy and smooth in the seat, his tweed jacket patched at the elbow and his thick beard made him look like a tramp.

As he peered excitedly out of the sooty window as the train rattled up the east coast towards the Borders, he knew Minn would accept him just as he was. He could not wait to see her face when he turned up on her doorstep with open arms and a knapsack full of drawings and a bottle of lovely perfume. The years in between would seem as minutes once they were together.

How could they have stayed away from each other so long? It was Ken Broddick's accident that had forced this separation. For all he'd fought in dirty skirmishes on lightening raids, killing soldiers, traitors, the shoving of her husband's body off the rock to the mercy of the sea was something he could not forget or forgive. They should have told the island constable and be damned. It was all his fault and the silence had gone on too long. This troubled his conscience.

Was this why neither of them was able to refer to that last meeting? Was it guilt driving this wedge between them, tearing them apart? They had punished themselves with silence for too long.

He was looking out over the grey North Sea coast with interest. It was no surprise that most of his artwork was haunted by the sea; that the upsweep of the waves, the swollen waters of Phetray found its way time and time again on to his canvas. The sea was his constant inspiration and his curse. He drew upon boyhood memories of canoeing along the coast; the rocky outcrop where Agnes had died was imprinted on his mind's eye.

All the momentous events in his life had taken place close to the shore. From memory he could picture the changing colours of his own familiar seascape. One day he knew he would have to go back and face those distant shores, but not now. Now he was in the lush green borderlands of Scotland within sight of drumlin hills, cavernous gullies where the Tweed rolled down amongst the pines and firs and grazing sheep and cattle fed on green pastures.

It was an alien landscape to an Islander used to flatness, white sands and a stretch of ocean. As he sat on the country bus twisting and turning on his way to Pitlandry he thought only of Minn's welcoming arms and the sight of her silvery mermaid hair. Now at last they could be together.

The driver dropped him off by the iron gateposts. He saw before him a long drive sloping down towards the river, lined by huge black poplar trees. Ewan strolled slowly down the lane sniffing the blossom, savouring the sight of the stone house nestling in the hollow, the roof of its one turret glinting in the sunshine. It was a scene straight out of a John Buchan novel: a 'Huntingtower' perhaps but he was no Richard Hannay in his shabby tweeds and knapsack on his shoulder.

No dogs barked at his arrival so he made for the tradesmen's entrance, knowing his place in such an establishment. The courtyard was full of motorbike parts and a man was tinkering with the engine of a Lagonda sports car. He looked up with a smile. 'Sorry, old chap, Cook's day off. No scraps today.'

Ewan nodded, realizing that the chauffeur thought him some tramp on the scrounge. 'I'm Ewan Mackinnon, a friend of Mrs Broddick ... she'll be expecting me.'

'Are you now?' replied the chauffeur, looking at him more carefully. 'Ah, the Highland laddie could it be? The wanderer returns. I think she was expecting you last Hogmanay.'

'I didn't get her letter,' he explained. 'I've been studying abroad. I've only just got back. Is she inside?' Ewan found the man's attitude vaguely patronizing and made for the door.

'Sorry, no can do. You're too late. She left for Edinburgh this morning on business. She was not expecting visitors.'

'But I sent a telegram.' Ewan looked crestfallen at the news. 'I'll find somewhere to stay for the night until she returns. I'm in no rush,' he insisted, having come so far he was not to be fashed by a delay of a few hours.

'So it seems. Pity ... I think you've missed the boat, the bus and the train there ... old boy. The Lennox family think the world of Brodie, you know,' said the mechanic as he continued polishing the bonnet.

Ewan assumed he was talking to the chauffeur, and didn't want to know his opinion of Minn. He was a bit too smooth and sure of himself, that one. He turned to the line of motor bikes. 'These are old army bikes. You were in the army?'

The young man wiped his greasy fingers on a rag. 'Tank Corps actually, but these are all surplus. Do you want to buy one? I can do you a deal. Mr Lennox can supply anything for the right price.'

'I bet he can.' Ewan sniffed, sensing some scam going on. 'You work for the Lennox family then?'

'You could say that,' the man replied, eyeing up the suitor with suspicion. 'What outfit were you in?'

'Navy. Special Boat Squadron.'

'Hush, hush, chappie, nice work. A frog-man?'

'Not exactly.' Ewan shook his head, having no desire to pursue this conversation. His service record was not for general knowledge. He turned to walk back up the lane. 'I'll call back later,' he shouted.

The man was following after him, scratching his head. 'Look, I don't know if I ought to be telling you this but Brodie ... er Mrs Broddick's away to buy some fancy rig out, for a special occasion so we've gathered. She and young Mr Lennox are very pally. Now he's a grand chap, heir to all of this. Mr Roddy was a pilot, one of the few ... quite the ace. He's got a DFC and bar. They're very close. Just thought I'd better warn you, old chap. The war's over and new beginnings all round, I say. Shame to disturb her and the kiddie too, such a bonnie bairn, bright as a button. She'll be getting a good education if the Lennoxes have anything to do with it...' The chauffeur winked.

'I didn't know she had a child.' Ewan's heart started at this news.

Harry tapped his nose. 'One of those post-war-time things. Don't ask me the details but let's just say the master adores the tiny mite. Shall I be telling her where you're staying?'

Ewan was too stunned to take in all the chauffeur was hinting. 'No, perhaps not. She's probably forgotten all about me. A lot

of water under the bridge and all that...
You're sure she's happy with him?'

'Delirious, old chap. She's a born lady, fits
in beautifully, the family think she's quite
one of them. But I can tell her you called.'

'No! Not if it upsets everything. She
deserves some peace. Her first husband
made her unhappy. I just hoped when things
settled down we could get back together
again. We were sort of engaged for a while,
you see. Thanks for being so honest with me.
Perhaps it's better to let sleeping dogs lie.
My timing doesn't seem to be very good in
these matters... Better to leave things well
alone this time.'

How could he forget his arrival on the ferry
boat in Phetray and the mayhem he had
stirred up there? There could be no second
mishap. Was it nearly three years ago?

'I'm sure young Mr Lennox will be giving
her everything she wants. Only the best in
this household.' The chauffeur smiled,
looking him up and down with undisguised
superiority.

'That doesn't always make a body happy
though, does it?' Ewan argued staring hard
at the mechanic with the plush accent and
silk scarf tied round his neck.

'Oh come now, Mr Mackinnon, ladies like
the good things of life and Brodie seems no
different from the rest.'

'I suppose so... Stupid of me to think she

wouldn't run with the herd. I'll be taking my leave of you.' Ewan reached out to shake his hand firmly.

'Yes, of course, you do that, sir, pleased to meet you, Mr Mackinnon.'

'And you are?' he asked.

'Just call me Harry. I'll show you to the gate. No, wait. Fancy a spin in the jalopy? I'll run you to the station. It'll be a long journey home for you otherwise.'

'Thanks, Harry, that's most obliging of you.'

'No trouble at all. Any friend of Brodie's a friend of mine. Fine lassie, a real lady. She'll make Lennox a very happy man.'

Ewan clung on to his seat trying to clear his head as the wind whistled and the sports car roared and spluttered round the twisty lanes towards Peebles. So that was why she had not written. Too much had happened since their last meeting. Now she was a mother and soon to be a bride. There was a baby and a new life to plan. Is that why she was desperate for him to come, so she could explain it all face to face and introduce her Mr Roddy, the air force ace?

You didn't waste much time, did you? his heart cried out in anger. Every time I leave you, you find comfort elsewhere. 'Frailty, thy name is woman!' Old Shakespeare was right.

He was rattled and shaken by the chauffeur's wild driving to the station, but a lift was better than shank's pony. There was no point in staying or going back to London now. It would be easier to head north to Glasgow. He might even look up Johanna Macallum and catch up on old times before he went on to Inverness to see his father. He had her address somewhere in his rucksack. Somehow he didn't want to be alone with this disappointment. He needed to talk it all out with an old friend, and Jo Macallum was a good egg.

His mind was racing. It had happened again, him hanging back sure of her loyalty and love but staying away too long, just as before. How could one compete with a Battle of Britain ace who lived in a woodland palace, offering security and a home for his bride and their love child?

All he had brought north in his knapsack was a battered sketch pad and the promise of foreign travel. Not much to satisfy the obvious ambitions of Minnie Macfee, he sighed with bitterness. Perhaps it was time to find someone else, who would be impressed by his world and show his faithless lover two could play at that game.

'Let me see you on to the train, Mr Mackinnon.' Harry the chauffeur lifted out the kit bag with a smile.

'There's no need. I can manage,' said Ewan surprised at such willing service.

'Anything to oblige the SBS!' Harry made

a mock salute to his passenger as Ewan made for the platform. The driver waved and smiled, emptying his pockets, throwing an undelivered telegram into the waste bin with relief.

It was a glorious evening as the bus cornered the lanes tightly, brushing against the leaves of overhanging trees. Minn looked up at the flashes of spring greens and the blossom dripping from the boughs like welcoming garlands. She would never tire of this journey from the bustling city out into the winding, rolling lanes along the river Tweed, which flashed and danced in the late-afternoon sunlight. She had sat down wearily after a successful shopping trip to Edinburgh, with a box containing a ball gown of midnight blue velvet studded with silver sequins.

It had been fun trying on all the gowns in the wholesale warehouses that Harry Lennox had managed to get her passes to view, but to watch the beautiful panorama unfolding before her with her daughter sleeping on her knee was a luxury no money could buy. It had been a lovely excursion.

Harry was waiting for her at the halt looking especially pleased with himself. 'Come and see my new sports car!' he said, ushering her into the passenger seat to view his Lagonda, carrying her sleeping child into the car.

'Do you like it?'

'Not another change of car! You never keep them five minutes ... but it's very swish.' She smiled indulgently. Harry and his sports cars were a family joke.

Anna was ready for her cot. Harry followed them both into the cottage, eyeing her box. 'So you made a purchase, good show. Can I come in? You will try it for me? I want to see you in all your finery.'

'When I've put Anna to bed,' she replied wearily, for it had been a tiring day spending his money.

'Why don't you call her Nancy?' he said.

'She's my child. I like Anna,' she replied.

'But Nancy suits her better, Nancy Lennox... How does that sound?'

Minn looked up at him shocked by his presumption. 'Don't be silly, Harry, she's a Broddick.'

'Is she? If you married me she could be a Lennox,' he whispered, staring at her.

'Are you drunk? Why should I marry you?' she said, shaking her head.

'No, I'm not drunk. Never more sober. Marry me and I'll give little Nancy the whole world as her plaything. She'll have only the best, and her mother too: fine clothes, horses and a respectable name,' he said, grabbing her hand and kneeling on the floor.

'You are drunk... Get up! I told you, I'm not free to marry anyone. My husband may

235

be dead but in the eyes of the law he's still missing. I'm not free to many anyone yet, and if I were...There's someone else...'What had brought this on?

'You can forget about him! I know he never bothers to answer your letters or contact you. What sort of relationship is that?' Harry knew how to press home a valid but painful point.

'He must be abroad still,' she argued. 'I don't know... My private life is none of your business.' How dare he question why Ewan had stopped writing to her when anyone could see she was still rankled by the long silence between them.

'Oh but it is, young lady. Ever since I saw you hanging out of that window with those golden pigtails I knew I was never going to let you out of my life ... ever ... even if it does take years! You're the one I want and what I want I usually get.' Harry was smiling wickedly, raising his brows in a challenge.

'I was taught want never gets. I'm not one of your black market, fallen-off-the-lorry bits up for sale to the highest bidder,' she snapped.

'You'll never get a better offer than this. I can give you comfort and luxuries. Think about it for Anna's sake. I'll be patient, I'll stay on my bended knee all night if I have to, but I'll not be thwarted by you or anyone. Go and change into your glad rags and

let me see what wondrous goods I'm buying.' Harry wafted her into the bedroom.

There was such a glint of lust and ambition
in his foxy eye as he appraised her body, her
posture and the flush of her cheeks. Her
fingers trembled as she unfastened her plain
clothes and fingered the exquisite fabric of
the dress, looking at herself in the mirror.

Why was he being so attentive? She could
hear him singing a nursery rhyme to Anna.
Perhaps she owed her daughter a secure
future. What if Ewan never came to call?
What if he didn't acknowledge the girl as
his? What if she wasn't his baby?

She made a grand entrance out of her little
bedroom, shaking with the chill and a
frisson of fear. Harry's eyes lit up.

'You pay for dressing, Brodie. I know that
we have a business partnership but it'll work
even better if you do me the honour of
marrying me. You always make me so proud
when I take you to meet clients, but I want
more from you. I want to see passion in
those icy blue eyes. I want everyone in the
room to see what a beautiful woman is on
my arm. You've tantalized me long enough.
I don't care a jot if your hubby's alive or
dead. Marriage lines are only bits of paper.
Who cares if we jump the gun? We can go
abroad. No one will know. You and I are
going places, my darling. Pitlandry House
will soon have served its purposes and I'll

take us south to England, the Continent, wherever. What do you say?' he whispered, his eyes sparking in the firelight.

'This is only the beginning, Brodie ... only the beginning of a wonderful life. Come here and let me kiss away your fears. I'm going to make you so happy.' Harry was drawing her ever closer into his perfumed net, reeling her like a fish on a hook into his arms with promises, promises.

She looked around her shabby little room with its pitiful furniture and homespun furnishings.

Do you want this for the rest of your life? Do you want Anna to miss out on everything a gentleman's daughter might expect from an indulgent father? Across the yard in the big house there were acres of space to furnish and all that her heart desired.

She looked up at the little figurine shining on the mantelpiece. It stood so forlorn, showing up all the rest of the room with its delicacy. If you say yes to Harry who knows how many pieces of china you can add to your collection, she thought.

As Harry crushed her in his arms she cried not with joy, but with anger for Ewan. Where are you? Why have you not returned for me? There was no warmth in her lips as she kissed Harry slowly, but he opened her mouth gently at first, pressing expertly enough to arouse a flicker of a response.

His eyes glinted brightly and she knew he was buying her compliance with promises of comfort and security. The part of her that still yearned for Ewan wanted to draw back from this contract but there was a needier part of her that snatched at this unexpected offer, knowing she was getting a bargain.

Harry Lennox was taking her to his bed just as she was, flawed, with a child, from an unpromising background, and asking no questions. He wanted her youthful body, her passion and commitment in return for his protection. Was it wrong to want calmer waters after all the storms of the past few years? Here she could be safe among strangers, here Anna was already happy. Only a fool would turn this offer down, but what if Ewan ever came to collect her?

There was no use depending on other people's promises, she sighed. You have to ride the wave, a daughter of the tide must take the tide when it comes and the tide was turning in her favour for once.

You don't love him, cried her heart, but this time she must let common sense be her guide. Harry was offering respectability at long last, a good name, a chance to do good in the district and to give Anna the best chances. He was offering her the Crannog and all those childhood dreams on a china plate. Only a fool would refuse him. This time she was deciding for herself.

So what if some of the friends and acquaintances he encouraged her to entertain were a bit shady, shallow, glittery: constantly on the search for the latest distraction money could buy. Would they ignore her obvious humble background once they were married? Did they even care?

Are you marrying Harry for his money, selling yourself down the river for a cabinet of porcelain, a wardrobe of furs and satins, or to protect Anna? How will I know? she thought, and does it matter?

Three

Phetray, 1948

In the summer of 1948 Eilidh Macfee made her summer progress from Phetray via Glasgow to visit Niall and his wife, Mima, in Rutherglen, then on to Pitlandry House, where she sat bemused in the kitchen gardens, admiring the rows of vegetables as Gil Chisholm hoed the weeds down neat rows. The annual holiday visit was always strained, this time not least because Minn was in early pregnancy with her second child and felt wretched and tired, and Eilidh was full of news from the island.

'It was such a swish wedding ... Factor Macallum's daughter and Ewan *dubh*, the minister's son. They went to France on their honeymoon and now he's back painting pictures at the Crannog, a gey funny way to earn a living.' Mother paused, seeing the look of surprise flit across Minn's face. 'Ewan's mother would turn in her grave to see him dressed like a tramp and no some minister of the kirk with a dog collar around his neck.

'Still, you've done better for yourself with Harry. A rising tide lifts all boats, they say. I always hoped you'd make a go of it with the minister's son, but who knows what the Lord has in store for us!'

Minn watched her own mother treating Harry and Anna as if they were minor royalty. Her English was halting and hesitant and the little girl hung back from her stern face, steel-grey hair and plain clothes. When Harry's friends called by they assumed she was Minn's old nanny and no one told them otherwise, but Minn was not proud of this deception.

It was when Mother sat in the sunlight sucking peppermints that Minn noticed how translucent and yellowish was the skin on her face, and her plump legs were now like candlesticks, so thin she had become. 'Go and see Doctor Murray,' she suggested.

Mother shook her head firmly saying, 'I'm fine enough. It can wait. This inland air is too dry for my taste. I miss the tang of salted ling in the wind. My stomach is not used to such fancy foods. The richness of it sticks in my craw. It's time to be away home, *mo ghaoil*.' There was a far away gaze in her dull eyes like a dog pining for its own kennel.

When the telegram arrived later in the autumn addressed to Mrs Lennox at Pitlandry House, asking Minn to ring Doctor Murray on Phetray urgently, it was not entirely unexpected. 'I think you'd better be paying her a call, Mairi,' said the doctor. 'She's no long for this world. This sickness can no longer be contained. She's asking for you to come back home one last time.'

Should I take Anna from nursery school? Minn wondered, but the prospect of them squashed into the stone cottage facing a dying old lady was unthinkable. She must face this journey alone. Harry would see to her with Edie Lawrie's help. They were settled at Pitlandry now and the house was being gradually renovated to fit their growing family. Her child needed familiar surroundings when there was sadness in the house.

Minn was four months pregnant by now, still feeling sick and queasy at the thought of a sea voyage, but once summoned she made every effort to catch the next flight from Abbotsinch Airport near Glasgow, and Harry drove her to the airport in his latest Bentley.

She looked down at her wedding ring of

242

white gold studded with diamonds. They had 'married' abroad discreetly in the autumn of 1947 and Edie Lawrie, who'd married Gil Chisholm, came to live in the cottage in Minn's place. Her life was now running a large household. Mother's death would be the last chapter of her old life on Phetray.

'I can come with you,' offered Harry, anxious for the health of his coming child. 'We can transfer her to a private hospital in Peebles, if you wish.'

'No, she would hate being among strangers. Better to go alone, I think. I don't know how long this will all take. I want you to be around for Anna and see to all the alterations in the kitchen,' she said looking round proudly at her new modern kitchen, with tiled walls and the latest kitchen range. 'I want everything shipshape for Christmas when Daisy comes. Make sure that the decorators finish on time. It sounds as if this is going to be my very last visit to Phetray.'

As the plane bumped in the clouds on this sad journey north, she could feel the old pull of the isles returning. She had not regretted her decision to live with Harry. Anna must have a father, someone to provide for and cushion her from the harshness of life. No one had ever provided for Minn, only a grumpy parent and an absent uncle. Her own children would have a better life.

She smiled thinking of Harry's persistence

in wooing her. He made her laugh, distracted her from her bouts of doubt and gloom. There was none of the old fear in making love with Harry either. He was experienced with women and it showed.

He knew how to climb the ladder of success. In uniform and a kilt he was passable. Most of all he belonged to the world she had always aspired to. All her life she had been preparing for this role, even at the Crannog, she mused.

Dressing well came easily for she had an innate sense of style and an eye for colour. She looked elegant in the new Dior fashions with their full skirts and nipped-in waists. Speaking with her careful cut-glass accent gave her a cachet among the Border county set, who were intrigued about her mysterious background but assumed she was one of them from her accent and elegant clothes.

She had started off simply as Harry's escort, his consort, and gradually become Brodie Lennox, his queen, his equal.

Any black market dealings were abandoned in favour of more respectable business acquisitions now. Harry sniffed out companies to be bought and sold on, developed transport and haulage links with the Continent. Harry had the knack of finding the right man for the job and placing him in authority, giving himself time and freedom to mix in the county: in the hunting, shooting and fishing fraternity who had contacts in London and within the right circles around Edinburgh.

Once she was his wife, she was invited to join the exclusive charity committees and the coffee-morning circuit, where she too could glean information to further their cause. Together they were a team and Harry adored his little girl.

In the early days she covered for him willingly, lied to keep his standing afloat, pretended and disguised their rickety finances when deals went wrong side up, flirted with disgusting men to keep them sweet. It had not been easy but Harry had delivered all his promises to her. He was a safe option and a sure bet. He would never let her down. The fact that she had never really trusted him was always pushed to the back of her mind. When his parents died within months of each other there was no reason to stay on at Pitlandry, but neither of them could bear to move south.

Sometimes she dreamt of Ewan and the gale of passion he could stir up within her. News of his wedding had only convinced her how right she had been to choose Harry, but she envied Johanna Macallum. The ring he had given her was confined to the back of her dressing table drawer in its maroon battered box. She could not bear to look at it. Anna would have it one day for her birthday.

In her eyes he had proved as unreliable as Ken Broddick. The fact that Ewan and Jo were staying on Phetray now terrified her more than facing her mother's death.

Mother was lying in the box bed by the fire, with kind neighbours keeping the peat fire banked up and steaming pans of broth on her new stove, but she was too sick now to eat much. It was time for Minn to roll up her sleeves and see to her comforts to make the last days of her life more bearable. They had begged her mother to let them build her a bungalow on the machair but she had refused all help but a little extra money for repairs.

Now it was a dark November night and the gales were howling over the damp machair. Minn stared around the room, sniffing that familiar fug of smoke belching back out of the hearth, wondering how she had ever lived in such a hovel. She tried to stifle such shameful thoughts as her mother lay close to death.

The two of them had never been close, not even when she was young, for Mother had seemed so grim and downtrodden, having to kow-tow to Uncle Niall's commands as if she was his servant, grateful for a roof over her head, not his sister.

In later years she had been in awe of Harry and Minn's way of life and an uncomfortable visitor at Pitlandry, but no one could say that her daughter hadn't been dutiful. She did feel guilty that she had not brought her down to Pitlandry to live in a modern cottage, to spend her last years in comfort, but Eilidh was stuck in her peasant ways and spoke such halting Highland English that it would have been painful for both of them. It would never have worked. In her heart she excused this lack of insistence because she sensed that Mother would have hated to be far from the sea and the people she knew, trapped in an alien land.

Sometimes it felt as if she had neglected her mother. All those years of poverty, of coolness and silence for being a bastard child of no consequence had driven a wedge between them. Now they lived in separate worlds. Now she wanted to cushion her from the pain and the draughts but it was too late.

'Come ... close ... Minn, *mo ghaoil...* Don't be weeping for me but for yerself... There's something that I'll be shedding from my soul afore I face my Maker...' Mother whispered.

'Wheesht, Mother.' The old language came back haltingly as Minn drew the wooden chair closer to the bed.

'It's time I spoke the truth to you. Hard have I been on you to protect you from the curses of leaving this island shore. Now I'm after thinking that ma task is done if I tell my story once only to you.'

'What troubles you? What secrets are these?' She could feel the heat of her cheeks as she thought of her own guilty secrets. What was there more to say on the matter?

'Closer in, child, so the spirits hovering don't catch my tale... About your father...' Eilidh gasped.

'Yes?' she replied, hoping to find the truth would be aired at last.

'It shames me to go to ma grave without unburdening the sorry tale of him. Don't get hopes up. The truth of it is no very edifying.'

'So who is the mystery man I've lived with all these years? I'd love to know his name.' Minn bent to hear the whispering lips.

'It is shaming me that I dinna ken his name. I was in service in Glaschu, a very respectable place in Kelvinside in the West End. I was sent as a maid at just fifteen. They were a musical family with this big pianny. I had to polish it every day. They said it was one of the last to come down the water afore the Great War ... a Winklemann. I can see they letters etched in gold. I had to sit underneath to polish its legs, big round curvy legs, fat as a beast. I knew every grain of wood on that wooden beast. I was the tweeny... You know how that is, up and down stairs, a wee dogsbody trying to keep out of sight of the mistress like some sea misty ghost on the stairs.' The effort of talking was exhausting her but she drew a deep breath.

'One night there was a concert at the St Andrews Hall and the pianny man came to tune the beast. Then the man came to practise on our pianny, to loosen his fingers on the keys, leaving his finger marks on all my polishing. He made fine music. I'll give him that. I was polishing the legs when he came in and hid under the beast out of the way, with the bangs and crashes in ma ears deafening me like the crack o' doom.'

Minn had never heard this tale before, and could picture how it was at the Crannog.

'The house fell silent when they all went to hear him play and we were made to wait up and see to the fires and the supper on their return. I sat at yon pianny and tried to make it sing for me but it wouldn't play. Then they came back with the pianny man and there was a fuss, more singing and playing and fizzy wine and they all said he was the maestro.

'He patted the beast and said it was a fine instrument and well cared for.' Eilidh was swallowing and Minn gave her a drip of water from the little funnel cup.

'I waited until they all went to bed to see to the fire in the music room. He was still pacing up and down, full o' wine and praising. I saw he was an older man with a moustache, very tall. I bent down to see to the coal bucket. He took me by surprise.'

Minn's heart was thumping as she saw the scene in her head in the half-light of flickering firelight and gas lamps: the rump of the young maid in her starched rustling skirt, round and inviting, the man watching her bend...

'He took me on the floor under the pianny. I was trapped like a ship in a glass bottle. He forced me open ... for his own relief, like a bull at a coo as if I was some beast of the field. I was so afeart. I shut my eyes to hide from this shaming under the roof of that damned pianny. Just a wee maid, I was, intact, innocent o' the ways of men, but no more after that night. You heard o' such things, but the shame of it... I'll say no more.'

'Oh, Mother, who was it who did this to you?'

'I've no mind of his name ... only his music and his pianny, but I ken he was from foreign parts. He spoke a gey queer English. His shadow was tall. I found golden hairs on my shirt. You must have his looks for they're no mine. I was so shamed when I knew my condition that I wrote away home and begged for my fare. I told nobody.

'He was the guest in the house, a stranger but no gentleman. So it makes no difference. I never clapped eyes on the beast again until you were born and I saw those blue eyes staring up at me. Gie me a sip of water.'

Minn poured from the stone jug into the

invalid cup with its tiny spout to aid the supping of liquid down her mother's parched throat. 'All this time I've let them think I fell to some fisherman as his whore. Then I hear you singing and carrying on, making music and growing like a beanpole. I wished you dead many a time but new life flies with its own wings, they say, and you've made your way despite your birthing to be a lady: one who can hold her head up in any company. I see you turn your nose up now at the bed on which you were born in such fear.' Eilidh lifted her head from the pillow as her daughter wept at this sad tale.

'All this time you've kept this festering in your heart. It wasn't your fault. You should have told me before,' she cried.

'Would it make any difference, *mo ghaoil?* What's for you will no go past you as you well know.' Eilidh sobbed in gasps and Minn grabbed her bony hand and cried for all the pain her mother had held in her heart.

'It tore at my heart to see you at a pianny singing and carrying on, knowing where you get all that music... What's done is done and can't be altered. I've said ma piece and that's the end of it. I can go now and it's time. I've had enough of this pain. It's been a hard life but the Lord is merciful. The doctor has eased my pain away. Fetch the salt and the earth.'

Minn wept softly as she searched for a

saucer and sprinkled on some salt and drew grit from the soil outside the door, mixing them together in the saucer to place on her mother's chest to settle her dying spirit the old way.

Why wait until now to tell me all this? her heart cried out with shame and pity. If only we had been closer and not such strangers. Poor lonely Mother, these last words on earth explained her strictness, her shame and her reluctance to let her leave Phetray.

'Has the tide turned yet? I shall go out with the tide into the sea without a shore...' Eilidh lay quietly with her face to the wall, turning from life, breathing in rasps now.

Minn dozed by her side, jolting herself awake to see if there was any change, holding her hand. In the early light she saw that there was no more breathing and opened the door to release Eilidh's spirit into the wind. The shoreline was littered with spoils from the sea and the tide was far out, carrying her mother's sad soul to *Tir nan og.*

There would be much to see to, visits to make and a funeral arranged. She would wire Harry not to come to the funeral. She would see to it all herself. In death as in birth there had only ever been the two of them. So now Eilidh would have the best of funerals. It was the only way Minn could soothe her guilty heart.

Underneath her fine clothes, cashmere and silks, the mink coat and the diamond watch flashing on her wrist, the handmade brogues, nothing was changed. Here on Phetray she felt still that bastard child, conceived in lust and born in fear.

Why had they never understood each other until it was too late! If only she could have admitted how right mother was to fear her own fate, how ungrateful she had been. If only they had loved each other, but there was no touch of love between them, even at the end they had kept their distance.

In the days that followed she was busy making arrangements, ordering provisions and a hearse, until Uncle Niall and his shrimp-like wife, Mima, came on the first boat from Glasgow. As male head of the household he wanted to make all the decisions. She retreated into the local hotel sick of watching Mima claw her way through Mother's trunk like a vulture, sifting out all Minn's expensive gifts: silk scarves and lamb's-wool cardigans, pretty stone brooches still unwrapped and unused, packing them in her suitcase to take home for herself.

Uncle Niall saw to the burial plot and the catering for the funeral tea. Harry sent a lavish bouquet by air from Anna. Mother might have been born in poverty but she was buried with no expense spared on Minn's part. Her presence on the island did not go unnoticed and many, more out of curiosity than duty, called to pay their respects.

Uncle Niall was just as wizened and dour as she remembered as a child, and his wife tried to pretend all the tasteful catering arrangements for the funeral tea were their own idea.

It was easy to slip back into the role of useless girl, but a Lennox woman was not to be ignored. The marble headstone would be finely engraved and erected exactly to her specification. The bed was made up for Uncle Niall, but thankfully they preferred to stay at the local tavern to see his old seafaring shipmates.

There was a crumb of comfort in sitting alone with the body until the day the men came for their dram and took the coffin down to Kilphetrish kirkyard to be placed next to Grandfather Macfee and his line-up of ancient relatives. Here they were warmed with another dram and then on to the Tulloch for Niall's wake.

The women in black and grey sat around the croft sipping tea and cracking to each other at a speed Minn was finding hard to follow. Her Gaelic was rusty, but fluent enough to overhear that Ewan *dubh* was back on the island with his wife.

Walking along the beach she bent westward into the wind, humbled by its force, pausing to catch her breath, heart thudding at the news.

Phetray was an island of winds that whistled, sang, roared as they pleased. 'Isle of the singing winds,' some bard had proclaimed. Now it was screaming into her ears, making them ache, 'There is danger here!'

How she needed to escape. The coastal path was tarmacked where once her bare feet had skipped along the rutted sandy track chasing the hens. The narrow lanes still stretched from Kilphetrish like arteries pumping the daily gossip from the harbour in carts and traps to the four corners of the island. Nothing was changed: the shimmering outlines of the purple isles across the white sand bay, the roaring tide and waves. Yet everything was changed. Ewan was here on the island and she was afraid.

Visiting old haunts and looking out at the grey water with aching eyes, she had forgotten how depressing the winter months on Phetray could be. Now she longed for the safe warmth of Pitlandry and Anna: the warmth of the kitchen stove and the chatter of children bickering over toys. She yearned for the satiny quilt of her eiderdown, the eagerness of Harry's embrace.

Pitlandry was her rightful home, where all things were possible because Harry was generous and careful for them. Ewan Mackinnon seemed like some far-distant ghost from a half-forgotten past. He had proved unreliable and cold. He was not the upstanding island son everyone thought him on Phetray where his praises echoed in every conversation. He was cruel and fickle and unreliable and she never wanted to see him again.

Four

Kilphetrish

There was a phone message left for Minn at the Phetray Hotel and a card with a small bunch of late roses from Mrs Ewan Mackinnon, which read: 'We were sorry to hear of your sad loss.'

She picked them up with trembling fingers. So they were both here. Word would have gone round the townships. As if reading her very thoughts the young manager called out her name.

'Mrs Lennox? A call for you.'

Minn ran to his office hoping it was Harry and Anna ringing to give her support after such a long day.

'Minn... *Ciamar a tha thu?*' said a familiar voice. How was she? After all these years, how could Ewan just pick up the phone out of the blue? There was no escaping this encounter and Minn's voice trembled.

'Ewan *dubh?* What a surprise.' There was no warmth in her voice or the English of response.

'Minn, it is you? I knew you'd come home... I was sorry to hear about Eilidh,' he was continuing as if he hadn't heard her coolness.

'Thank your wife for the flowers. It was thoughtful of her,' she said.

'Johanna has a kind heart.' There was an awkward pause. 'How long are you staying?'

'I leave tomorrow on the boat. I can't face flying back at the moment,' she replied, trying to sound cold and indifferent.

'Mistress Macfee must have been glad you came to her at the end,' he said.

'I know my duty.' She bristled at his insinuation. 'What brings you back to Phetray after all these years?'

'The call of the sea, the turn of the tide, a chance to take stock and think about my work before we are off travelling again. I've always worked better in the open and on the move.'

'Is Johanna happy to be back?' Minn was keeping her voice smooth.

'She's resting. We've a child on the way. You know how it is in the early days,' he offered.

Minn patted her own stomach and smiled briefly. 'I do indeed. I can hardly keep anything down myself at the moment,' she replied.

'Are you still in the Borders?' he continued.

'Yes, we decided to stay on there. It suits the family,' she added.

'How many are there of you now?'

'A little girl and one on the way. We are hoping for a boy this time.' She was shaking. Why was he asking these questions?

'Mr Lennox must be a proud man. It's a fine spread you have there,' Ewan answered.

'How do you know? You've never seen Pitlandry,' Minn gasped. What was Ewan hinting at?

'I have so... I came to see you.' There was a deafening silence. Minn felt her stomach churning and her legs shaking.

'When was that?' she said, suddenly feeling queasy.

'Last year, in the spring after that dreadful winter. I was in Europe and missed most of it, but when I found your letter I sent you a telegram and came on the next train,' he said.

'I received no telegram from you. Not one word. You came up to Pitlandry and I was never told? Who did you see there?' Even her voice was trembling now.

'The chauffeur. He told me all about your pilot and your little girl ... discreetly, of course,' he answered, and Minn felt the shock waves down her body. She wrapped her fur coat around her to shield herself from this blow. His words were making no sense.

'What chauffeur? There was no chauffeur

then. In fact, I did most of the driving my-self,' she snapped.

'He was mending a rather splendid Lagonda, if I recall correctly, a ginger-haired chap. He told me all about your engagement to the air force chappie.'

'You're talking double Dutch!' Minn was shouting down the phone. 'I was never engaged to a pilot! Who told you this?'

'Harry, the chauffeur. It was he who told me all about the Battle of Britain hero, Roddy Lennox.'

She could hear the sneer in his voice. There was another silence.

'I think you've made a mistake, Ewan. Roderick Lennox died in the Great War. Harry is his younger brother. I married Harry eventually, when you never came. And did Harry tell you I had a child by his brother too? Oh God, the bounder! I knew he could bluff, but this ... it takes my breath away!' Minn's voice was trembling as she tried to make herself understood. 'And you believed him? I wrote to you and waited and waited but you didn't come. I thought you didn't care. Oh, Ewan. He's cheated us. He must have taken the telegram and waited for you. Then he told a pack of lies and when I was low he pounced. He asked me to marry him.'

The phone line began to crackle. She was trying to grasp what Ewan was saying.

'Sorry, Minn, my timing was always a bit

off... I was frightened of getting in the way again like I did with Ken. After Ken's death... Do you blame me? I just thought it better to disappear. He took me to the station and saw me off. I fell for his story hook, line and sinker! I thought he was a good chap going out of his way to do me a favour.'

'The only favour Harry ever does is for himself. Oh, Ewan,' she pleaded. 'I can't believe it. You were in Pitlandry and I never knew it and here's me thinking you didn't care. I never stopped hoping but I thought you no longer remembered all our promises,' she whispered, thinking fast. All the years rolled away and she could see them together once more alone on the shore.

'I've always loved you, Ewan. Harry could never make me feel what I felt for you. These years have made no difference, have they?' There was no stopping her now.

Ewan's voice was shaking as if he had been taken by surprise. 'But we're both married now, Minn. It alters things. Johanna is a good wife to me and there's a baby on the way.'

'I know and I bet she's not a bit like me, is she?' Minn answered, shocked at her own desperation. 'After what we've both heard we can't just leave it like this, can we? Harry has lied and cheated. I owe him nothing. How could he do this to us?'

'Because he loved you and bagged you for himself. He was ruthless but he's got what he wanted now,' said Ewan, and his answer sounded final. She was too angry to let him go.

'All these years he's let me think ill of you, making it easy for me to give in to him. If I'd known you were still waiting I'd never have married him. You must believe that!' she cried down the phone.

'But you did marry him, Minn, and I thought I was doing what was best for you. He suggested that the Lennoxes could give you all the things I couldn't so I let you go. It seemed the fairest thing to do after Ken. His shadow has loomed large over our lives. I never want to destroy anyone again.'

'Shush! Walls have ears here! If only you'd trusted me. I wrote because I had so much to tell you about us, so many things to explain,' she pleaded, pacing up and down and around the phone cord, banging her hand on her head.

'Where does the baby fit into all of this, or was that another figment of his vivid imagination?' said Ewan.

The moment had arrived at last to tell him the truth about Anna.

'I was coming to her. Oh, Ewan! She's such a beauty... I want to tell you about her but I want to tell you face to face. Meet me at the beach tomorrow morning. No one will see us. I have to tell you about Anna,' she whispered.

'I'm not sure that's wise, Minn. I don't want trouble... It's been over for us a long time now.'

'It can't be over for us, we've something binding us together for ever. You have to understand about Anna. I want to explain it all. Surely you still feel something for me deep down ... please, for auld lang syne!' she was pleading.

'You're distraught... It's your mother's death affecting you. Once we walk down that road there's no saying where it will end ... in tears and guilt like the last time, or have you forgotten?' His voice was trembling too.

'You sound so hard and cruel. It wasn't my fault Harry messed up our reunion. My head is bursting with regrets. You've no idea what the past few days have dredged up for me, and now this,' she pleaded. 'Just come to our *traigh* tomorrow morning, please.'

'But if you'd truly wanted me, Minn, you'd have kept on waiting and turned the Lennox fellow down. If you truly loved me you'd have not left one pebble on the beach unturned until you had traced me. I think that Harry's offer was always too good to turn down. Look at you. It is said you are a lady now with fine furs, a queen on the island.

'It's been noticed, girl, how you never brought your daughter to see your mother but kept away for fear of getting her shoes muddy. There are many eyes and ears on

Phetray who'll be telling the truth and shaming the devil. You took Harry's offer as you took poor Ken Broddick's offer. I realized a long time ago that you and I were not meant to be.' He paused. 'Perhaps it's our punishment for what we did to Ken. There's no going back to the way we were. We've both changed. Johanna is a good friend and I won't betray her loyalty, however many promises you and I made in the past, Minn.'

'But it's not fair. I waited when you went missing. I waited for you after the war,' she argued.

'Not for long enough. You've always liked your comforts, and the temptation of an easy life was just too much. So go back and enjoy all your comforts. It'll make this disappointment more bearable,' he sneered.

How could Ewan be saying these words?

'Go to hell Ewan *dubh*, you black heart! Why did you ring me then? Was it just to taunt me with all of this? It's not fair!' Minn was sulking, her lips pouting into a tight ball.

She could hear the laughter in his voice. 'If I could see how you're sounding it would no be a pretty sight, Minnie Macfee! You made your choices and we've all got to live with them as best we can. Go back to Harry the chauffeur and wring his neck or squeeze him dry. It's far too late for us now.'

'But I have to tell you about Anna...' Minn was screaming down the phone. 'Come to the beach tomorrow,' she ordered, but the phone had gone dead.

How could that man say such things, insult her with such venom when her mother was not cold in her grave? Where there was hate there was also love, she mused. Perhaps he was as shocked and stunned by her presence on the island as she was by his. He wanted her to flee from its shores but she was going to go to their beach for auld lang syne and he would come.

She tossed in her narrow bed listening to the sound of waves pounding on the shingle. He must come. What they had to say to each other must be said face to face. Ewan was no coward. He would come and she would feel his arms around her once more and the scent of his breath. This was their special island and he had always belonged to her here.

She ate no breakfast and walked along the coastal path in the wind and the rain. Her shoes were soaking in the boggy machair but Minn drew strength from fresh air. It was a longer walk than she recalled and she was tiring but she could have made her way blindfold such was her confidence that he would be waiting there once more.

Beach of the singing winds was calling them both, carrying their old loving promises across the air into the ocean. Today Ewan would hear the truth at last and they could begin afresh putting all the past misunderstandings and mistakes behind them.

She could hardly wait to see his handsome face, and he would see how sleek and smart she was, how well dressed in a cashmere suit and furs. How grown up she now was.

She waited on the sand by the edge of the sea watching the roaring waves and listening to the howl of the wind through the rocks. She waited by the iron gate on to the machair and found the boulders where they had first made love. She waited and waited until she knew it was time to walk back for her luggage but still Ewan did not come.

Later, as she hung over the rail of the steamer chugging out of Kilphetrish harbour to plough its way back to Oban in the choppy winter sea, she wept. The seagulls screeched overhead as the islanders waved off the boat in time-honoured fashion. There was no one to see her humiliating departure. There was no one left who cared if she ever returned.

In her belly were the first quickenings of life like the flutter of butterfly wings. 'New life flies with its own wings,' Mother had once said ruefully, but she would be carrying this child now with little joy.

How could she ever forgive Ewan's cowardice? How could he walk away from meeting her? Perhaps he now thought her foolish and extravagant, vapid and shallow. Perhaps he no longer desired her, thinking her fickle and mercenary in marrying for money. Perhaps it was true. There was a fatal weakness in some of her decisions, but it was his staying away that shamed her most. Was he afraid to see her?

How could she have thrown herself at him so eagerly after all these years? The bond between them was shattered and for Ewan there was no going back, for Jo's sake. He was an honourable man and she was a faithless woman.

Now she was leaving Phetray with a cold steel plate of armour round her broken heart. Never would she return to this shameful island and all the broken promises. Her throat was dry and her voice had cracked when she had tried to sing a funeral elegy for Mother. No love song would ever pass these lips again, she thought. Her ears would be deaf to the siren sounds of music.

She was after all a bastard child, not of Phetray, but some mongrel mixture born of such a cruel mating. That must be another secret.

Minn turned away from the retreating grey shore to face the open sea ahead. From now on she was going to live life to the full as Harry's lady. With a vengeance would she see to it that he gave her everything she desired in payment for his treachery.

Never would she tell him of this discovery, but it would lie between them in the sheets like a brick wall.

Ewan paced around studio half the night. You must be off your head to make contact with her after all these years, he thought. Why was he considering meeting his old love on the *Traigh gaodh nan seinn?* Only a fool would meet that sea *cailleach* again.

He was ashamed of his outburst over the telephone, words spoken in anger to a woman still in the throes of grief. Hearing the shock of her revelation about Harry Lennox's treachery had slowly dammed the torrent of his own spite. They had both been duped by this man's cunning deception. Now he must be strong for both of them and walk away from temptation, turn his back on her pleadings, to the awful truth of their betrayal without a backward glance, for Johanna and their baby's sake.

He had slammed down the phone on Minn in fear, not hearing out her story about her bairn. In truth he had fled from her voice, from the power of her presence on the island and her eagerness to meet him once more. The impact of that smile would never change. He would be as helpless as on the very first day that they had met.

She was a dangerous woman, he argued to himself, a magnetic force, pulling him like the tide into treacherous waters. There was his wife to consider. He loved Johanna's gentle ways, and there was a new life to prepare for. Johanna was the one who had comforted his disappointments, built up his confidence, stuck by him in college, supporting them financially in this time.

Surely he was man enough to face that siren and stand firm by his principles and walk away from her wiles. Surely old friends could be sensible and rational and considered in all their actions when they met. What was the harm in bidding her farewell one more time?

He woke early to do the morning chores, seeing to the fire and the stove as usual, combing the beach for firewood along the shoreline. He often took his sketchbook to the far end of the island to capture a scene, to finish off some detail. Johanna was feeling sick and rose slowly in the morning to ease her discomfort. She would not worry if he left her for a few hours. It was after all her suggestion that they contact Minn before the funeral.

He had stayed away from Eilidh's funeral and the burial out of respect. Surely there was no harm in visiting Minn now to pay his respects.

Deliberately he rode out on his bike in the opposite direction from their appointed meeting place. He took his sketch pad out to the north shore to the circle of standing stones to catch the morning light on the gnarled stones, to sketch in the final details for a study of rocks and fortresses he was making. He listened to the gulls screeching and sipped from his hip flask, gathering courage before he would face his old lover for the last time.

Time always flowed freely when he was at work, and it was only when he saw the light had shifted that he paused to glance at his watch. It said ten o'clock but he could tell by the sun that it was nearer midday. He shook his wrist but the minute hand was still. The damned thing had stopped and he hadn't noticed. He had only the sun to go by and he was late, far too late.

He should have been relieved that fate had intervened once more to prevent their meeting, but Ewan was cycling like the furies towards her, along the flat tracks that curled and turned through farm yards to find a short cut, carrying the cycle over the bogs and marsh land, heading ever westwards towards the beach of the singing winds.

Perhaps she would still be waiting. Perhaps it was not as late in the day as he feared. On he cycled into the wind that tore at his flapping windcheater and baggy corduroys, pushing him backwards not forwards.

Now it was imperative that he made the rendezvous with Minn, imperative that they make one final farewell and finish the business between them begun so long ago.

Puffing and winded he sped down the hidden valley, but knew in his heart she was long gone. He heard the distant hoot of the steamer leaving Kilphetrish harbour and sat down with his head between his hands.

Alone he faced the grey-green crashing of waves pounding the shore, flinging their spume in a welcome spray. The sea did not care. The sea was a fickle mistress of fortune, swayed by moon, wind and tide. The sea had taken their dead and not thrown back the evidence, and the sea had stolen his little sister without mercy and crushed her on its rocky heart. In his fevered brain Minn and the sea were one and the same to him.

For days after her departure he hunted on the shore for a sighting of Minn while knowing in his head that she had left the island for good. He took his sketchbook down to the water, walking for hours, sifting through ideas for a large seascape upon which he could express all his anger and sorrow, a canvas on which to vent his frustration and fury in some meaningful madness.

He must work through the night to erase Minn Macfee's hold on his heart, making huge waves to drown out her face from his mind for ever. With the help of whisky and cigarettes he saw before him a terrible sea hag with gorgon hair and grasping claws. Then the vision changed into a beautiful mermaid sunning her body on the rocks, luring him towards her with siren songs; the arching waves were in her hair and the sea in the colour of her eyes. With this vision came the terrible sight of shipwrecks and the broken bodies of mariners flung on the white sand. Agnes drowning, her body bloated and her eyes picked clean flashed before him. Life and death, lust and love, passion and betrayal were in his brushstrokes that night.

As dawn rose it was finished. Ewan looked upon the sight of his creative wrath and was satisfied.

Part of him stood back to admire the effect. It was rougher and more alive than anything he had ever painted before. There was a new confidence to his style with a careless but powerful use of colour. There was something new growing from all this hurt and he liked the effect. He would experiment again with the same textured effect.

This painting would never be for sale but would lie hidden, its face to the wall of his studio, gathering dust, as a warning: a constant reminder of the futility of love. It would not be for public viewing. He could never inflict the grief of his lost passion on anyone, especially not Johanna. She would be hurt by these feverish outpourings if she knew how much loving Minn was his muse. Minn would always have a corner of his heart but her face must be turned to the wall.

The canvas was laid to rest covered in brown paper on the shelf where it must stay to remind only him of his own frailty, weakness and his lost love. It was signed and dated. The title was scribbled on the back of the canvas: *Traigh gaodh nan seinn.* Beach of the singing winds. 1948.

This canvas would be the first born of his grieving and Ewan would insist that after his death it must be burnt and the ashes scattered with his own at sea. Perhaps now he would find some peace.

Five

Pitlandry, 1950

'You ought to be doing something with that voice of yours, Mistress Lennox,' whispered the choirmaster, Archie Carswell, after the rehearsal in Pitlandry parish church. 'It's far too good for this wee choir. I know someone in Edinburgh who'd loved to take you on. It's a solo voice, a Kathleen Ferrier voice lying undiscovered in this backwater,' he sighed.

There was much talk about the discovery of this Lancashire woman whose prodigious talent was taking the operatic world by storm.

'Thank you, that's most kind of you, but no thank you, Archie. Coming to the choir each week suits me fine. What would I want with singing lessons?' Minn brushed off his compliments with a weary smile.

'With respect, I disagree,' Archie argued. 'A voice like yours should be used, stretched and trained to give pleasure to others not stuck in a pew and brought out only Sundays.'

'Now when would I be getting time for trips to Edinburgh with two children, a house to run and husband who's too busy for his own good?'

'Mr Lennox is in London again?' Archie asked with deference, and she nodded. 'I'd love you to do the Introit solo for "Lead me Lord".'

'I'm not sure, since Hew was born... I'm not sure,' Minn sighed, torn between her lethargy and wanting to please Archie to stop him pestering her again.

If only she didn't feel so tired and indecisive. The truth was that since her return from Phetray after her mother's death everything was an effort and the thought of standing up in front of the congregation, having to learn a new piece of music, was something she could do without.

'I'll think about it and let you know,' she

said hoping that he would now forget all about his request and she could just nestle behind the stone pillar with the other sopranos unnoticed.

There were so many alterations to oversee while Harry was away on yet another of his trips south: the new kitchen, and the stable block to be converted into a huge garage for the Pitlandry fleet, an expanding range of expensive cars.

Harry's motors were like his baby son, cosseted and preened over, his pride and joy. Only behind a wheel driving fast did he seem to relax.

Minn drove a large shooting brake, a belated present for her birthday. At the time it felt more like an afterthought for Harry's collection than a real expression of love to her.

Since Hew's birth in the summer of 1949 their marriage seemed to be limping along. The birth of a son was the pinnacle of success for Harry but Minn felt so lethargic and depressed, unable to snap out of the doldrums, uninterested in the growing success of the Lennox Corporation.

Her world was shrinking to the nursery and schoolroom and taxiing her daughter to an exhausting array of lessons, pony club meetings and birthday parties. Harry spent more and more time in London and Edinburgh developing his ventures and she had no energy or desire to accompany him to all the dinners and business gatherings. Since her return from Phetray they both were busy avoiding each other.

The doctor had suggested she took herself off abroad into the sun to lift her spirits, but the thought of being stranded on some foreign beach seemed more effort than it was worth.

Since that fateful return from Mother's funeral it was as if the two of them inhabited separate worlds now: she and the children lived in the Borders and Harry joined them at weekends for parties, balls and hunting in the season. Outwardly nothing had changed, inwardly she was in turmoil.

They were seldom alone for there was always some business visitor dragged up north to sample the splendours of Pitlandry hospitality and some good shooting. Harry would stay up late at these boozy functions, with the sort of businessmen who bored Minn rigid. Then he would stagger home legless at dawn, sleeping in his dressing room so as not to disturb her fitful sleep.

Life went on at Pitlandry House at its own pace in tune with the seasons. She never tired of its woodland beauty. She found she relaxed best helping Gil Chisholm in the vegetable garden digging over the fine tilth, planting out and planning new borders. Alone in the enclosed world of their kitchen garden there was no time to brood while Hew sat in the bucket pram, as had his sister before him, throwing his toys out on to the path for her to retrieve.

He was the image of his father with foxy hair and bright eyes and she adored his chubby arms around her neck. Anna was growing fast and about to start in the village school. She wore dark pigtails and an intense look in her eyes signalling determination to master every move with her pony, Dusky.

Sometimes when Anna frowned there was a v-shaped furrow over the bridge of her nose and for a second Minn would think she recognized something but then stop herself. It was no good moping about what had happened in the past: better to let things be now.

Singing in the church choir was another simple pleasure and now Archie was going to spoil it by suggesting she did a solo or took her musical interest seriously.

The ache in her heart for what might have been with Ewan had dulled over the past year. There was no point in telling Harry his deceit was unmasked. Why rake up old bones; better to leave them buried with her dreams. Yet it had brought up all her doubts about his honesty and destroyed her trust in him. What else did she not know about?

Now there was the joy of children, of course, but what about when they were sent away to school? Sometimes the emptiness inside her felt like a pain.

To the outside world Mairi Lennox had everything. She appeared like an elegant white swan gliding calmly through her commitments to the village: Women's Rural, church, charity work without so much as a ripple on the surface, but Minn knew otherwise. Underneath all this graciousness and geniality was a darker unknown part of herself paddling like fury to keep afloat, with all those shadowy secrets that hid in the recesses of her mind.

Strange how the world she had coveted in the Crannog all those years ago no longer satisfied. Why when she had everything around her was she not content? Why was it when she looked at Harry, with his moustache already peppered with grey, his agate eyes and slight paunch, did she feel a growing sense of panic?

The minister had preached last week something from St Augustine about taking what you want in life but being prepared to pay the asking price for it. She had craved security and comforts all her life but there was little joy now in their acquisition. Even her collection of china no longer interested her.

No one had warned her that a cabinet of cold porcelain figurines was no substitute for real love. Ewan's gift of the shepherd and shepherdess still stared from the shelf, unmoved by her restlessness. He no longer cared so why should she?

Perhaps what she needed was another interest, something to take her mind from everything, and listening to music was a great comfort to the soul. Should she take up Archie's suggestion? A trip on the train to Edinburgh, shopping on Princes Street might shake her out of this lethargy. She might have tea with a friend.

What friend? Who are you kidding, she thought? Most of the wives she met with Harry were acquaintances, strictly for business with no common points of interest.

If one was as rich as one's friends then she was a pauper, she sighed. To have a friend you have to be a friend and she was too wrapped up in the children and the house to take time to make any. She felt alone now in this marriage with just hired help and the children for company.

Edie and Gil Chisholm were the nearest she had to loyal friends, but they knew nothing of her private turmoil.

Perhaps a proper assessment of her vocal chords by a professional teacher would put paid to all this nonsense once and for all. Archie would be satisfied when he heard that his prodigy was after all just a middle-of-the-road mezzo-soprano.

The morning of her visit to Moira Sanderson in Elgin Square Minn dressed with care, not knowing how to present herself before the teacher: country housewife in tweeds, smart girl about town in a shapely two-piece with a peplum jacket and straight skirt or casual in a swagger coat, slacks and scarf? None of these seemed right somehow.

Minn the singer was plain Minn Macfee of Phetray and she would have worn a kilt and a Fair Isle jumper, her hair brushed back into a chignon and a beret. The songs she would sing would be the old ballads and she knew them by heart.

She had taken herself far from the island but no one could take the Hebridean childhood out of her soul, haunted as it was by such yearnings for escape. In her heart she was still that scraggy child singing by the shore in a dirty dress and bare feet. She would dress simply in a tartan and cashmere with a string of fine pearls just to give her courage.

She caught the early train with instructions left for the children to be good for Edie and a belated call from Harry wishing her luck for the audition. She was hours too early for her appointment and hung about the shops in Princes Street. The rationing seemed worse than ever and there was nothing to tempt her in the shop windows but paper displays.

Since the war everything looked shabby and tired, the buildings needing paint and shoppers all greys and duns with no colour anywhere.

There was plenty of time to stroll through the gardens and take in the latest exhibition at the Scottish Royal Academy. Here she could feast her eyes on some colour.

It felt so peaceful to walk through the Grecian splendour and the cool stillness of the viewing rooms after the bustle of the busy streets, her feet echoing on the marble floors.

There was a mixed exhibition of young Scottish painters and sculptors. She glanced at the catalogue, recognizing Willie Wilson's work, Joan Eardley's paintings of the east coast and Ian Fleming's stone harbours and harled cottages. The theme of the exhibition was Seascapes and Sky. Then she saw a canvas and her heart stopped.

It was a violent seascape of crashing waves and a shoreline on which a coiled lone figure was lying on the sand with dark hair streaming out like seaweed, naked, vulnerable against the power that had thrown the body back to the beach. She sat down breathless to search out the artist in the catalogue and saw the title. *Agnes*.

The signature was so familiar that she found she was shaking at the imprint of a memory she could never quite recall.

There were two other canvases by Ewan Mackinnon, both of Phetray, one of an upturned boat used as a shed by the beach, every detail lovingly coloured.

Ewan, dubh... Ciamar a tha thu? How are you doing? Can I never be free of you her heart cried as she sat transfixed by the oils, feeling the island tugging at her heart again. How could she be living so far from the sea? His pain and anger were in that canvas. Here were the rich blues and greens and greys, the white sands and all the colours she missed. She could feel the island's breath on the salt air, taste the smoky tangle of shingle and rocks as she sat lost in time and memories until jolted back by her watch.

It was time to run now to find the house and the stranger who would listen to her singing. Her throat was dry with emotion. How could she sing after such a shock? It was impolite not to turn up, but if only she could catch the first train home and forget those haunting images.

Moira Sanderson was tall and elegant in a jersey wool dress that emphasized her willowy shape, not at all the teacher that Minn was expecting. By the time she found Elgin Square she was breathless and pink.

'I'm sorry, I'm late. I went to the exhibition and sort of lost track of time. I do apologize,' said Minn, aware that her hair was sprouting out of its chignon and her

281

cheeks were aflame.

'Sit down and tell me a little about yourself, Mrs Lennox. Archie tells me you have a voice worth hearing,' the teacher said, ushering her into a large drawing room with a grand piano in the corner.

'I can't sing now. I've had a shock,' she replied, feeling the tears rising in her eyes. 'Forgive me. I had a baby last year and I've not been myself. I greet at the slightest thing and I hate to be late. This is a terrible mistake. I'm sorry to waste your time,' she said, rising to leave. 'Please excuse me.'

'I'll be the judge of that. Sit down and take some deep breaths. There's plenty of time to sing, but tell me more about you. I see you're wearing tartan; which one?' said Moira, sitting down, unperturbed by Minn's anxiety.

'It's Macfee, my mother's family. I'm from Phetray. I never knew my father,' she said, aware of the big piano and her mother's last words, feeling it was better to leave her history at that. 'I sang a little as a child. I like music, any sort of music, but I've no training.'

'You sang in the Mod?' Moira asked.

'No, I'm ashamed to say.' How could she explain that the likes of her never were entered into a competition?

'Then sing me something you would have sung then ... in the Gaelic,' the teacher asked.

282

'I can't remember... I brought some ballads,' she offered half-heartedly, pulling out a few scores from her shopping bag.

'Sing me something you would have sung as a child, anything will do, a lullaby, a waulking song, come on, don't get upset. You've had a shock. Sing me something that tells me how you are feeling.' The teacher was trying to coax the music out of her. It was not going to be easy.

Minn stood up and looked out across the beautiful square and the grand houses opposite. It was a city landscape of grey stone and porticos. She thought about Ewan's pictures hanging in the gallery. He was an important artist now.

Then the memories of Phetray and the little girl who used to sing by the shore to the seal, the old Colonel, all those years ago came flooding back. If only you'd known then what you know now, she sighed to herself.

From somewhere deep inside came this groan of sorrow, of yearning for home, anguish for her lost love, and she sang the lament for the drowned brother: *'Cumha Iain Ghairbh Ratharsair'*. She sang through her tears in a language she thought she had abandoned and it soared across the room up into the high ceiling, out of the open window so people stopped and looked up to see who was singing, and then she stopped.

'I can't go on. I'm sorry. I have to go,' she wept.

'I've heard enough to know we must work on that voice and share it, Mrs Lennox. I can train people to breathe and enunciate but I cannot teach what you have just shown me. Your voice is rich and pure and unspoilt. Don't waste your gift. Let me bring out its depth and tone. It would be a privilege to help such a sound go out into the world,' the teacher said, touching her arm. 'Who is the musician in the family to have passed this on to you?'

'I don't know, perhaps my father,' she said. 'I'm sorry to have wasted your time. I can't sing. I won't train. I have a family. It's all too late now,' said Minn desperate to leave the room. 'It hurts me to sing. I have nothing to give.'

'Oh but you have, and it's never too late to sing but training is hard and needs practice. Come back to me when you have the time,' said the teacher, reluctant to let her go.

'It's not that... I haven't the heart for it. There's no songs I want to sing. It is like bearing my soul and I couldn't do that. Archie Carswell meant well but it was a mistake. I do apologize,' Minn cried as she rushed down the steps and on to the pavement, blinded by tears.

'Let it be for now, Mrs Lennox. The time'll come when the songs'll return to you. Your voice will have its day and I shall look forward to seeing you then.' Moira Sanderson waved from the door.

Minn sat on the train going home. How could she have been so stupid? If she had stayed at home she wouldn't have known about Ewan's success and those terrible reminders. It was safer to go home and get on with her own life with her children and try to make up to Harry for not loving him.

One evening in September when the leaves were thick on the lawn and the rains had turned them into slippery, squelchy mulch, she dined alone listening to the wireless. Anna and Hew were asleep upstairs and Edie had retired to the new cottage. Harry was out at some golf club dinner and Hew was wailing from the sound of their little battery alarm.

He was not going to settle until she took him into her bed. She often slept better when his little body was curled up beside her. Harry would return when the spirit moved him. She did not hear him come back.

They all slept in late, and Harry came thundering through into their bathroom with a hangover demanding the keys to her shooting brake, muttering something about 'Taking your car this morning, darling. Must dash!' Next moment he had gone, leaving her to rouse the children for her own dash to Anna's school along the narrow twisty lanes that edged the Tweed.

Minn refused to drive the scarlet Jaguar, Harry's latest toy. It was fast and sleek but she found its speed deceptive and unnerving. She didn't trust her turning on such slippery lanes.

Minn dropped off Anna by the school gate, stopping off on the way back at the post office for some stamps where she found herself standing in the morning queue behind whisperings and tuttings of village wives on their way home from the school gate.

'Good morning, Mistress Lennox ... fine the day?' They turned to acknowledge her but carried on with their gossiping. She was used to being treated politely and kept at a distance but the shop was full of the dramas of some road accident and voices were loud with anxiety.

'Shame about the Prentiss boy ... knocked right off his bike in the early hours. He's away to the big hospital. The bissom didna even stop! Terrible isn't it, Mistress Lennox. Yon lad works in the mill, home frae his shift on his bicycle... Found by the road unconscious. Some beggar must have knocked him off and kent fine what he'd done!' said the postmistress with indignation.

'Who's the boy?' Minn asked.

'Maggie Prentiss's son ... just married and

286

a bairn on the way... Works for Galbraith's woollen mill. His mother's in an awful state.'

Minn knew Maggie Prentiss from the Women's Rural. She always won the competitions for the best sponge cakes. All the way home, Minn had a growing feeling of unease... Surely not... Harry wasn't involved? What human being would hit and then run?

The roads were narrow and a cyclist on a pedal bike even with a dynamo lamp would be difficult to spot, like a pinprick in the dark. She found herself making excuses for why somebody might not stop to see what they had hit in the darkness, unless... What if the driver was going too fast and couldn't stop? There would be skid marks and telltale signs, broken glass. What if the driver was drunk at the wheel?

Minn parked the estate van in its usual place, puzzled and not a little troubled as to why Harry should borrow her car this very morning. She peeped in the garage for the Jaguar but it was not in its usual berth. Perhaps Harry had parked it round the back in the courtyard so that Gil could give it a clear, but it was nowhere to be seen. Perhaps it had merely broken down in the lane, but she knew she had not passed the car.

Not to be thwarted in her search, Minn made for the back of the house to where the cobbled road petered out into a track alongside the old hay barns. There were tyre marks leading up to the door and her heart was thudding when the side door opened. She peered through the darkness with the help of a shaft of light from a glazed roof tile. There under the grainy spotlight was the Jaguar parked neatly with its face turned into the wall.

Now her heart was thudding with apprehension and dread. It had been well hidden from view. Few people ever bothered to come to this barn. She needed more light on the situation, so lifting the heavy bars from the byre doors she swung them open to let in the morning light and examined the front of the car carefully. Once glance told her all she needed to know: the nearside passenger light was cracked and the paintwork was dented and scratched.

This car had been in an accident recently and it must have been Harry who had left the injured lad on the roadside to take his chance. He had just carried on regardless because he was drunk, but he had been mindful enough to hide the evidence from view.

How many times recently had Harry returned the worse for wear? How many times had she warned him about his responsibility to set an example? How many times had her husband argued that he could hold his liquor, that he was a careful driver when he knew he'd been drinking? He knew when he had had enough, was his boast.

What if Maggie Prentiss's laddie died? What if his car was identified and Harry was sent to prison for manslaughter? What would happen to the business, the house, their children? Myriad questions spun around her head and she felt that old sickening fear returning.

What should she do? Ring the police with her suspicions? Testify against her husband? The evidence was there for all to see. Minn closed the door trembling, feeling sick and ashamed. Harry had done many things, but to let a boy die?

By the time he came home that evening she was shaking with fury, waiting for his explanation. 'Why did you take my car this morning?'

'The Jag's playing up,' Harry lied, confirming her worst fears.

'Where is it then?' She was not be fobbed off.

'In the garage for repairs,' he snapped, his hand already stretching out for the whisky decanter.

'No! It's not, you liar! How come it's hidden in the far byre with a broken light and dents? Did YOU knock Maggie Prentiss's boy down this morning?' she screamed, pulling the glass out of his hand and smashing it on the floor.

'What on earth are you talking about? Look at the mess you've made,' Harry bluffed.

'You know exactly what I'm talking about. Did you knock a man off his bike in the small hours and leave him for dead?' she said with ice in her voice.

'Keep your voice down, the children will hear. There was a bump. I hit a rabbit, that's all,' Harry whispered.

'Did you stop to find out? No ... you were too drunk and you swerved and sped on your merry way. It was Maggie Prentiss's boy and he's in hospital. For all I know he may be dead. Everyone knows how fast you drive, as if you own the road. You were drunk. You're always drunk these days!' Minn spat out her words.

'And whose fault's that? There's precious little to come home for these days ... not since Hew was born,' Harry snapped back. 'You turn your back on me every night.'

'Go on, blame me, change the subject. Did you hit the cyclist?' Minn persisted.

'I don't know. I saw the damage when I got back. I didn't stop. I was afraid. If I lose my licence how can I do business?' he whined, and she could see for the first time he was owning his crime.

'Ach away with you, you can afford to hire ten chauffeurs if you need to. You have to report the accident to the police and cut down your drinking sprees. You have to stay home and be a responsible citizen. Take responsibility for your actions, and don't you dare blame me.' Minn was furious, her eyes flashed icily at her husband. 'You disgust me ... leaving a young man to die on the road.'

'He's not dead,' Harry croaked. 'I rang the ambulance from a call box as soon as I realized what had happened, if you must know. He's got a broken leg and concussion. He landed in the ditch and it broke his fall, thank God!'

Minn paced the floor, speechless at his confession. She could see the shame and agitation on his red face; the veins on his nose were standing out. This was her husband; a liar, a cheat, a coward, a weak man who drank too much, and she hated him. 'So what are you going to do about it?'

'I don't know.'

'You must own up to it at once. Claim you think you hit something last night. The longer you leave it the worse it looks,' she pleaded.

'What if I've to go to court?' he argued.

'That's the least of your worries. You must apologize to the Prentiss family, make it up to the couple. Say you were tired and half asleep after a long drive and you didn't realize. Please, Harry, it's the only way to square it with honour.'

'Do you really think so? Don't be naive! It's already far too late to report the accident. It looks bad. Better to say nothing. I can make it up to Donnie Prentiss in my own way. Just leave it at that. I've learnt my lesson.'

'Well if you won't I will,' Minn replied, her voice trembling as she made for the telephone. Harry grabbed her arm roughly.

'Let it be. You can't testify against me. Just hold on and think it all through. It has implications for you and the kids if I'm sent down. I promise that I'll never drink and drive again.' Minn turned and glared at him. 'Look, you've got to trust me. I know what's best for this family. I've learnt my lesson. Let me make it up to the Prentiss family in my own way. There's no permanent harm done. It was just a little fall from a bike. His lights were faulty, I'm sure,' Harry argued.

'How can I trust you, Harry Lennox? Everything you've ever done has been a lie, and worst of all I'm stuck here because of your lies,' she answered, suddenly feeling strong.

'What on earth do you mean by that?' He looked like a little boy trying to fake his lying.

'Who was it who told Ewan Mackinnon that I was about to marry Roddy Lennox and that my love child was his? Who was it who let him think he was talking to the chauffeur and who made damn sure he was driven at top speed back from whence he came? Who made sure I never saw the telegram he sent? You sent him away and let me think he didn't care. How can I ever trust you after that?' she said turning away to stoke the fire.

'That was a long time ago. You were unhappy. He had hurt you and I wanted you. All's fair in love and war, darling, and I loved you the first time I set eyes on you. Don't blame a man for loving you,' he said trying to sit close to her, but she edged away.

'It's not love to deny someone their true happiness or to deny them the chance to choose. You cheated me as you cheated the government with your black market racketeering. Don't think I don't know how you kept this show on the road. I don't trust you and I never will until you own up to what you've done. For once in your life be a man and do something the honourable way and stop drinking so much.'

'My cars and my wines are all the comfort I get in this cold house,' he said. 'Show me some affection.' He grasped her but she struggled.

'Not now, not until I'm sure you mean what you say,' she said, standing up. 'I'm tired and I want to sleep alone. The rest is up to you.'

In the days that followed the accident Minn picked up the phone and dropped it many times. She watched for a blue police car coming up the drive bringing a summons to their door but as the days turned into weeks nothing happened. Donnie Prentiss came home on crutches to the arrival of a brand new bicycle presented by Pitlandry Men's Forum, whose president just happened to be Harry Lennox. Minn recognized her husband's handiwork in the gesture.

They maintained the usual outward appearances of unity for the children's sake but Minn had never felt so utterly alone or ashamed of her own cowardice. She could no longer live this lie, cushioning her misery with fine clothes, furniture and collectibles. This marriage was a sham. Even their wedding certificate was not worth the paper it was written on, since Ken Broddick was still officially declared missing.

Did that make Hew a bastard like herself? She couldn't stand for him to bear that stigma. How would she ever learn to lead a single life or trust in her own decisions? Would Harry go on supporting them? How would she survive all the lonely weekends when there were no footsteps in the hall bringing flowers and wine and gossip on a dark night? How would she fill the gap with only the children for company?

A mother divorced, alone with children,

was a social outcast. Her own mother had taught her that. Was she still a timid Highlander at heart?

As the week went on and neither of them picked up the phone Minn could not sleep or eat or be civil to Harry. If the boy had been killed, what then? Would she have had the courage of conscience to have done something? She couldn't be sure. It was like leaving Ken Broddick all over again and the fear of poverty was lurking at the back of her anxious mind. How could she live with herself? What example was it to their children?

The more she rejected Harry's advances, the more she drove him from her bed, the worse it would get. He was right in that one thing. She was unfaithful, for she was still in love with Ewan.

This strange affair was haunting her mind. It was the worst betrayal of all, which would wound Harry all his life: an affair of the mind that never ended because it was never properly fulfilled, she mused.

She had tried to put Ewan out of her mind, living this insular life, distracted by theatre, music, fine art and family. There was no time to think about lost love if she was busy with the children or being entertained.

Yet in the early hours, in the twilight between waking and sleep, night and morning, when she was so vulnerable he came to her, the dark man of her dreams. In the dream she ran towards him with longing, calling his name into the wind. *'Cait'a bheil thu a dol?'* Where are you going? but the grey haar thickened, screening his face from sight. Then she woke with tears streaming down her face, a stab of pain in her gut and the realization that her marriage was a bed of sorrows, a bed of thorns, and it couldn't go on.

Minn rose early and began to pack. They would need warm clothes.

PART THREE

Is it not sweet to hear the breeze singing?
As lively it comes o'er the deep rolling sea;
But sweeter and dearer by far 'tis when
  bringing
The barque of my true love in safety to me.

One

Phetray

They bent westward into the wind round the edge of Kilphetrish Bay with its curved expanse of white sand. There was a thin line of blue on the horizon and Minn hoped that the worst of the storm that had trapped them indoors all day in the empty harbour hotel was over now.

She held on tight to Hew's hand as he waddled in his siren suit and new shoes while Anna sped out of the doors like a young calf let out in the spring fields for the first time. It was a world of wonder for a child to run free on an empty beach staring up at the neat thatched cottages and pointing to the roofs netted and roped with stone weights against the gales that had lashed the coast since their sudden arrival two days ago.

The stone manse stood firm close to the village school, silent because it was midterm and the children were helping with the potato harvest. Older familiar faces passed them by, glancing in their direction, curious but polite. Their names tumbled out of her memory and she nodded back. Soon it would be round the island that Minnie Macfee was back for a visit with her children; a gey strange time to take a holiday, tongues would wag.

Was it a holiday, an impulse break away from the strain of the past weeks, or was she fleeing from a stale marriage and Harry's weakness? She didn't know and didn't care. It was enough just to sniff the wind and such familiar scents: a tangle of clover and thyme, salt and seaweed. There were terns diving overhead, lapwings chewitting in protest, and the kittiwakes soared as she carried Hew down from the coastal path across the wet machair towards the rocky outcrop close to a ruined harbour.

From the pasture and track they were turning from modern times to more ancient territory where the past was harder to ignore. Here tramped the Duke's men to clear the land for sheep and pushed her poor forebears to subsist on the shoreline. Here the sons of Phetray boarded men-o'-war, pressed into service never to return. Here the bodies of luckless mariners were carried shoulder high for burial, up the old gangway encrusted now with barnacles. It was as if her sturdy brogues footed themselves to this shore.

'Come away from the water,' she cried out as Anna raced ahead. The girl turned and gave her such a look of defiance it shocked her. She darted across the rocks, muffled in her thick coat and woolly hat like a rubber ball. Hew strained at the leash to follow her, struggling out of Minn's grip, wriggling.

'It's time to find Granny's house,' Minn shouted. 'First to see it is king of the castle!'

Anna turned, curious, making her way back as they trod gingerly across damp boggy grass, avoiding the steaming cowpats and cattle and the dips where in summer the yellow flag iris bent to the force of Kilphetrish Bay.

Why had she never brought Anna when her mother was alive? Why did she wait until there was no one here to greet them to ask Uncle Niall for the loan of the cottage for a week or two?

She had written to him asking if they could stay on Phetray, not waiting for his reply. The key would be where it always was, hung on a hook in the old byre. Here no one had need to lock their door. There were no public crimes, just the odd misdemeanour, a bit of drunkenness and a few secret lusts that were held in check by the kirk elders.

As they came ever closer past the little clachan of cottages she could hardly breathe for emotions flooding like the racing tide as the house of her childhood came in view, standing alone from the others; the vegetable patch overgrown, the thatch in need of repair, the thick walls standing sentinel.

'This is Granny Eilidh's house. This is

where your mummy lived when she was a little girl,' she whispered to Anna. 'We're going to stay here for a little while,' she added.

Anna looked at it puzzled. 'For a holiday?' she asked.

'Perhaps,' Minn replied, pushing the creaking door into the byre where once the cow snuffled in a warm mixture of dung and straw to find the dusty key for the lock. It was rusty and wouldn't turn. In frustration she turned the knob and the door just opened.

She stared into the little living room. There was still a scent of peat and smoke, like the scent of a rich malt whisky. She fingered the gernel kist that kept the oats and flour dry and the shelf above the fire where the wooden framed photograph of Uncle Niall in his uniform stood stern over their daily living like the eye of the Lord.

Minn was lost for a second reliving that last visit, the stink of a leaking paraffin lamp, the big black Bible in the corner open for evening prayers and her mother's last confession. She saw the razor strap hanging on the hook behind the door and remembered the skelpings. Her eyes filled up with tears.

'It smells in here and it's dark. Where's the light switch?' Anna sniffed, turning her nose up. 'It's like a doll's house. I don't want to stay in here.'

'Come and see the little bedrooms,' Minn

replied pointing to the door that opened into the bedroom with its brass bed and chest and the other little box room that had been her own den when Uncle Niall was away at sea.

'Look, here's the spinning wheel. Do you know, when I was small we gathered all the fallen fluff off the sheep and spun it into wool to knit our clothes. Wasn't that clever? And we even collected up the cowpats and dried them to put on the fire,' she said.

'Yuk! Cow poo! Mummy, that's horrible,' Anna said.

'I see I've grown a little snob, young lady,' Minn snapped. And who's to blame for that? she thought.

Even she could see it was all too damp and fusty to live in straight away. It would need a good spring clean. The fire would need building up to heat the iron range for hot water.

'Do we have to stay here?' said Anna, unimpressed.

'It'll be like *Little House on the Prairie*. We'll light a fire and air the house and find the hot water bottles and buy some groceries from the store and have lots of fun,' she said briskly.

'When's Daddy coming? Why can't we stay at the hotel?' Anna was not for bribing.

'He's busy at work. I told you before. This is our special adventure, just the three of us to see if we like it. Don't you want to play on

303

the sands and see where Mummy was a little girl?'

It was going to be hard work coaxing the reluctant child who always took her daddy's side of the argument. Anna was spoilt and used to the easy ways of Pitlandry. It would do them all good to do without comforts for a while, to be alone together and explore the island. Surely there would be a car to hire or a pony and trap. That would be an adventure.

'I want to go outside,' yelled Anna, dashing through the door again, her dark pigtails down her back, into the sunlight.

Standing in this ghostly half-light, Minn saw herself as a child, impatient, darting like a stoat out of a dyke, and Mother's voice calling her back, *'Cait'a bheil thu a dol?'* Where are you off to now? Anna was no different and she smiled.

'Don't go far,' she yelled. 'You can play on the grass but not by the rocks. It's dangerous and slippery! Come and help me make a fire.' There was no reply, as she watched Hew sitting on the wooden floor contentedly pulling at the old rug.

She was going to need some help to make the cottage fit for them all to live in. As if in answer to prayer an anxious voice shouted at the doorway in Gaelic.

'Is that you, Mistress Lennox?' Outside was a familiar face from her past; a face older, leathery and wind etched: their neighbour,

Peggy Sinclair.

'If I'd known you were about the place I'd have opened it up for you. The house's lain empty since your poor mother passed away. I've not see Niall this past year. We heard you were back on the island with yer bairns. Come a way in with the wee boy for a warm up and a blether. You're brave to weather the crossing at this time of year,' said Peggy ushering them to her own warm cottage.

So her arrival was news already, and they were itching with curiosity. Peggy would ask gentle questions and form her own opinion as to why the wealthy Mistress Lennox should come back to Phetray at the time of the storms. It would be passed from the store to the Tulloch and the outlying farms that the Macfee girl was back to claim the cottage.

'We flew in from Glasgow,' she offered, knowing it was best to give a little true information. 'This is Hew Charles, Mistress Sinclair, and Mor-Anna has gone off to find her bearings. Thank you for your kind offer. A cup of tea would be a Christian act on this cold afternoon.'

'And Mr Lennox, he'll be coming at the weekend?' asked Peggy.

'No, he's far too busy,' she replied a bit too quickly.

'And you'll be going back after the mid-term?' Peggy sipped, her ears flapping.

'There's no rush. Anna's not in school full

time yet,' Minn said feeling the heat of the peat fire on her cheeks. How cosy and warm these houses could be when the thick walls were heated through.

'She's a big girl for her age. She'll be your first husband's girl?' Peggy asked.

This inquisition had gone on long enough. 'Thank you for the tea but I must get on and open up the house. There's plenty of dry peat in the byre I notice. I'll take the children beachcombing in the morning,' she said, standing up to check Hew, who was just about to pull the tablecloth on to the floor. 'I'd better find Anna before she gets into mischief.'

'She's away playing with Jessie Munn, see. Does she have the Gaelic?' Minn shook her head, ashamed that she had not passed on her mother tongue.

'Children learn quickly when left to themselves. They teach it in the school now. In my day we were only allowed the English in class, but you'll not be stopping that long will you?' said Peggy.

You nosy wee *cailleach*, she thought as she whisked Hew out of the door. It had brightened up and so had her spirits. With Peggy's help they could make the cottage clean, dry and lighter.

'It must be our season for visitors this autumn,' smiled Peggy Sinclair. 'There's been a big gathering at the Crannog all summer, a bunch of artists from Glasgow taken over the big house as some school, comings and goings. The Macallum girl has been rushed off her feet cooking for the lot of them, and now back in the village school teaching...'

'Jo Macallum, Johanna. I thought they were abroad now,' said Minn, stopped in her tracks by that name.

'Aye, Mrs Mackinnon now, of course. Ewan *dubh*'s the assistant warden at the Crannog. Made a name for himself in Edinburgh by all accounts, and here with a bunch of students.

'Most of them are on their way back now for the course is over. It's nice to see the old place being used like the old days. You'll have to pay them a visit while you're here. You were all pals as I recall.' Peggy smiled, knowing full well that the whole island knew about Ewan and Minn before the war.

She stepped back blindly from the path, waving and calling Anna back from her playing. He is here on the island, her heart cried, shocked by Peggy's news. She leant on the gate to recover herself.

He is here. Why are you so helpless when you hear his name on the wind? she cried. Was there no escaping the torment of greeting a face that haunted her dreams?

She had come here for peace of mind, for time to rethink the future. The letter left for

Harry was terse and to the point, giving him no chance to persuade her to stay.

Dear Harry,
Tell Edie and Gil I've gone to Phetray for mid-term with the children. I can't stand the atmosphere. Need some time to clear my head. Don't come rushing after us. We'll be fine in the cottage. I'm trusting you'll take the time to sort out the Prentiss affair while we're out of the way. Can't go on like this.
  Brodie

How could she find peace of mind now, trapped by the storms, by all the broken promises the two of them had made on this cursed island? There was so much still to say and yet nothing to say. It was six years since they had last met face to face.

Why was she feeling as if this impulsive flight with her children, this voyage of her heart was ending here on this shore with the tide out and the ferry boat cancelled for a hundred years, with no means of escape? How could she face him again?

Two

The Crannog

'They've all gone at last,' sighed Ewan Mackinnon, assistant warden of the Crannog summer school for artists, as he made his way down to the old boat house on the beach that served as his temporary studio.

The experiment was over; the students returning back to their colleges seemed satisfied by three months retreat. His head was spinning with all he had learnt from Sandy Thompson, a brilliant maestro who'd torn his work apart, made him reassess his ideas and left him raring to start on some fresh abstracts.

Phetray was free of its annual visitors, the Tulloch bar emptied of the English crews, and the peace of his beach walks with Cullein, the terrier, was uninterrupted by strangers.

He needed time to process all that Sandy had suggested about his work: how to capture the tones and textures of harbour scenes, how the houses here grew out of the landscape. He wanted to capture the isolation of his community, the vibrant colour of

309

it all so that he could go back to the mainland and continue his studies with all these visions still in his mind's eye.

His head was spinning with ideas. What was needed now was peace and solitude.

Not that Ewan had any quarrel with the sons and daughters of Phetray for returning each season when the schools were closed. The annual invasion of swallows flocking back to their breeding grounds with new bairns and aged parents, cramming on to the decks of the *Pride of Argyll* ferry for a first glimpse of Kilphetrish harbour and Sandy 'the polis' waving them ashore was only to be welcomed. They were family, inborn bairns, but they were all but gone now before the gales stopped the ferries.

His head was spinning with ideas and he wanted no disruption to his quiet routine, for there was real work to be done. Jo had taken up a temporary post helping out with the infant school. She was a great help to the cook at the Crannog but needed to fill her time in her own way until he was ready to return south.

It had not been easy for her this last year. They had been travelling to Italy when she'd lost the baby suddenly without any warning; the wee boy was born too soon to live. She named him Andrew John after their fathers and they buried him in a little hospital close to Milan. She took great comfort from the busy cemetery with waxed flowers and pictures.

'He'll not be lonely there,' she wept, and Ewan felt it was all his own selfish fault for dragging her off on one of his restless sprees. She was a saint to put up with his single-minded determination to cram years of neglected education into a few months living out of a suitcase.

Taking the post on Phetray seemed only fair so Jo could be close to her family and recuperate. They were told there was no reason for them not to conceive again, but nothing was happening. This time they would stay until she was ready to leave. He owed her that but he felt uneasy staying on.

The past cast its long shadow. Women and islands could drive a Highland man mad, was the old saying. Jo seemed to enjoy living in such grand houses and meeting all the artists. She acted as temporary housekeeper to a bunch of absent-minded scruffy students of all ages, shopping, giving orders to the cook, but she was happiest around children.

Ewan parked his battered old bike on the gravel, making his way down to the boathouse set neatly on one side of the cove. Here he could work free from interruption.

Jo would call down after school to bring tea in a flask, he smiled to himself, unlocking the boathouse and setting up his work for the day. He lit up his pipe and looked out over the beach, to an expanse of colour as far as the eye could see: a delft-blue sky touching an opalescent sea, silver sands and pea-green machair dotted with chestnut cattle.

Some would call it predictable, a choc-olate box landscape, but he was not going to paint like a photograph. He wanted to capture the scene through sunlight, capture the essence of light on the sea. His quirky seascapes were beginning to fetch a decent enough price to keep his shelves lined with books and a bottle of best Islay malt whisky.

Phetray was more of a connoisseur's taste: an island flat, delicate, full of light. In June it shimmered with sunshine, in winter it was wild and windswept. There was not the hilly grandeur of a Skye or the ruggedness of some of the inner isles. Far out on the dis-tant horizon those landscapes shimmered as its backdrop. It lay like an emerald in the ocean, brilliant, filled with white spume, home to myriad flowers and rare birds, oceanic shells, all the colours of the rainbow.

It was criss-crossed by just a few roads strung with old black houses and crofts, always a breeding ground for artists and craftsmen, naturalists and seafarers. Traders across the centuries had left their mark on Phetray culture, its language and its poetry, and he was proud to be an adopted son.

After all the wanderings of the past year he

was strangely content to return, if only the memories of his last visit would die down. How could he forget what he had said to Minn Macfee.

A shadow crossed his canvas, disturbing concentration for a second, and Ewan swung round in frustration only to see Jo in her thick coat and headscarf waving a flask, standing in his light with her arms folded.

'Oh, it's you, Jo!' he snapped. 'Shouldn't you be at school?'

'Have you forgotten it's mid-term. School's out and I've been down to the post office.' She smiled, waving some mail in front of him.

'Huh! Is that all you've come for... It could wait... I want to get this finished.' Ewan was putting the final touches to a seascape of sand, rock and waves. After Sandy's eye had roved over it he was no longer satisfied with the finished effect.

She shook her head. 'I've heard some interesting news. I just thought you'd want to know,' she said.

'What do I want with gossip?' he sneered, continuing with his brushwork, standing on the planks under the upside-down boat with a glass hole in the upturned hull to capture the northern light.

'There's smoke coming out of the Macfee croft,' she teased.

'You came all the way down here to tell me

Niall Macfee is in residence?' He laughed.

'That's where you're wrong. Peggy the postie had it on good authority from Sandy the polis who heard from Effie in the Co-op store who saw Alice Munn, who's Peggy Sinclair's neighbour, that Minn Macfee is cooried up in the cottage with her kiddies for mid-term.'

'So?' Ewan paused, unimpressed.

'Apparently she flew in without any warning and they had to air the house in a hurry while they were staying at the hotel,' she added.

'Is the Lennox chap with them?' Ewan carried on fiddling about.

'Apparently not, he's away on business, abroad or in America. You can take your pick. Anyway we must ask them up for tea,' Jo replied.

'What ever for?' snapped Ewan wishing she would leave him to his work.

'Ewan, you were engaged to the girl, we were all at school together and the whole island knows about it, so don't be mean.' She smiled, her grey eyes flashing with a twinkle of mischief. 'It'll set the cat among the pigeons if we do. Everyone wants to know why she's back and living in a wee house.'

'Johanna Mackinnon, you're getting as bad as the old *cailleachs*, and here was me thinking what did I do to deserve such a paragon of virtue? Now leave me to my work and find some dusting,' he said as she picked up an oily rag and threw it at him.

'Oh don't take it all so seriously. I'm only trying to be polite.' Jo smiled. 'I'd like to see her children and catch up. I feel bad we never saw her when her mother died. It'll be very strange for her after a big house. She might like to see the Crannog again before it's closed up for the winter.'

'Please yourself,' Ewan muttered, feeling a wave of anger surging through him, tightening his chest.

Jo stood inspecting the state of the boathouse. It smelt of oils and dried spirits, with crumpled rags curled to a crisp. Through the sunlight of the open door she could see a stack of canvases, shelves of tools, frames lining the walls, an easel, and Cullein, his biscuit-coloured Cairn terrier, snoozing in the corner.

This was the working, living, messy studio of an artist. A shaft of sunlight glistened on the whisky bottle and she picked it up in disgust, shoving it in his face.

'I'm going to pour that stuff in the sea. If your teetotal father could see the state of you...' Jo pointed to his baggy checked shirt. 'It's about time you changed that rag.'

'Don't you dare touch that bottle. It's a fine peaty malt from Islay. What pleasure is left if an artist can't have his dram after a hard day's work? Don't you be such a fishwife, nag, nag nag.'

'And just what's this officer's camp bed doing back in here? Have you been sleeping rough at night? People'll think I've chucked you out of my bed.' She winked.

Trust his proud eagle-eyed wife to miss nothing. He knew her chunnering was meant well, but he did his best work in a cramped guddle. It suited him sometimes to carry on painting into the night, to sit by the shore with his pipe and watch stars across the stretch of sky he knew so well. Sometimes he was just too bushed to walk back over the rocks and machair to the big house. Sometimes he was too unsteady on his feet to attempt the journey. Sleeping rough alongside a bottle of 'Ardbeg' had always soothed his spirits. He liked to be close to the sea.

'You shouldn't doss down in this hut like some tramp. I'm told you get too drunk to make it back some nights. How are we ever to make a child?' Jo argued.

'Have the old *cailleachs* of Kilphetrish nothing to do but clack their false teeth so you come running with their cracking?' he winked.

'The sea's rough now and it's too cold for nights under the stars. What if you had an accident?' she snapped.

'Then it's no far for you all to be dumping me back into the sea.' He laughed away her worried look.

'Enough of this morbid talk... Why did I have to marry such an irascible man? Irascible, reclusive, stubborny *bodach*; that's you!' She laughed. 'You shame me dressed like a tramp, your hair down to your shoulders and a beard like Moses. Minnie will think you're some dosser when she sees you! Honestly, have you seen yourself in the mirror lately? How long since those bespattered cords saw a scrubbing board and washing line? I want them off you and in the tub.' Jo tugged at his britches.

'Hush, woman, and let me get on!' he said, knowing there were still so many ideas in his head, so many moments he wanted to imprint in his memory before they left the island and the weather closed in on him.

Jo still did not understand how fiercely he was driven. How could she understand how he had been given life when so many good men had perished in the war? The past was never far from his thoughts, invading his dreams with bitter memories.

The sea was a cruel but stalwart companion and he wanted to record its moods and secrets, capture the elusive power of its hold over him. Here on Phetray he felt closer to its essence. It was here that his passionate affair had begun.

Jo was sensing defeat and sighed. 'I don't know why I'm bothering. You never take a blind bit of notice of what I say. I might as well be invisible; perhaps Minn Macfee will put a clean shirt on your back and a decent shave on your face.'

Ewan put down his brush carefully, looking up with his leathery face creased into a v-shaped frown, his eyes spearing her with anger. 'And why on God's earth should she be doing that then?'

'Haven't you been listening to a word? I'm going to ask her round for tea. Don't make me ashamed of you. You couldn't get enough of her once upon a time,' she added.

'That was a long time ago. We were still bairns. I don't care what I'm wearing. I never have. Life's too short to be a fashion plate,' he snapped back.

'Well there's no fear of that then. I'll leave you to it.' Jo was making tracks across the powdery sand back to the path.

'Aye, I've heard you... Don't go making any show for that jumped-up madam,' he shouted, throwing his brush across the boat-house. His face was drained, his weather-beaten features cragged, hewn and gnarled. 'I'll be making myself scarce. I'll not be wanting to make a spectacle for her amusement,' he muttered spitting his pipe out wearily.

Suddenly the sky above darkened as black clouds banked up over the sea. Ewan shivered with the chill on the breeze, uneasy at the news. Surely not ... in the name of God! After all these years, the wanderer was returning to haunt him once more.

He was in no hurry to go back to the house. Cullein wanted a run along the beach. In the grey light the machair was dotted with a thousand stars, the last of the summer flowers still blooming: clover, vetchlings, harebells and wild thyme, shimmering with raindrops. He swigged the last of the malt in his flask in a gulp of frustration.

Who was it said that whisky took the fire out of fever and the ache out of loving? The wind was beating his cheeks like whipcords. Her presence on the island was making him edgy.

He could sense her on the wind, Minn ... his signpost and his muse, hewn like him from these hard rocks.

She was the one love that had almost broken his heart. He ached to see her but hurt pride would cage up this longing. He would never go to her again, to that sea *cailleach* who cast a spell over him. He must steer clear of her wily magic.

The thought of her would distract him, for with her name came back so many memories. Thinking about her was an indulgence he could ill afford when there were so many other visions in his head.

'Go away!' he shouted. 'Don't bother me!' he yelled, and Cullein stopped in his tracks and sank on the sand dejected.

'Not you, old *bodach*... Not you.' He

picked up a stick and threw it.

One man, his wife and their dog was the best life for him. As he stood watching the dog tearing across the beach in pursuit of his master's command he heard the siren voice calling to the seals and saw again the girl in the faded frock, barefoot on the shore. Their lives had been so inextricably bound together by the sea and the tide. How could what was begun with such innocence cause so much heartache unless there was some curse in the wind?

Three

Kilphetrish

At first light Minn woke with a start. Where was she? She could feel Anna's bony legs lying across her stomach, but her own feet were cold on the stone bottle. She swung herself gently out of the bed feeling giddy with hunger and fear. What had she done bringing her children into this cold damp place on a whim? Her feet were used to soft rugs and polished floors not rough mats and overcoats thrown over the bed for warmth, and she had to see if Hew was still breathing.

She tiptoed into the tiny box room where

he slept tousle-haired under the borrowed plump eiderdown from next door. Her children had survived the night and the fire was still in. She hadn't lost the art of fire making.

In fact it had been fun to clean off the salty dust, beat the rugs and air the rooms, buy in provisions, get the range fired up and give them an evening wash in the old zinc bath, wrap them snugly in the warmed beds and settle them down with a story. It was like pretending to play 'wee hoosies' when she was little in her den with Agnes.

She sat down in the wooden chair in the half-light alert to the rattle of the door in the wind, the draughts creeping through a loose window and all the noises of a house waking up for the day, looking up at the weathered rafters. Everything seemed so small and cluttered. How had three of them managed to live in the one room?

As the parings of light slid through the curtain she fingered the arm rests polished with the elbows of many generations. Time stood still in this ancient place; its fusty scent was unlocking the floodgates of recognition: Mother sitting by the fire knitting at speed, Uncle Niall peering from the mantelpiece, and she felt small again.

The past was all around her and there was no escape. Minn was afraid. What am I doing? What am I trying to prove? she thought.

The whole island knew she was back, curious as to why and anxious to let her know that the Mackinnons were also here.

She was told about Ewan's course at the Crannog, that Johanna had lost her baby abroad and that he was exhibiting in the Scottish Academy and in Glasgow. The artist was up for the Guthrie Award.

It felt as if at every door and stopping place someone would accost her with their pennyworth of knowledge about the happy couple while trying to prise out of her just why she had returned so late in the season. The Lennox family was a nine-day wonder and if she kept them all out of sight then curiosity would soon fade. The islanders would never change, she smiled.

Yet knowing she could bump into Ewan at any moment tinged every hour with danger. What would he look like? Would he acknowledge her? Did it matter if he ignored her? She could hardly breathe.

All the old sadness and yearning, buried deep for so long, was rising up to the surface. This was her first courageous act for years. She was so alone in her marriage, filling her days with meaningless activities.

How could she ever forgive Harry for cheating her into marrying him and being weak. How could she forgive herself for being weak and taking the safe option?

'I don't like you, Minn Macfee,' she whispered into the smouldering peat. 'I don't like who you've become, trying to pretend you could ever be a lady. Here you'll always be an oat bannock not a white pan loaf...' She smiled at Mother's words echoing in her head. Mother was right after all. She mustn't ever take those humble origins out of her heart, but part of her was missing Pitlandry and her comfortable home.

'Who're you talking to?' Anna crept behind her rubbing her eyes.

'Just to some old ghosties, Granny and myself,' she answered, feeling a sadness wash over her that she had not been closer to her own mother.

'What are we going to do today? Can we go down to the beach exploring?' said Anna. 'What's for breakfast?'

'One thing at a time ... porridge first. I'll show you how we make it over the fire. I've soaked the oats in the pan. Then we'll get washed from the kettle and the bowl and go and buy a postcard for Daddy if you like, from the stores,' she added, seeing the look of delight on Anna's face.

'When are we going home?' said Anna.

'We'll see. Aren't you enjoying our stay?' Minn sighed.

'It's cold and wet and I want to see Dusty.' Anna gathered all the bowls on to the table. 'And there's no toys here.'

'We can make up our own games and play

sandcastles. I can find a pony for you to ride, if you like. When I was little we had to amuse ourselves.' She couldn't resist the jibe. How lucky her children were and how different her own circumstances had been.

'Did you have a friend like Dusty?' Anna said.

'No, but I had Agnes Mackinnon, my best friend at the school.' She felt her voice trembling.

'Does she live on the island now? Can we visit her?' Anna asked, and Minn shook her head.

'Not exactly but I can show you her name and tell you all about her later, if you like,' she offered and Anna smiled, her dark eyes flashing. The day was planned and her daughter was content.

Anna was not an in-born bairn. Her world lay a hundred miles away from here. It wasn't fair to drag her children out of their home on this wild goose chase. What dream was she chasing here? What fantasy was she acting out in forcing them to live as she had lived? Did she really want to stay in the cottage, deprive them of their father, put them in the village school where they would have to master a foreign tongue? Was this her plan?

Are you jealous of your own children for being loved and pampered and cherished? In this house of stone there was little praise and encouragement for you, no hugs and kisses.

Only Ewan treated you like a princess and you let him go. After him no one was enough, not Ken or Harry, but they seemed to be right at the time. Are you punishing your children? The fear stabbed her.

Anna and Hew were already bemused by their mummy speaking another language and the change of surroundings. Hew was still young enough to adapt but Anna wanted her daddy. Only he wasn't her real father. Was it possible that her real father was here and there was unfinished business between them? Had fate drawn them back together to sort out this one last thing remaining between them? This time she would not be gainsaid. This time she would tell Ewan the truth and shame the devil no matter what. Then once her duty was done she would be free... Free from what?

For once the storms relented and the wind died down enough to walk upright. The sun shone out of an ink-blue sky and for a few hours they could pretend it was still high summer and race along the white sands collecting the fine shells thrown up from the Gulf Stream, purples, pinks, cowries, while searching for messages in bottles. Anna wrote her name on a slip of paper and they launched their message out on the tide. Then, borrowing Peggy's go chair they pushed Hew along the tracks towards Balenottar village and the crossroads to the little cemetery where Agnes lay.

They picked the last of the autumn flowers and Anna ran ahead to look at the weathered gravestones. She knew about death because her kitten had died and horses had to be put down and Gil's sheepdog had grown old, but not about little girls who died before their time.

'How did she die?' she asked.

'Drowned in the sea in an accident,' Minn said, picking her words with care.

'What's an accident?' her daughter asked.

'Something that just happens all of a sudden,' she replied. How could she explain all the reasons why Agnes drowned and she did not.

'Did it hurt her?' Anna asked, and Minn tried to be honest.

'I don't know. We were swimming when we shouldn't have been swimming and the sea took her away and then brought her back, but she wouldn't wake up.'

'Did she fall asleep in the sea?' Anna looked at the faded gravestone and then skipped around it. 'Does she know we're here?'

'I don't know, but every time I come home I have to pay her a visit and tell her all my news just in case.' Minn swallowed back her tears. No matter how long she lived on this earth she would never forget Agnes. 'And now I've brought my little girl to see her.'

'I'm not a little girl. I'm a big girl,' sneered Anna, running off. 'Let's go down to the sea and play accidents.'

'No you don't. You hold my hand near the water, young lady. One accident is enough in a lifetime,' Minn shouted, but the wheels of the pram rutted in the damp sand. 'Come on, time to head home for tea and we'll bake drop scones on the griddle.'

Anna was staring out at the sea, transfixed by the huge rolling waves surfing down on the pebbles.

'Why does it make that noise? Is it an angry sea?' she asked.

'It does it at this time of year because summer is over and winter is coming.' Minn laughed. 'I suppose it could be angry. I've never thought of it like that.'

'I think it's crying cos it's lost its daddy,' Anna said matter-of-factly, skipping along loppity, happy to be close to water.

In that instant, in that joy, Minn knew that her child was another daughter of the tide, a child born of love, not rape. She had to be Ewan's daughter, tall for her age and slender. There was something of Agnes in that skipping, and her heart skipped a beat. If only she could be sure.

Slowly they trundled their way back to the warm fire, stopping to let Hew toddle along and roly poly in the sand like a puppy. It was good for them to be in the fresh sea air.

When they returned there was a battered car outside the machair and Peggy Sinclair was waving from her cottage door.

'You've a visitor, Mrs Lennox. I told him you were away out with the bairns for a walk.'

Her neighbour was peering into the window pointing.

'I hope I did the right thing...'

'Thank you. You are very kind,' Minn said, closing the door. Perhaps Ewan had called on her at last. 'Ewan?' she found herself calling around, knowing full well it could not be him. Peggy would have said it was him.

'Ewan,' she sighed, shaking her head.

'Sorry, old girl, only your husband,' said Harry, rocking himself in front of the fire.

'Daddy, Daddy, Daddy!' Anna flung herself into his arms. Minn let Hew waddle his way into the open arms, but she was wary. He gathered them in with a smile.

'Harry, I told you not to come...' she whispered.

'I'm not surprised, living in this hovel,' he whispered back. 'What on earth possessed you to bring them here?'

'I wanted them to see where I come from, where I belong,' she snapped.

'You don't belong here. You never did. You couldn't wait to get rid of your accent. Who are you kidding?' He laughed. 'It's time to get back on that plane to Glasgow and stop all this foolishness.'

She shook her head. 'Not yet. I need time and you know damn well why I left you,' she whispered.

'All sorted, I promise you. I went to see the Prentiss boy. I explained I thought I'd hit a deer but realized it was more serious. I offered him compensation. They were very understanding. I said ·how upset you were that I might have not realized it was Donnie at the time. It' s all sorted now.'

'What's sorted?' asked Anna.

'We're all going back to the Phetray Hotel for the night and tomorrow we're back home to Dusty.' Harry winked. Minn could have hit him, looking so smug.

'I'm not ready to go back yet,' she said, suddenly weary from all the walking. 'I want to stay here a little longer with Hew. Anna can stay with you just for tonight.'

'Oh by the way, this was shoved under the door, letter from lover boy,' he sneered, handing her a note. She opened it, bending into the fire for the light.

Sorry to have missed you all. Would you like to come to tea on Friday at the Crannog?
Yours,
Johanna Mackinnon

Minn sat down suddenly exhausted. The invitation was not a surprise. Johanna must be as curious as the rest of the island. She had sensed one of them would have to make contact. There was no refusing and no excuses. This appointment must be kept, and she threw it to Harry.

'See... Just a social call. I'd like you to see the old house. Don't rush off. Let's make it a bit of a holiday for the children's sake.'

'In this weather? Come and have a proper meal at the hotel at least,' he replied, but Anna was tugging at his arm.

'Mummy's going to make drop scones and I'm going to help her and you can too,' Anna ordered.

'But not until she's changed young Hew, I hope. He stinks to high heaven.' Harry laughed.

'Then pump us up some more water from the well.' Minn pointed with a sigh.

It was all beginning again, her boat was leaving the jetty bound for who knew where? With children aboard as ballast how could she not steer a clear course?

Four

The Crannog

'I want you shaved, dressed and smartened up by three o'clock,' ordered Jo, plonking Ewan's breakfast on the table.

He was in no mood for interruptions after a fitful night and carried on with his outline sketch barely looking up to greet her. 'What's so special about three o'clock?' he teased, knowing full well that she had invited Minn and her kids. 'Are we expecting a royal visit?'

'All I'm asking is a pair of trousers without paint on them, trim your beard and be civilized, I'll do the rest,' Jo replied, ferreting in a box to find some old photos. 'Look, I brought these from home to show us all at school. I thought her little girl might be interested. What's her name?'

'How should I know... Anne or Nancy, something like that... Suit yourself. I don't know why we have to go through this charade. I don't want to see Minnie Macfee or her wee brats!' he snapped, feeling mean, but Jo had no right to invite them without his say so. She was stirring up trouble.

'Ewan! What's got into you? You've been like a tiger on the prowl all week. If I didn't know you better I'd say you were scared to face her. It must be six or seven years since you two last met. She'll want to see these pictures.' Jo sat down and slid them across the table.

'There she is sitting with Agnes on the front row looking wild and woolly, the one with galoshes two sizes too big? They say down in Kilphetrish that she's very smartly dressed even to go to the store, in a gabardine mac and silk head scarf... There's you standing on the back row scowling and me in front with pigtails.' She smiled, hoping to soften his moodiness.

He picked up the school line-up, faded and cracked with age. How could he forget that summer, the summer Agnes drowned and Minn lived? They were all blinking into the sunlight, windswept and tousled, so full of life and energy.

There was Robbie Colquhoun, who was killed in Africa, and Murdo Murchison, who was lost on HMS *Hood*, and Lachie Sinclair, who died in a Jap POW camp, and Agnes who never made it to the next school term; so many gaps in the line-up now.

He had forgotten how pretty his sister was, so dark like himself. There had been no photos of her in the manse. Mother hadn't been able to bear looking upon her face but had brought her out only when there was company in case people would talk. Why should he be remembering that, except that today the Lady of Pitlandry was paying them a state visit?

'I'm away to my work,' he said, rising from the table. 'You can ring a bell but I don't want any interruptions. I'll take the bike across to the far end. This is the last day of your holiday, I should have thought you'd want to be enjoying yourself not entertaining my old girlfriend,' he quipped.

'Your old fiancée, Ewan. You dumped me for her as I recall, at the regatta dance.' She grinned wickedly.

'And I lived to regret it, *mo ghaoil*,' he said, pecking her on the cheek. 'I wouldn't swop you for a hundred Minns.'

'I'm glad to hear it. Who else would put up with your moods and the wanderings of a man who lives in his head, lost in a world no one else can share?' she said, her soft hazel eyes twinkling with mischief. 'I'm going to enjoy playing the lady of the manor myself, serving tea in the drawing room, baking fresh scones and biscuits for the small fry and showing Mistress Lennox around the very house where once she scrubbed the stairs. There'll be no airs and graces after that little exercise.' She winked. 'But I want you by my side to show just what she's missed all these years. Three o'clock sharp and no excuses... I'm depending on you so take a watch. I know how you lose all track of time, and keep out of the Tulloch.'

'Yes, Sergeant!' Ewan saluted and clicked his heels. 'I'll be there.'

'Why won't you come with me, Harry?' said Minn as she was changing Hew into his one clean outfit. There was no washing machine here to keep her children pristine, just a bucket for soiled nappies and water from the well. She was running out of clean clothes and longed for a soak in the giant bath at Pitlandry. 'I want you to see the Crannog and us to meet the Mackinnons together. Don't run out on me now,' she pleaded, but for once Harry was not for turning.

'I've no mind to see Mackinnon again,' he said.

'I wonder why? I've told you he knows it was you he spoke to. It was years ago,' she replied, surprised by how important it was for him to be by her side when she met Ewan again.

'You can take the baby, Brodie, and I'll take Anna out of your hair. We'll hire some ponies and trek down the coast,' he offered, and Anna was jumping up and down with excitement.

Since Harry's unexpected arrival the child had never let him out of their sight, hanging

334

on to his arm so the two of them had not had a minute alone together until the children were asleep. Then it was awkward in such a confined space.

'Oh yes, Mummy, you promised I could ride,' said Anna.

'But I really wanted to take you with me to show you everything,' she said, torn by her desire for Ewan to see her daughter and perhaps wonder at this new-found resemblance to Agnes. It was all part of the plan she was carefully constructing in her mind so that when they were alone she could drop this bombshell and test his reaction.

She would engineer being alone with him somehow. Harry was to be the decoy, who would tour around the gardens with Johanna and Anna while she spoke to Ewan. Perhaps it was a silly fantasy and best forgotten as no one wanted to play ball.

She was nervous about going back to the old house where she had been both happy and sad. At least pushing Hew in the go chair would give some solid support to lean on. He would be the distraction with his sandy gold curls, but it would remind Johanna of what she had lost and Minn didn't want to hurt them by parading a baby in front of them. Perhaps Peggy would be persuaded to mind him for a couple of hours.

She dressed with care in a heather tweed suit and warm cashmere jumper in a soft shade of blue and matching scarf. It would be cold and draughty in the Crannog. Her gabardine was splattered with salty mud and stains but it would keep out the chill. Harry was taking the hired car so she would have to walk, as she had done all those years ago.

How strange it was coming back as a parent, feeling almost middle aged and staid in her brogues with her hair whipping her face in the wind. After nearly a week on the island she still felt a stranger, an off comer, a visitor politely welcomed but kept at arm's length. They knew all her history and the islanders were suspicious.

Peggy told her the rumour was that the Lennoxes were coming to buy the Crannog, and Harry's sudden arrival only confirmed this theory.

'Why should we buy the Crannog?' she said, amazed at such an idea.

'To pull it down and make a hotel or live in it in the summer,' Peggy said, fishing for facts. 'So it's not true then?'

Minn shook her head and smiled. Islanders never change, but she had changed. Once upon a time when she was scrubbing out the stone pantry floor and picking up Lady Rose's smalls she might have dreamt of buying it to lord it over everyone just to prove that the Macfees were as good as anyone, but those days were long gone.

Now she would be happy to put in proper

sanitation in the old cottage, running water and electricity, smarten it up as a holiday home for the summer months; but it still belonged to Niall and Mima and was only on loan.

What was happening to her plan to stay here and put the children in school to test how she could live simply without Harry's money? It was fading fast in the harsh reality of life without running water and comforts. Harry was doing his best to be attentive and had not touched a drop since his arrival. He was sober, thoughtful and the children were happy to see him. He was keeping his end of the bargain but what about her?

All she could think of was seeing Ewan again, holding his hand, feeling the grip of his fingers, looking into those dark eyes and wondering if he still found her attractive. It was wrong, it was ignoble, it was not fair on his wife, but she felt the pull of him even now and her steps quickened to the gates of the house so carefully avoided until this moment.

She was struck by the stone grandeur of the old keep, a fortress jutting out on stilts from the little loch by its side. It had been won on the turn of some roulette wheel in the eighteenth century but its origins were steeped in the violent history of the island. There were thick castle walls at the heart of it but the outside was softened by rebuilding in the Georgian style, elegant sash windows that were a devil to clean from the inside and four flights of stairs, each step of which she had known from their splinters and creaks.

It would make a fine hotel suitable for sailing and fishing and shooting, but dependent on ferries and air and decent weather. She thought of how Pitlandry nestled into the woodland, grew out of the landscape, but this house was the tallest on the island and could be seen for miles, standing sentinel like a barracks. She would not want to live here.

She walked up the gravel path slowly, taking in the loch and the overgrown garden. The paintwork was flaking on the windows and the door was in need of some good oil. Pulling the ring bell, her heart thudding with anticipation, she stood on the steps trying to look composed.

It was Johanna who came to the door, smiling, older, paler, thinner but still the factor's daughter, the upright head girl of their schooldays.

'Do come in.' She paused, looking behind her visitor. 'You've not brought your children?'

'Harry came earlier than we thought,' she lied. 'He wanted to take them both out. Hew is quite a handful at the moment and needs a sleep,' she lied again as she was escorted though the familiar front hall to the main staircase, where there were blank spaces and no portraits. It had seen better days, she thought, thinking of how once there were bowls of flowers and sparkling paintwork.

As if reading her thoughts, Johanna smiled. 'It must look very different. It was the officers' billet and after the war lay empty. The art foundation rented it for students and as you can see they've bashed it around a bit.'

Minn glanced around still nervous. There was a charm about its shabbiness, the smell of cigarette smoke, bashed leather chairs, the dull panelling on the walls and the remains of art work lying around. It had a lived-in, relaxed look as if all the frosty corners of the Struther family were knocked away.

She followed Johanna as she climbed up to the drawing room on the first floor, where Ewan would be waiting no doubt.

'Are you staying long?' asked Johanna as she opened the door.

'I'm not sure.' She smiled back surveying the room at a glance. 'Harry will have to go back to his business, of course, and I can't keep Anna out of school too long.' Minn paused. 'I had forgotten how wonderful the view is from here.'

She rushed across the empty room to peer out of the window. She fingered the same old brocade curtains lined with hand-woven blankets to keep out the draughts. How she had struggled with those shutters when she was small. She turned expecting Ewan to walk through the door but no one came and Johanna sat down, poking the fire.

'I expect you're wondering where Ewan is?' She looked up at her guest. 'These artists sometimes don't know what day of the week it is, never mind the time. Ewan is hopeless. He won't be long and then I'll bring some tea.' She smiled and the corners of her mouth twitched.

Minn could sense the tension, the embarrassment and the gaps in their polite conversation. She hardly knew Jo Mackinnon. They'd never mixed in the same circles when they were young, and there was that night before the war... She was older and cleverer. She went to college and was a teacher. The only connection they had was Ewan and he was late. Johanna was cross and trying not to show it. It was up to her to put his wife at ease.

'This must be a wonderful place for artists to study,' she offered. 'Are you staying through the winter?'

'Just until New Year. Then we hope to go abroad again to Paris. There's so much Ewan needs to learn. His training has been very bitty what with the war and everything. I am just holding the fort in the school until Miss Ferguson recovers from her operation. You'll recall Betty Ferguson in the school; she went away to Glasgow to train as a teacher at Jordanhill.'

Minn nodded politely, recalling a little shrimp of a girl in glasses with a crooked leg who was always into her books.

'How's Ewan?' she braved. 'I hear he is doing well with his art.'

'Ach, you know Ewan,' Johanna sighed. 'He lives his life like a clenched fist, in and out like the tide, always full of ideas. He gets cranky when he's not working. I expect that's where he is now, up to his boots in mud, stuck on a rock sketching.' Her laughter was brittle and false.

'I was sorry to hear about your miscarriage,' Minn offered, feeling the tension mounting in both of them.

'It wasn't a miscarriage,' she whispered. 'It was a stillbirth, just one of those things. We were in Italy. Andrew is buried there. They say time's a great healer but...' Johanna was trying to swallow back her emotion. 'Oh, where is the damn man?'

'I'm sorry if I upset you by asking. Perhaps I'd better go, perhaps another time is better. I don't want to intrude. It was very kind of you to invite me considering...' Minn rose to leave but Johanna barred her way.

'Considering what, Minn? Considering that it's Ewan you want to see not me. It's you two who are the friends. We were hardly to be bosom friends were we? How I hated you over the years for letting him down like that, hurting his feelings. You bewitched him

341

on that night of the regatta and then you dropped him for the Lennox heir,' she snapped.

Minn stepped back in shock. 'It wasn't exactly like that. Didn't Ewan tell you?' She paused, seeing the look of confusion on Johanna's face. He had not said a word about Harry's deceit.

Johanna continued. 'He came to me limp and broken in Glasgow and I was there to comfort him. Don't think that I don't know I was second best. I've felt your presence in his canvases, in his dreams. Following an artist isn't easy. They've no interest in mundane chores; it's living out of a suitcase, always on to the next idea, the next scene. Perhaps if we'd stayed here Andrew would have lived. A child might have changed him.' Jo was staring out of the window down the empty path.

'You have everything and still you come back for more. No wonder Ewan is staying away from the power of you... I'm sorry,' Johanna cried. 'I've been so rude. I don't know what came over me.' She pulled out a handkerchief to cover her tears. 'I can't let you leave after such a tirade ... since the baby I've not been myself.' She sat back on the sofa exhausted by her outburst.

'Let me make you a cup of tea. I know the kitchen like the back of my hand,' said Minn. 'There's not a nook or cranny of this place I've not swept, dusted and polished.

'One of the reasons I came back on this whim was, like you, I've not been myself since I had Hew. There've been problems at home. I needed to get away. Life isn't smooth waters even when there's the cushion of a few bob in the bank, believe me. I had no idea you would be here. It's not true, you know. Ewan loves you, he told me as much. You are a good wife to him. I would have been a selfish demanding *cailleach*.'

She sped downstairs, shaken by Jo's outburst. The tea was laid out in the kitchen, easy to find, with its familiar cupboards and floors and scents. She carried the tea with trembling hands on a tray as she had done for Lady Rose.

'I'm so sorry, Minn. I never meant to say any of this,' Johanna apologized. 'When did Ewan tell you about me?'

'Tears are better out than in, my doctor tells me. Ewan phoned me after Mother died to apologize for not attending the funeral. We spoke on the phone and that is all,' she lied with conviction. 'I'm sad of course that I won't get a chance to see him. There was one little matter I did want to clear up but it can wait.' She smiled, sipping the tea. 'It was like old times bringing the tray up here, but I'm sad to see the china's seen better days.'

They made polite chatter, glanced at the

old photos carefully displayed, worked their way up the three-tiered stand of scones, tea bread and fancies until Minn glanced at her wrist watch and made to leave.

'Thank you for being honest, Johanna. Not everything you think is true. I have my side of the story but it's better to let the old dog slumber. Ewan and I share the blame for Agnes's death and we'll have to live with that for the rest of our lives,' she tried to explain. The rest of their history was not for sharing. 'Good luck and safe travels.' She reached out for Johanna's hand. 'It was kind of you to ask me in. No one else on this island has bothered,' she said.

'They're afraid that you're too grand now for us,' Johanna said. 'You haven't changed you know, not deep down, and I'm sad that Ewan couldn't be bothered to give you the time of day. It is his loss,' she added.

Minn sobbed all the way back to Kil-phetrish, great gulps of tears. How could he be so cruel? There was unfinished business between them. How could he still stir her heart like this? Why had he humiliated her in front of his wife. Why was he afraid to face her? She stopped suddenly in her tracks. Only the heart sees clearly, she thought. In another time and place Jo and I could have been friends not rivals. There was only one reason why Ewan was avoiding her now and

Jo knew it too. The power between them was still there.

'How could you let me down like that?' Jo screamed at her husband when he arrived ten minutes after Minn walked back down the drive. 'What's your excuse this time?'

'None. I told you I'd no mind to meet that woman again,' he snapped. 'It was all your idea so I left you to it.'

'And what a fool I made of myself, breaking down in font of her, blaming her for ruining your career, losing our baby, spoiling this island,' she sniffed.

'You did what? You hardly know the woman! Damn and blast you, I just want some peace and quiet to get on with my work and you stir up a hornets' nest. What's got into you?' Ewan was furious, guilty, ashamed and embarrassed all at the same time.

He had spent the afternoon lurking in the studio watching the clock until he was sure the Lennox woman would have left for Kilphetrish. He was not proud of his action but it was for the best all round.

'You think I don't know what a spell Minn Macfee holds over you? I wanted to show her who was boss here. I wanted you there by my side to prove that you are mine now, but without moving a finger after six years she has you running scared, so scared you can't even put on an act and give me some support.' Jo was sobbing. 'How do you think that makes me feel? It's not over between you and her and it never will be until you do something about it. She has a part of you I can never share and you cut me out of your feelings.'

'I'm sorry, Jo. Come here. I didn't think. If only you'd said what you were feeling.' Ewan gathered her into his arms.

'It's not what you think. When I see Minn I see Agnes and the war and other things I've never told you about. She's part of all that and I want to shove it all in the past not dig it up again, but I see I've been a coward and I'm sorry.'

'Sorry is not enough, Ewan, not this time. Now's your chance to sort it out in your head and give us all a chance. Let it all go and face her, for my sake, for our sake, for our future's sake,' Jo cried into his chest.

'It's not like that,' he said, puzzled.

'Oh but it is, Ewan. It's her or me. I can't share you with her any more,' Jo sighed.

'But I've not seen her for years. How could she threaten us?' he asked. They were treading in dangerous waters now.

'She's in your head and your heart, in everything you create I see her influence. I can't compete with your dreams unless I know what they are. You have to choose. Take her with you and get off this island and set me free to find my own life or let her go

346

and bring all of yourself back to me.'

He had never seen Jo like this before. Her eyes were steeled, icy with fury and pain. How had it come to this when he had done nothing but stay away out of courtesy? How had he got it so wrong?

The very act of avoiding a confrontation with Minn was the one thing that confirmed to Jo that he still preferred the past to the present, and it wasn't true.

He loved Johanna and he had loved Minn but they were different loves. How could she ask him to destroy his muse? It was like asking him to stop painting and drawing and destroy his imagination.

'Tell me what to do, Jo,' he asked. 'I would never hurt you.'

Jo shook her head and stared up at him. 'If I have to tell you that then what hope is there for us?' She turned and left, banging the door.

Ewan stared out of the window watching the dark clouds banking up over the sea. Storms were gathering for a flood tide. It was too late to do anything about it now.

Five

Kilphetrish

The storm raged for two days and nights. Minn had forgotten just how the Atlantic Ocean could rattle the island to its very foundations so that few trees could stand the gales and the houses grew with their backs to the west like tombstones. No one could stand against its power or sail over water or fly in the air and the planes were grounded and Harry felt trapped and restless, eager to take them back south.

He insisted that they hole up in the Phetray Hotel together, fearful the roof of the cottage might collapse.

'It's been there for a hundred years or more. Houses are built to stand up to the weather here,' Minn argued, but for the sake of the children she left the cottage and enjoyed her first decent bath for days.

They played tiddly winks and Ludo and paper games. Anna was full of pent-up energy and wanted to race around the shore but it was too windy for her to be let out. On the third day the storm eased and Harry went racing to book them tickets for

Glasgow but the flights were still cancelled and he could hardly contain his fury.

'Of the islands in all the world, why did we have to land up here? This is the most godawful dreary place on earth. No wonder you wanted shot of it,' he snapped.

How could she tell them that she had enjoyed the storm, the windows battered by rain, the howling gale in the chimney. It was part of her childhood, complete with smoking chimney and soot and stew over the fire.

Together they were safe, a family once more, and she could shove all thought of Ewan's rejection out of her heart for a few hours.

If he could not be bothered to give her a minute of his time then she could not be bothered to write to him about Anna. Two could play at that game, but Johanna's words stung her for being half true.

Once she knew Ewan was on Phetray she had wanted to see him for old time's sake... 'Auld Lang Syne'. She found herself humming the tune. 'Should old acquaintance be forgot and never brought to mind...' she sang to herself and then stopped.

'Go on, Mummy, sing us another song,' pestered Anna as they amused themselves around the piano. She sang the 'Skye Boat Song', 'We'll Mak the Keel Row' and 'Road to the Isles'.

Hew clapped his chubby hands and tried

to join in and Harry stood back silent.

'It's time you took those lessons in Edinburgh, Brodie Lennox. I shall organize some soirées for my clients and you can sing for your supper,' he laughed.

'Don't be silly. Who'd want to hear me caterwauling?' she said, flushing at the thought.

'I've paid good money to hear worse,' he laughed.

'Thanks very much but I'll keep my singing to the bath from now on,' she replied.

She was just about to start packing when Mrs Stewart said there was a call come in for Mistress Lennox.

Minn hoped it wasn't bad news from Pitlandry. 'Hello?' she said, for the line was weak.

'Is that you, Minn? It's Ewan. I gather you want to speak to me about a matter.' The line went quiet. How dare he pick up the phone as if they were old chums and he had not avoided her yesterday? She wanted to be cool and cold and collected.

'I could have said my piece yesterday and two years ago for that matter, if you had deigned to put your face round the door,' she answered, her voice shaking.

'I know, sorry, I know, but we can meet up now,' said Ewan.

'What, in this weather? I'm not traipsing back to the Crannog on a wild goose chase

350

again for you to be away at your scribblings and getting an earful from your wife,' she answered.

'You've every right to be angry. I gather Jo went over the top a bit. She's very upset,' he said sounding contrite and anxious at the same time.

'We're going home tomorrow if the plane can land,' she said.

'I wouldn't bank on it,' he said. 'I can meet you at your cottage or the hotel?'

'No, I don't want an audience of eavesdroppers. On the beach for a walk for auld lang syne,' she replied.

'At the beach of the singing winds?' he offered.

'No! Not there,' she snapped back. She would never go back to their old trysting place. 'Balenottar will do. Halfway between your place and mine will be fine, and don't keep me waiting. It's cold.' She put the phone down sharp.

'Who was that?' Harry sidled up to her, putting his arms around her waist.

'It was Ewan. He wants to meet me.'

'What does he want?' Harry's voice hardened.

'How should I know?' she snapped back.

'Are you going to go?'

'Of course. There're things he should know,' she added.

'Not all that business about Anna, is it?

351

Leave it be, Brodie. You said yourself you weren't sure. Don't bring up all that stuff again just when we were getting along fine,' Harry's eyes were glinting with anger.

'Harry, nothing's fine until this is all sorted, all out in the open. It doesn't go away for being swept under the carpet. I have to see him one more time, just to be sure...' she said, hoping he would understand.

'To be sure you want to come back to Pitlandry or stay on this godforsaken island mooning over lover boy?' The gloves were off now.

'Do you mind if we go somewhere less public to have a row? *Pas devant les enfants.*' She stared at him.

'I need a drink. I'll see you later.' Harry turned his back on her.

She caught his arm. 'Come on, sit down, calm down. I'm only going for a walk with him not jumping between the sheets. He has a right to know about Anna one way or the other,' she pleaded. 'Then it is finished.'

'It'll never be finished between you two. Don't think I don't know why you've hung on here. I'd have given you three days on Phetray if Mackinnon wasn't here. Don't think I don't know that I was always second best, a meal ticket, an also-ran. No wonder I drink,' he whispered, watching Anna turning to see what they were arguing about. 'If she is his bairn he'll want to be seeing her and interfering and I'll never be rid of him. He will be the spectre at the feast, the ghost who hovers over our bed. It's been good us all being together these past days. Don't spoil it all just as we're going home. Let him go, stand him up. You had years to tell him and you didn't, so why now?'

'Because my silence has gone on long enough. You'll have to trust me. I know what I'm doing,' she whispered back, mouthing the words.

'Do you? Do you really know what you're doing, opening all this up again? I don't trust him,' Harry replied under his breath.

'It takes one to know one. You took your chance and betrayed my trust but I'm not like you. I keep my word. If there was any other way I'd take it but it has to be face to face. I have to know,' she cried.

'Know what?' he shouted.

'I'll know it when it happens,' she whispered. 'I have to go.'

'Where are you going, Mummy? Why are you cross?' Anna climbed on Harry's knee.

'We're not cross, darling. Mummy is going out for a walk.' Harry tried to smile.

'Can we go too?' said Anna.

'No, dear. I have to meet someone,' Minn replied. She was not going to lie to her child.

'I want to come with you. It's dry outside now,' Anna argued.

'I know and Daddy will take you both out

when Hew wakes up. Be a good girl.' Minn rose to find her coat and hat.

'Where are you going?' Anna whined.

'To Balenottar,' Minn said, wishing her daughter would shut up.

'To see Agnes Accident?' shouted Anna. 'I'm coming with you.'

'No. I don't want you to come this time. This is grown-up's talking. Stay with Daddy, he'll buy you some sweeties from the store if we've any coupons left.' Minn smiled but Anna was scowling, that familiar V furrow over her brow with a turned-down mouth that made Minn laugh.

'If the wind catches that sourpuss face you'll be stuck with it for ever, young lady!'

'I hate you!' shouted Anna from the door.

'And I don't like you when you sulk,' snapped Minn, turning herself to face the westerly.

It had come at last, this final summons. No more shilly-shallying, coxing and boxing around the island. This time there was no escaping the moment and her heart leapt with excitement. When I see him I shall know, she sang, and marched herself down to the grey wet road.

Balenottar Point

It was time to go and sort this business out

354

once and for all. Ewan was in no mind to be lingering on a deserted beach as he strode down the coastal path, but he was dressed with care in his khaki corduroys and Harris tweed jacket, feeling the security of his second best pipe in his pocket, and he had trimmed his beard.

So what if the mountain was coming to Mohamet at long last? He was doing it for Johanna and for no one else, and for the hurt he had caused her yesterday.

If he had not been so thoughtless this visit would have been unnecessary. It was cold and windy and the sea was restless, swollen. There were far better things to be doing on this dull afternoon.

Yet his steps quickened at the thought of meeting his old lover face to face again. He did want to explain why he had missed her last time through no fault of his own. He could make a hundred excuses why he had flunked coming in for tea at the Crannog and she would no doubt see through them all.

What a square dance they had led each other over the years, going round and round in circles, forwards, backwards; swing your partner, change your partner, round you go. Ewan smiled to himself.

Now they would take up their positions as polite strangers, bow one to the other, circle around and then walk off in opposite directions for ever. So what was he worried about?

If only it were that simple, he chunnered to himself. If truth were told, since he had heard Minn was on the island part of him ached to catch a glimpse of her again, but the sensible bit of him had scuttled into the safety of his studio to keep out of her way. How could she be on Phetray without them meeting?

Minn was Phetray, part of the mystery and magnetic force that bound him to this island, part of the gravitational pull of this sea and this tide force.

Don't be so whimsical, he argued to himself. Phetray was a lump of rock set in a rough sea, and the woman had not lived here for years. They were both married to others and there was nothing binding them but sad memories and a brief fling. They were grown up now with responsibilities for others. How could he even think such things?

And yet ... when he saw the outline of the lone figure walking towards him in the distance his heart leapt with recognition and excitement. His steps were quickening with anticipation as if some old memory of running towards her was still informing his feet. It was an effort of will to slow down and saunter as if he didn't care that she was drawing ever closer and he would see the face of a thousand dreams, those sea-blue sapphire eyes, the sunshine hair, the body that would never disappoint him. His hands were shaking and he shoved them in his pocket to find his pipe and pouch. A man needed support at a time like this.

The old spark, that damned eternal spark, was still lurking to ignite the unwary and he must shield himself from weakness with the thought of Jo waiting anxiously for his return, trusting in his decency and honour.

How he wanted to feel indifferent towards the Lennox woman, immune to her physical presence, bored by her intellectual inferiority and ignorance of his artistic world, angry at her tainted wealth, but most of all unmoved by the sight of Minn Macfee standing now before him.

He was washed away on the tidal wave of her scent, the salt-tangled freshness of her features. She had not aged but seemed younger, more vulnerable, breathless, her eyes averted for a second and then flashing out a shy smile as she held out her hand to him like a polite stranger. This gesture stung him more that he could say. He was speechless and nodded like some dumbfounded schoolboy on his first date. The dance had begun.

She looked up at him, unprepared for the impact of the surf roller wave hitting her, making her step back, reeling, from the shock of seeing the dark man of her dreams once more, wild haired, standing with the same half-smile and wide grin, taller, broader, with the same confident stance: his legs apart as if grounded, anchored into the sand. His beard made him seem even more distinguished. Time rewound its tape and it was as it always was. Nothing was changed.

Oh, Ewan, she thought, I've dreamt of this coming together so many times, imagined me telling you the full truth of our story, written a hundred letters of explanation. How many times has your name been on the tip of my tongue? Why does courage fail when I think of breaking the long silence between us?

It seemed like a full five minutes before either of them could speak, but it was only seconds when Ewan laughed.

'So we meet again, Minn Macfee. I was hoping to catch you singing to the seals but... What made you want to come back here to this beach to talk after all that happened?' He stepped back, mirroring the distance she had made between them.

'I don't know. It felt right to meet out in the open where it all began.' She hesitated, knowing Balenottar Point was windswept and the rollers were heaving and crashing down on the shingle. 'How are you, Ewan?' she whispered.

'I'm fine, and you didna bring me all this way to talk about my health. And for your information I did try to contact you yon time after your mother's funeral. My watch stopped. I mistook the time until it was too late. I meant to come but you and I have ebbed and flowed like the tide, waxed and waned like the moon, but never in unison, never together in the same place at the same time long enough to straighten things out or to connect,' he said, pointing in the air with his pipe.

'We managed it once or twice or does my memory fail me ... on a certain beach under the stars?' She smiled. Had he forgotten their old trysting place? 'Now we stand like strangers landed up on the shore listing into the wind. It could all have been so different,' she said, piercing him with her fiercest gaze, willing him to make it easy for her. He said nothing as he turned his face from her.

Don't tempt me, Minn, thought Ewan. Don't dazzle me with your glamour and beauty. Don't do this, reminding us of what might have been if only we were free to love. Perhaps it's the arrogance of a first love that it thinks it can outlive all other loves, that it can be picked up anytime and any place. You and I are different people, older now. We've separate lives and histories.

Ewan sensed he must be hard for both of them, step back from those piercing eyes and the scent of her, step back from the brink.

'So what was there of such importance that you needed to tell me before you left the island. What is there to speak of now after all this time, *mo ghaoil*, but the weather and our health,' he snapped. Flippancy was always a good defence.

There was a deafening silence for a second as she brushed back a strand of golden hair from her face and drew a gulp of air as if summoning courage to make herself plain.

'There's something I should have told you long ago and didn't. Even now, Ewan, I'm after wondering if I should,' she said, looking into his face, trying to read his mind. He had forgotten how intense Minn could be, how determined to succeed, how ruthless she was in stunning his will power, how dangerous it was to be alone with her.

'Spit it out then. It's too cold to be standing,' he said, looking at his watch, trying to unnerve her with his careful indifference.

'After you left Phetray there was a baby...' she began, but he snapped her off in full flight.

'Ah-ha, the wee love child that Harry passed off as his brother's bairn.' Ewan felt his lips curl up into a sneer.

'He told you a pack of lies, as well you know. What I didn't tell you was that–' Minn stopped short, distracted by a moving figure, a small shape jumping across on the rocks jutting out towards the needles of Balenottar Point. 'What the devil! Look, Ewan! There's a child playing on the end of those rocks... and it's Anna,' she screamed, running as if her life depended on it.

'Come down from there this minute. What's she doing up there? Harry is supposed to be looking after them. Anna, you naughty disobedient *cailleach*, you come down off there this minute and I'll be giving you such a skelping,' she screamed like a fishwife, but Ewan grabbed her arm.

'Whisht, don't startle her. She must have followed you. Why?' he asked, working out the best way to approach the child, as she was stranded on the edge with the racing tide flooding and swirling into the bay. In a few minutes she would be sitting on an island of slippery rock at the mercy of the swell as it broke on the Needles.

'I took her to see Agnes's grave. I told her the story and she wanted to play "accidents", the minx. She wanted to come today but I turned her back and she's followed me. Look at her now with no sense of danger, waving as if this is some picnic. Oh, Ewan. I'm not dressed for the rocks but if I have to scramble up barefoot... We have to get her down. Oh dear God! Not again, not Agnes ... not our daughter... We have to save her! She's our daughter!'

Ewan was racing ahead not listening to Minn's pleas to the Almighty to save the child. He had long ago stopped putting faith in that higher authority. All he could see was a little girl, not yet frightened, about to be trapped by the sea. Once she was stranded she would freeze with fear and cold. He had to reach her first before the tidal waves lashed over her. The sea witches of Balenottar Point were about their mischief again.

Minn was gasping for breath, running against the force, loosening her coat, anything that might hamper the task ahead. Where the hell was Harry, dozing in the bar while Hew slept? She could kill him for being so careless. Now was no time for blame. Ewan was already yards ahead of her, tearing off his jacket, making for the gully and protecting himself against the force. Why was there no one around when you needed them, fishermen, coastguard, not a single passer-by?

There was no one to stop this tragedy happening all over again. The sea wanted her child. You can't have her! She screamed into the wind. We'll defy you. Take me if you need a sacrifice but this child is the future of this island, fruit of these very rocks, a daughter of the tide, an ally not enemy, so be gentle with her.

Suddenly she was back on this beach so many aeons ago, swimming with Agnes, losing her grip, losing sight of her friend, her limbs heavy and weary and the fear pumping all the stuffing out of her body, and she tasted the salt and ling and the fear, for the first time remembering it all.

'Climb back, Anna, Mummy's coming. Go back where you came from, it's not too late. We'll soon reach you and the sea hags won't have you. If you climb higher up, the sea *cailleach* can't reach you, the green hag who haunts this tide, this hungry tide will go away empty handed. Mummy's coming...'

The wind was carrying her voice away from the rocks and out of earshot. It was hopeless to out shout the sea. She dared not look but look she must and face her fear if they were to save their child.

This was all her doing, the lingering obsession that had brought them both here. If only she could have walked away from the temptation to see Ewan again. But no, the pull of curiosity was too strong. She'd wanted to see if the passion was still there, the look of longing in his eyes, she'd wanted to tempt him again and now she was paying the price of her silly fantasy. You can't turn back the clock, she cried. We are not as we were nor ever can be, you fool, she thought.

She sank into the wet sand on her knees.

'Save my child and I'll never trouble this island again. Take me in her place, if you must, but don't harm Anna for the sins of her silly mother. As God is my witness I'll do anything, but save my child, Ewan,' she prayed, with tears streaming down her face.

Then she began to climb with smooth hands not used to gripping wet rock, slime and lichen: hands grown weak, not the callused hands of her youth when she could skim over these rocks like a goat, but manicured useless fingers that felt out the ledges slowly.

She would clamber up behind the child and guide her back to safety, coax Anna back into the safety of her arms, away from the treacherous gullies and crevasses that were as deep as hidden wells. At least her shoes were tough, with low heels, and gave some purchase. Together they would make a team and pull the child to safety.

Then she caught a glimpse of Ewan waving, shaking his head as she tried to clamber up the rock, and signalling. Go for help, summon the lifeboat, find a lifebuoy or a fishing line, anything, he signalled. He was far away from her now like a dot scrambling up towards the lump of rock where Anna was cowering down, aware at last that she was in danger. She could read his thoughts, hear his commands. He would save Anna as he had saved her all those years ago.

Ewan knew what he was doing. He would rescue the child while she must run and do his bidding. For a second she lost concentration and shifted her balance, losing her grip so she began to slip, grasping at the rough slime, plunging backwards on to the sand.

Winded and shocked by the fall she knew she was stranded. Her ankle was suddenly numb. It wasn't working. Trying to stand only made it worse. Just when she was needed most she busted her ankle and would have to hobble up the shingle to the path, crawl if needs be, but she knew where there was the one telephone on the counter of Balenottar post office.

If she had to crawl on hands and knees she would make that village and raise the alarm. Tying her scarf tightly round her ankle she forced herself to stand, and hobbled, wincing with pain and frustration. Where was the island girl who once could race barefoot over rocks? Where was Minn Macfee in this feeble useless body, and where the hell was Harry?

Then she saw the black saloon heading down the bumpy track and knew the cavalry was arriving in the nick of time. Now everything would be all right. She sat down on a boulder, waving furiously. Harry jumped out of the car.

'Is she with you? I've been searching with Sandy here. The blighter darted off while my back was turned.'

'Where's Hew?' she cried, trying to hobble forward.

'He's fine, in the bar fast asleep. Where's the young madam, scaring me half to death...? Harry saw the look on Minn's face as she pointed to the rocks.

'What's happened? Oh my God! She's stuck on the rock and the tide's nearly covering it...'

'Ewan's swimming up to hold her. We've got to do something and quick or we'll lose them both to the tide,' she screamed. 'And it's all my fault.'

Harry was running and Sandy was running and she was stuck with only an old umbrella to lean on as she jumped into the car. She would drive for help, drag out every man she could find and summon the villagers before it was too late...

Ewan was climbing, gripping on to the tiny crevices, shinning up, edge by edge, to where the girl sat shivering. 'Lie flat,' he ordered her. 'Cling on to the rock and it will hold you,' he added, trying to coax her to move, but she was terrified. All he was thinking about was getting up there before the tidal waves washed over her, sweeping them both out to sea.

Minn would be running for help, gathering nets and lines and men in boats who would risk themselves on the swell for a child.

He looked up at her face, the dark frightened eyes and the frown. She didn't look like Harry or Minn with that sodden black hair. Anna was little more than a baby with long legs, a fearless madam to get herself out into such danger. She began to whimper and shiver, eyeing him with a fierce curious gaze.

'Stay down flat. I won't be long. Mummy's gone for help,' he panted, for the exertion was tiring his limbs. It was years since he had tried himself against the rocks with the SBS.

You're unfit, man, gone flabby with all that sitting, he thought, but his will of steel would give strength to his muscles. He knew this coastline only too well, and this time the sea mustn't take this child as it had taken Agnes.

He looked up and for a flash of a second he thought he saw his sister lying flattened on the rock, her face looking down at him. For a second it unnerved his concentration to be seeing a ghost. Was this all a bad dream? Was he swimming out again after his sister who had died on these very rocks?

The wind biting his fingers, whipping his face was no apparition. This was real and he was losing his grip with such fantasies, but if he could save Anna it would be one back from the dead, a life saved, a fresh start, a debt repaid. No more hankerings after the past and possession of Minn. He would be free of the guilt for ever. This was his plea bargaining to himself as he clambered the last few feet.

One more lift and he would have her within his grasp. There was barely enough room for the two of them but once he grabbed her he was not going to let Anna go. He edged himself slowly on to the tiny island and smiled at her.

'I'm Ewan, a friend of your Mummy, come to get you back home, but first you must do everything I say.' He smiled, holding her into his body, rubbing her arms to keep her warm.

'Why is the sea hurting us?' She looked up at him in all seriousness.

'The sea is the sea, Anna, it does what it always does. It takes its orders from the wind and the moon,' he replied, looking up with relief to see a line of men edging towards them slowly, dodging the crashing spray as best they could.

'Look who's coming! There's Sandy and Archie Kinnoch.' He pointed. He could see Harry Lennox following behind, carrying what looked like a net. There was a crowd gathering on the beach. Word would have got back to Johanna on the island bush wires and she would be worrying.

How could he ever think of betraying her trust? How could he ever snatch at his own happiness without ruining hers?

Yes, there was still the Minn of his dreams

but she was changed by motherhood and other experiences he would never want to share. We were never meant to be together, he thought, as he held her daughter tight.

This obsession to possess her again would be an all-consuming drive if he gave into it. He knew that from his art. It was enough to have one demanding mistress in his life, not two, and where would that leave Johanna?

Pursuing his old love meant hurting good people and innocent children. How could he have ever have dreamt of betraying his wife? All that mattered now was saving this child and getting off this damned uncomfortable rock and back to his studio. This was all his doing. His timing was always out of kilter when it came to Minn Macfee. Now timing was of the utmost if they were to get off the rocks safely.

'What took you so long!' he shouted to Sandy. 'Can we fix up a line? I can't risk her in the sea.'

'I can swim.' Anna was coming to life as she saw Harry Lennox hovering anxiously. 'Daddy!'

'Not in this tide you can't, young lady. Is there another rope and a buoy? Tie the rope round the buoy and throw it,' Ewan ordered, thinking on his feet. If he could loop it through the other rope and make a swing he could carry the weight of this little girl, sitting on the buoy while she was thrown across the flooded gully to safety.

'Is there no other way?' shouted Harry. 'She'll need coaxing. We've brought some nets.'

'There's no time to scramble the nets, just let's try it before the waves push me forward.'

'What about you, Ewan? They've called out the lifeboat, but with this sea...' Sandy shouted.

'Just get on with it, now,' he screeched as he secured the buoy to the rope. He turned to Anna. 'Now we're going to play a special game of swing the boats. I want you to sit in the buoy and hold on tight.' He smiled, edging her towards the lifebuoy. 'Then I'll lift you up and slide you across the little sea to your daddy, very slowly. Don't look down, look across to your daddy and cling on tight, promise me?' He was mouthing the words above the roar of the water crashing on the rock.

'Are you coming too?' she asked.

'When you're safely across I'll come across on the rope,' he replied, hoping there would be enough time to jump on the rope and abseil his way back down. 'Let's do it now.' He wrapped the rope round his body. Never had he needed to be grounded into these rocks as he did now. It was going to take strength, luck and cunning to outwit the treacherous seas.

Slowly, with her eyes clenched shut, Anna clung astride the lifebuoy at an angle as they winched it across the raging water, swinging.

Ewan was straining every muscle to hold her against the wind and the slippery surface, while arms were flung out waiting to grab the child as she slid ever closer to the next slab of rock. For a second the rope slid into a grint of rock, dangling her out of the edge, stuck rigid, but Archie Kinnoch was already dangling down, unhooking the rope.

Ewan could feel his strength giving out. 'For God's sake grab her now. I can't hold on much longer!' He was kneeling, bruised and battered, when he felt the sling on the move again. He thought he saw her red coat bundled on to the rock but he wasn't sure for a huge wave crashed over his head and he was flung over the edge into the raging sea.

Exhausted, stunned by the cold water, thrashing blindly as the water rose over his head, he bounced up towards the surface where for a brief second he bobbed and thrashed his way in the direction of the shore.

So it's come at last, the final challenge. Even in extremis he was arguing with himself. You can't fight this, forwards or backwards. You're trapped by the force. You can't last five minutes in this chill. You're doomed. You're doomed if you give in to defeat, he argued with himself, floundering to gain some control. You're a sailor with a few tricks up your sleeve, fight to the end. Don't let the sea *cailleachs* drag you under, make a fight of it to the end. You don't want all your past life to float before your eyes.

Lifted and thrown, sucked in and out, he was running out of steam. Damn the mighty swell. He was not giving in yet. Ride it like a horse, whispered a voice in his head. Ride the waves, Ewan, but then the sea would have the last word. The sea would decide his fate. Agnes, Normandy, Ken Broddick and now this. Let the sea decide.

'What's happening?' yelled Minn, hobbling as best she could back towards the beach, where the villagers were gathered. She had driven from Balenottar like a mad woman to the Crannog. Someone had to tell Johanna. She didn't feel the pain in her ankle, only the terror of being away from the scene a second more than she had to.

Johanna was already tearing down the lanes on her bike. She had thrown the bike down in the hedge, jumped into the car and driven while Minn tried to explain about Anna and Ewan and the rescue attempts.

'The wee girl's saved, dragged over on a rope. The lifeboat's out on the water. They're doing what they can,' said her neighbour, Hector Sinclair, coming up the shingle to meet them.

'Is Ewan with them?' Johanna was searching the rescuers.

'He got washed off the rock, Mistress Mackinnon. The boat's out looking for him the now.' Hector was straining to catch a glimpse of the lifeboat chugging over the waves from Kilphetrish harbour.

Minn felt sick, grabbing Johanna's arm to steady herself. 'He knows the sea and its tricks. All those years as a commando, he'll know what to do,' she said, trying to be hopeful.

'He's not dressed for the sea or hadn't you noticed? He was out to impress an old flame,' Jo snapped. 'Why did you have to come back?'

'I'm sorry.' Minn fled from her anger. 'I must go to my daughter.' She limped as best she could across to where Anna lay swaddled in blankets. She could not see for tears of relief and fear.

She scanned the waves for any sign of life but there was nothing visible. The men were hanging off the rocks, dangling ropes and throwing lifebuoys into the water, fishing nets, anything to give Ewan a fighting chance of survival.

'Live, Ewan, live. You don't deserve to die. You don't deserve this after what you have done for Anna, for your child and mine, a child of love and promise. Live and we'll never bother you again, live and I'll make no claim on you. Live and I'll let you go for ever, set you free to love Jo and the children that will surely come from you both. Live, Ewan,' she willed him. 'Surely there's some old training you can use to ride the waves. The tide is coming in not out, ride the tide back to us. Come back to us now. Come back to your wife and your daughter and the woman who will love you for the rest of her life. Come back to us, Ewan!'

Every fibre of her being screamed the silent prayer as she hugged her baby and Harry and all the rescuers. 'Live, Ewan, oh live.'

The fight was over. For what seemed like hours Ewan had thrashed against his fate but his limbs were numb with cold and he was tired, so tired. It was time to admit defeat and let the sea have its wicked way with his battered body, time to launch himself forth to the *Tir nan og*, land over the horizon, land of the ever young, time to lose his grip on life and see all the deeds of his life before his eyes, but the voice was still ringing his ears, 'Ride on, ride on, you're not dead yet. Live, Ewan. Live, live, live...'

'We can see him!' shouted Sandy. 'Out there, look, by the reef. How the hell has he got that far out?' The policeman was jumping up and down, waving to the lifeboat chugging inland, signalling for them to turn round. Someone set off a flare to warn them. The boat chugged up and down, ploughing the sea like a furrow, throwing lines to the body floating aimlessly now on the water. Then they gathered him in their net like a huge seal, scrambled him over the side.

There was silence on the rocks, a dull sickening silence as they waited and waited. Johanna was wrapped in blankets. Minn sat with her back to the sea. She could not bear the suspense.

They are trying to pump the water out of him and life back into him but it's all too late, she thought, knowing the procedures. There was still danger, for the lifeboat was being thrown by the waves ever closer to the rocks.

Then the flare went up and everyone cheered.

'What's going on?' whispered Harry as Minn tried to scramble to her feet. 'He's alive. Thank God, he's alive. He's breathing not drowned. Oh, Harry,' she said flinging her arms round him with relief. 'Ewan lives! How can we ever thank him?'

Suddenly the pain in her ankle shot through her body and she was frozen to the spot. This was the moment she had been dreading, for the bargain she had struck must be fulfilled.

Johanna must have the hugs and kisses and the tender nursing of him. Johanna must have Ewan to herself from now on and they must quit Phetray without any fuss. No second chances, no regrets, no hankerings after lost love. It must be over.

'Did you tell him about Anna?' Harry asked, suddenly looking weary and worried and aged.

'No, I tried but he didn't hear. What's the point of raking it all up again? You were right, but I'll tell Anna in my own time when she's old enough to understand.' She sighed. There was no going back on her word.

'The sooner we're off this island the better. We've stayed far too long,' Harry said, his businesslike briskness covering the emotions they were both feeling.

She looked at her husband. The strain of the past weeks was beginning to show, his hair was thinning, his body thickening. She had chosen him for better or worse. Their children needed him and in a strange way she was going to need his protection and his arms for comfort. How could she think of ever abandoning them all?

'Let's go back on the ferry, over the water for old time's sake, slowly with dignity so I can get used to the leaving of Phetray for good.' She sighed.

'You'll be back.' Harry smiled, putting his

376

arms round her shoulders, but she shook her head.

'I don't think so, not for a long time,' she said, watching the lifeboat making its way to safety with its precious cargo aboard. Half her heart was in that boat but no one must know. The happiness she would find now was in making her family contented, but would it be enough for a lifetime?

The airplane was too quick a leaving, she needed time to think, to hang over the side and say farewell to her lost dreams.

Six

SS The Pride of Argyll

So this is how it's going to be? I must get used to this empty numbness. She gulped, watching the island disappear until it was a long flat line on the horizon. Reaching out over the rails for that very last glimpse, standing with one leg strapped to the knee and a pair of crutches for support, Minn was determined not to miss a second of her leave-taking.

This is how grief felt when there was no hope.

For once Harry was sensitive to her need to be alone on deck, for once he was not trying to fuss over her. He was taking charge of the children below deck.

She was grateful that he had taken Anna to the little makeshift hospital next to Doctor Murray's stone house to be checked over again. She was shocked but unharmed, being made of sturdy island stock.

Minn had hung back, afraid, for Ewan was being kept under observation there, still unconscious, suffering from chill. He had been so close to drowning, but the signs were good, and what he needed now was rest and peace.

How do you say thank you to the man who has saved your child's life? How could she tell him he had repaid the debt they owed to Agnes tenfold in saving his own daughter without creating a fuss?

In the end Harry took both the children in to see Johanna, who had not left Ewan's side all night, while Minn was examined and strapped up for the journey home. It was better to stay out of sight.

There were no bones broken but the real agony she was feeling would respond to no pill but time. The pain in her ankle would pass but now she could hardly breathe for the ache in her ribs, a wave of gratitude, anger, frustration and loss flooding over her. Not to be able to say farewell, not to be able to explain why she must never see his dear face again. So many things were to be left unsaid. How could she risk a scene by his bedside or harm his progress? The vows she had made were sacred. She would go quietly.

Ewan was her crime and Ewan was her punishment. He was out of reach now.

In the purple twilight between the daylight and darkness of this autumn afternoon she stood on deck, a lone figure staring out to sea with eyes wide, dazed, bewildered and hurt like a frightened child, an exile watching the island waters roll into the sea as it beat on to the side of the ship, eyes searching for something that was no longer there.

It came to her in the silence that this was the best it could ever be. What comes round must go round and in coming back to Phetray she had rounded the circle, but why had it taken half a lifetime for them to pitch up at the right place at the same time?

She sensed with all her being that her place in a corner of his heart was secure, but there was space now for Jo to have the rest. Her own heart must be given to her family from now on. She was finished with passion and all that sensation. There would be no more of that.

The two of them were like the tide, ebbing and flowing, pulled endlessly back and forth but never quite returning to the same place, like sands shifted this way and that by the currents and the forces of the wind.

Nothing stayed the same unless it was dead. If only Ewan had drowned it might be easier to mourn his passing. She sighed. How could she even think such thoughts? But to know that they must live on without ever seeing each other again was the ache that would never go away. It was hard enough to know that Jo would have a lifetime to explore all the joys of this talented man while she must make do with Harry's limited appeal So be it, that must be her choice. That was the price of Anna's rescue.

They were yesterday's children, marooned on shifting sands on separate shores. Anna and Hew were the future. They must come first from now on. They must not suffer. How could she ever have risked their happiness chasing after her own selfish dreams?

The weak sun was almost gone, with just enough light to torch the sea into a shimmering silver foil. The colours made her think of Ewan's bright canvases. He would be free to fill his life capturing the beauty of the islands in his pictures. He would go on to greater things without her distracting him. It would be easy for him to forget her. But what about me? she cried.

Oh, Ewan, heart of my heart, my disease and my cure, our time is over. I will always love you but there's no honourable life now for us to build on; no more letters or meetings, no re-entering into your senses, no taking you back into mine. It is over but the yearning for you will never go away. How can I bear to think of what might have been? We have to live with what is, and help to make what shall be.

Anna and Hew are my choice now. Harry and I will make the best of our marriage. There can be no more failure and lies. Oh, what am I to do if I'm not to limp through the rest of my life?

Fill the gaps, redirect your wandering heart back to hearth and home with all your mind and strength, learn to sing another song. There is always the comfort of Pitlandry waiting in all its autumn glory, there might be other children to suckle. She watched the shearwaters skimming over the surface of the waves.

There was something else, too, something that Moira Sanderson had said all those months ago about singing the songs of the heart, ringing in her ear.

Could she go back to Moira? Should she train her voice to sing the auld songs, the songs of the Gaels, to find solace in making music?

Sing the songs of the tide, the songs of the heart, songs of grief, the seagulls called. Take your passion and out of it will come songs of hope and love, for love is the sea without a shore; loving never ends. It would be a lonely journey, walking the pain and grief with invisible crutches.

Count your blessings, *mo ghaoil*. Children are a great distraction and solace. She smiled, hearing the lilt of her mother's voice in the singing waves as she bent over the rails to hide her tears.

There was a life waiting across the water.

'I'll try,' she whispered back into the wind. Just for now, though, she needed to be alone to practise carrying all these tormented thoughts with dignity. Minn turned her face towards the harbour with hope and began to sing:

'Blow the wind southerly, southerly, southerly,
Blow the wind south o'er the bonnie blue sea...'

Glossary

buth – shop
bodach – old man
cailleach – old witch
caileag – girl
carageen – seaweed
dubh – black
machair – grassy shoreline
mo ghaoil – my girl
Teuchtar – Highlander
traigh – beach
Traigh goadh nan seinn – Beach of the singing winds
Tir nan og – Land over the horizon; another world
uisge beatha – whisky